"Hey," Doyle said, tu... halted, suddenly awa... up beside him with...

The big man held the baseball bat in both hands, one hand on the grip and the other on the barrel. Mortie punched Doyle in the face with his fist around the bat's grip. Anger darkened his big features. "You're out of here, little man. You want to do it on your own, or do you want me to drag you out by your heels?"

Doyle wrapped his hands over his head. "Slow down. If it's all the same to you, I'll just show myself out."

"Next time I see you around here, I'm going to break something." Mortie paced him, following him to the door.

"I don't want to hurt her," Doyle said, thinking maybe Mortie would wait till he stepped outside to hammer him with the bat. Maybe the big man had a thing about somebody bleeding on his floor. "I want to help her."

"Hannah's had enough grief," Mortie said. "I'll be damned if I let her go through any more."

The big man stepped forward suddenly and rammed the barrel of the bat into Doyle's stomach, driving him through the doors and off the edge of the boardwalk.

Angel™

City Of
Not Forgotten
Redemption
Close to the Ground
Shakedown
Hollywood Noir
Avatar
Soul Trade
Bruja

Available from POCKET PULSE

The Essential Angel Posterbook

Available from POCKET BOOKS

ANGEL™

bruja

Mel Odom

An original novel based on the television series
created by Joss Whedon & David Greenwalt

POCKET PULSE

New York   London   Toronto   Sydney   Singapore

Historian's Note: This story takes place during the first half of *Angel*'s first season.

An *Original* Publication of POCKET BOOKS

 POCKET PULSE published by
Pocket Books, a division of Simon & Schuster, Inc.
1230 Avenue of the Americas, New York, NY 10020

™ and © 2001 Twentieth Century Fox Film Corporation.
All rights reserved.

ISBN: 0-7434-0701-6

First Pocket Books printing August 2001

10   9   8   7   6   5   4   3   2   1

POCKET PULSE and colophon are registered trademarks of
Simon & Schuster, Inc

Printed in the U.S.A.

This book is for Tara O'Shea for her enthusiasm and support and funny e-mail for the last few years.

For Micol Ostow, who always has a kind word and has been an absolute pleasure to work with.

And for all my nieces and nephews who want to see their names in a book . . .

In Minnesota:

Gale Olson, Teneil Olson, Sierra Olson, Amy Eich, Heidi Seibels, Paul Seibels, Shailyn Peterson, Samantha Murray, Tommy Murray, Johnny Murray, Eric Anderson, Kayci Anderson, Julie Olson, April Olson, Candice Walburg, and Wayne Walburg

In Oklahoma:

Imoneta Odom, John Ross Odom, and Justin Odom

Acknowledgments

As always, this book couldn't have been possible without the keen insights of Lisa Clancy, my editor. And thanks again to Joss Whedon and company for creating such wonderful worlds to "borrow" when I feel like playing in darkness.

PROLOGUE

Southeast Los Angeles

Father Carlos Oliveria swept the floor at the head of the church where he'd delivered the funeral eulogy only an hour before. All the mourners had gone now, but the sadness lingered no matter how hard or thoroughly he swept.

"Father Carlos, that floor can't possibly be cleaned any better."

The old priest glanced at the chubby woman standing by the altar. "Ah, and Albula, what would you have me do? Carry my sorrows home this night?"

Albula Cabrera put her hands at her hips and cocked her head to one side. She was in her middle fifties now, and silver shone in her black hair. Once, Father Carlos remembered, Albula had been one of the children he'd taught in the Sunday classes.

1

"No, Father Carlos," Albula said, "you shouldn't go home, either, for I know you will only fret about this poor boy there as well. You must leave him in God's hands now."

"*Sí*, I know this, Albula." Father Carlos was reed-thin, and despite the church mothers' efforts to keep his clothing in good repair and good fit, his black shirt and pants still bagged on him. His hair was long gone, leaving only an iron-gray fringe that matched his goatee. Age spotted his dark skin, hung wrinkles around his mouth and eyes, and reduced his neck to wattles that some of the younger children in church had said reminded them of a turkey's neck.

"Do you know what you should do?" Albula straightened the hymnals in the row beside her. "I think you should go to a movie. One of those reruns that you enjoy so much. I'm told *Casablanca* is showing again this week."

"Perhaps in a little while." Father Carlos glanced around the church. He'd grown up in the church, brought by his mother and sometimes by his father when his mother insisted the family all go together. When he was little, he'd chafed in some of the same pews that still filled the small room before him.

The old priest stared at the wreath that the funeral home had provided. The wreath was a modest one, white roses on greenery, standing on three spindly legs. In the center of the wreath was the boy's picture.

Cristofer had only been eight when he died, but the picture was one from school, showing him nearly a year younger. In the picture, Cristofer's smile was broad and innocent, showing the two missing upper front teeth and one below. He wore an L.A. Lakers T-shirt, which had been his favorite basketball team. His grandmother had apologized for the picture, saying that she didn't have a recent one of the boy large enough to put on the wreath.

Father Carlos gazed around the small church. The stained glass windows showed scars from the years. In places, thick glue lines showed when the sun hit them right, and even now the streetlights from outside showed the different colorings where the churchwomen had tried to replace the pieces that had been lost.

Feeling someone else's eyes on him, Father Carlos glanced at the entrance. With the seasons so moderate in the Los Angeles area, the church had never been wired for electricity, depending on the wood-burning stove in the basement for heat and candles for light. Few candles burned now, and the shadows masked the woman.

She wore black, and a veil hid her face. She stopped at the first row of pews ten feet from the priest. Her gaze locked on the picture of the boy in the wreath.

"What can I do for you, my child?" Father Carlos kept his voice low. Albula quickly and quietly made herself scarce, retreating to the back of the church.

The woman stood silently. Her black-gloved hands clenched and unclenched, shaking. Then she blew out a tight breath. "I need to make a confession, Father."

"Of course." The priest crossed the room and put his broom against the back wall. He brushed at his clothing, then gestured her to the confessional booth to the right of the pulpit.

The woman turned from the memorial wreath and walked into the confessional booth. She closed the door and the sound echoed within the empty church.

Father Carlos entered the other side of the confessional booth and sat on the padded bench. He took two measured breaths, thinking to himself that he knew her voice but was unable to attach a name to it. He reached up and slid the small covering from the screened partition between the two booths. "You may begin when you are ready."

"Forgive me, Father, for I have sinned."

"What is the nature of your sins?" Father Carlos asked.

The hesitation was painful. "I killed my son."

The reply shocked the old priest. Coming as it did on the heels of the boy's funeral, Father Carlos

4

prayed that God would give him the strength he needed to handle the woman's grief as well as his own. "There is forgiveness for everyone, my child."

There was no answer.

Suspicion filled Father Carlos. He glanced through the screened partition.

The other confessional booth was empty.

Stepping from the confessional booth, the old priest surveyed the empty church. The woman hadn't had time to leave that way. His head swung around, glancing to the left of the pulpit. The curtain covering the doorway leading to the basement stairs swayed.

"No!" Father Carlos gasped. He hurried after the woman, knowing there was only one thing the grieving woman could possibly want in the basement. The secret that lay below had been kept within the church for hundreds of years, since the early days of California. And that secret had been responsible for the deaths of hundreds of innocents.

He hurried through the curtain, spotting a flashlight beam ahead of him. The woman had come prepared. His hand found the smooth wood of the stairway banister and he descended the wooden steps as quickly as he could. Then, when he was close enough, he saw that the flashlight sat on one of the storage boxes of clothes the church mothers had gathered for the bazaar next week.

Where was the woman? The question barely

flitted through the old priest's mind before he heard a scuffing noise to his left. He turned, catching just a glimpse of the shovel before it caught him full in the face. He heard his nose break, and pain filled his senses a split second before they left him.

CHAPTER ONE

Angel pulled his black Plymouth Belvedere GTX convertible to the curb and glanced at the two-story building half a block down on the other side of the deserted two-way street. The neighborhood looked like a war zone, complete with uncertain flickering streetlights and bars over the windows of empty buildings.

"So this is the building, is it?" Doyle leaned forward slightly in the passenger seat.

The building resembled a fireplug squatting between another two-story building on the right and a three-story building on the left. Green letters on white paint spelled AKHURST HARDWARE.

Angel took Cordelia's hastily scribbled note from the pocket of his black trenchcoat and checked the address by the dashboard lights. "Yeah." He put the note away and scanned the building. Plywood covered the windows and someone had painted smiley faces on all the first-floor ones. "She told me that Devin Matthews called and I needed to check out this address." He switched off the ignition, got out, and strode across the deserted street.

"Okay, fine. We've got the right place. Now, do we have a plan?" Doyle asked as they reached the midpoint of the street. He was thin and wiry with black hair that seemed permanently mussed. His complexion was sallow from too many nights and not enough days. He wore a light jacket over a green bowling shirt and khaki pants.

Angel reached the other side of the street and stepped into the alley beside the target building. "Pizza guy."

"Angel, man, come on," Doyle groaned. "Twenty minutes we spent driving over here—and I'm not saying you didn't drive like a bat out of hell itself, I'm telling you—and in all that time all you can come up with is 'pizza guy'?"

The shadows seemed to crawl into the alley from the street, masking the other end of it. Angel glanced up through the metal fire escape ladders on the three-story building next to the one they wanted to enter. Only a few stray cats moved on the landings. He scented the air. As a vampire, there were a lot of things he could smell.

"You had the same twenty minutes," Angel pointed out. "Have you got anything better than 'pizza guy'?" He turned back to his Dumpster-diving, finding plenty of garbage but no empty pizza boxes. His irritation grew for a moment, then his curiosity started chiming in. *Why aren't there pizza boxes? With these guys, there* should *be pizza boxes.*

"You see there, I didn't know planning this job was going to fall to me," Doyle said. "If I had, maybe I would have paid a little closer attention to who was asking us to come out here."

Angel glanced at Doyle and saw that the half-demon wasn't kidding. It wasn't unusual for Doyle not to pay attention if a situation or problem didn't directly involve him. In fact, in a time when it seemed everybody wanted to be involved in everyone else's problems, Angel had found Doyle's attitude a little refreshing—except during those times that he had to recap situations in the middle of potentially dangerous action.

"Devin Matthews owns a video game design company outside L.A.," Angel said. "Calls it Brutal Dog Productions. He came into the office last week and said an ex-employee ripped off some of his game engine designs before he left. He's now creating games and posting them on the Net, charging fees for access to the games. So far, there hasn't been enough Internet exposure of the game engine to impact prospective sales of the games Matthews has in development. He hired us to recover his stolen game designs and put his ex-employee out of business."

"So this video games thief is supposed to be here tonight?"

Angel nodded. "Matthews has been trying to hack the Web server that posted the games. When he peeled back the shell companies and fake addresses to locate the physical address, he was supposed to let me know."

"And that was the subject of Cordy's note?"

"Exactly."

Doyle glanced over Angel's shoulder into the Dumpster. "All this looking around and you haven't found any pizza boxes?"

"No." Angel stepped back to show him.

"Now you see there, that's strange. Computer nerds and pizzas go together like a shot of whiskey and a beer chaser." Doyle looked back at Angel. "Curious that there aren't any pizza cartons. Or Chinese take-out. Or golden arches. Or diet soda cans."

"That's what I was thinking."

"You know what we're needing here then, don't you?"

"What?"

Doyle walked out of the alley and headed down the sidewalk. "A little bit of improvisation, that's what. Kind of like the method con. Without props, you see."

Angel followed, scanning the building. Power

lines ran to the building's roof. Shutting down Internet access temporarily would be easy enough. However, getting the software back could be difficult. Devin Matthews hadn't been certain how many copies of it might have been made.

Doyle walked to the front door without hesitation. A steel security door covered the entrance. "And there's quite a door," Doyle commented. "Looks new. Notice how there's no graffiti."

Angel noticed. The door did look like it had been recently installed.

Doyle took a deep breath, adjusted his coat, ran his hands through his hair, and pressed the buzzer. "Now pay attention here and I'll show you something. Technique." He glanced back at Angel. "And try not to look so damned suspicious."

A sinking feeling grew in Angel's stomach. "What's the plan?"

"Me," Doyle answered. "Got to be one of the ten simplest plans in the world."

"Me?"

Doyle nodded and frowned. "C'mon. You got a guy inside here doing something illegal, right? He knows people are after him, 'cause he's doing illegal stuff, right? However, no man—or criminal—is an island. Do you see?"

"Maybe," Angel agreed cautiously.

"Stand back," Doyle said. "I'll show you how these things work. A guy goes into hiding, see? He's doing illicit business and what-have-you, but he still needs things from the outside world. There's always guys these guys have to rely on if they want to remain anonymous."

"Who's there, man?" a voice demanded from the small speaker beside the security door.

"Me," Doyle said, making his voice hoarse and furtive.

"Who's me?"

Angel thought quickly, realizing they should have walked around the building first and found out how many different ways out there were. How long did it take to grab everything inside the building and run? Especially software? If the people inside got away, Angel was certain Devin Matthews wasn't going to be a happy camper.

"Guy who's got your delivery," Doyle said, "that's me."

"It's about time," the voice grumbled. "You're late, too, so that means the pizza is free, dude. And don't be expecting no tip." The speaker died in a staticky discharge.

Angel looked at Doyle. "Me?"

Doyle shrugged and held his hands up. "Me could be anybody. Tonight, *me* happened to be 'pizza guy.' So who are we going to find inside the building?"

"Tech heads," Angel said. "Computer gamers. Maurice Welker was a lead designer for Brutal Dog

Productions. Devin Matthews said the guy was a hothead."

"A hothead as in somebody who gets royally pissed, or are we talking about a guy who'd push you off a rooftop? There's a lot of leeway there, you understand."

"As in hard to get along with." Angel watched a car roll slowly by. "One day Welker stopped showing up for work and Matthews discovered his game engine designs had been copied."

A Papa Georgio's Pizza light glowed on the top of the car. The brake lights flared and a white, pimply face pressed up against the driver's-side window.

"He could be a problem," Angel said. "Go pay for the pizzas and get him out of here."

Doyle reached into his pocket and came out with a single bill. He glanced hopefully at Angel. "I bet it's more than five bucks."

Angel took folded bills from his pocket and peeled off a hundred-dollar bill.

Doyle intercepted the pizza guy, made the money/pie exchange, and was headed back toward the building in less than a minute. The delivery driver didn't hesitate about hurrying back to his car and driving off.

"I'm thinking," Doyle said as he rejoined Angel, "that I've already come up with a refinement on the 'pizza guy' con. Next time, you can always order a pizza and have it sent to the address. You know, that way you won't have to be rummaging through Dumpsters."

Locks ratcheted on the security door from the inside. Then the door swung open a few inches. The guy who answered the door was thin and pale. His shaved head gleamed from the light behind him, showing an intricate design tattooed onto his head. Piercings decorated his lips, ears, and eyebrows. He wore a peroxide-blond French tickler, wraparound amber-tinted sunglasses, and a Punisher T-shirt.

Doyle held up the pizzas.

The guy looked at Angel. "*Two* pizza guys?"

"What I'm doing," Doyle said, "is breaking in a trainee."

The guy's pierced eyebrows raised. "A trainee?"

"So what were you thinking? That pizza guys just fall out of trees?" Doyle asked.

"I've seen some that looked like they did." He reached for the pizza boxes.

Angel pulled the box back. "No money, no pie."

"It won't take just a second."

"In the meantime, I have to stand outside here? No. I want my money. And your pies are getting colder by the minute."

The guy looked slightly irritated. "Come on in. I'll take you to the guys who ordered the pizza. They can deal with you because me, I didn't order any pizza."

Angel felt the barrier over the door drop away

and he followed Doyle inside. The open warehouse floor had been divided into cubicles. No lights were on, but the soft blue-white glow from dozens of computer monitors left pools in the darkness. Angel scented the air, drawing in the stink of unwashed humans, blood, pizza, stale beer, Chinese food, incense, citrus . . .

. . . and something decidedly demonic.

Dozens of eyes watched him from the cubicles. Some of them held curiosity and wariness, but others gleamed with predatory alertness.

"You guys don't look like pizza guys," the pierced guy said as he threaded through the irregular path leading through the cubicles. "And, like, aren't you supposed to have protective wrap on the pizzas? To keep them from getting cold?"

"Just took it off. Left it out in the car so it'll still be warm for next trip." Doyle lifted the pizzas. In the gloom the steam wafted from the cardboard boxes. "See? Still steaming."

Angel glanced from side to side as they passed the cubicles. Devin Matthews didn't know how big Maurice Welker's operation had grown in the last three months. Judging from the state of undress and verbal content spewing from some of the cubicles, the underground computer network was also pushing bandwidth of a decidedly adult nature.

"What do you think?" the tattooed guy asked, waving at the cubicles. "Quite a setup, huh?"

"What do you do here?" Angel asked.

"Man, we do it all." The guy seemed really proud of his job. "We contract out for telemarketing, offer adult bandwidth that will blow your mind, host websites, and rent you cutting-edge, pay-for-play online games billed directly to your credit card that are the bomb."

Doyle looked around. "I'm looking around here, and I'm thinking maybe two pizzas ain't going to be enough, you know?"

"Man, that's no problem. Not everybody here eats pizza."

A cubicle door on the right opened and a horned Fyarl demon dressed in a lime-green Speedo stepped out. A cordless phone headset clung to the side of the demon's broad head. He wrapped long-taloned fingers around the pencil microphone by his fang-filled mouth. His mottled gray-pink skin glistened in the computer monitor lights. "Hey, Randy, we got any more beef jerky?" he said in English. "I ran out of mill worms." He shook an empty container.

"Aren't you supposed to be working?" Randy pointed to the small camera mounted on top of the computer monitor. At the moment, a rather unlovely view of the Fyarl demon's backside occupied center stage on the monitor. "The client is paying to see your body on the camera."

The Fyarl demon grinned, still holding the pencil

microphone. "The client is seeing my body. She says this is my best side. Want to hear?" He offered the headset.

Randy held his hands up. "No way, man. I'm going to try to eat something later."

"Well, either get some beef jerky out here or I'm going on break in the middle of this phone call." The Fyarl demon stepped back into the cubicle and slammed the door.

Randy looked back at Angel and Doyle. "Performers. They're all prima donnas." Then, as if realizing what the two "pizza guys" had just seen, he shook his head. "Don't let that look fool you. That's Bill. Bill's into special effects in a big, big way. I mean, that horned demon thing? Looks pretty authentic, doesn't it?"

"Very," Angel agreed. Although he'd already seen several large demon-friendly operations in L.A. and expected there would be several more, he was still surprised to see them in action.

Randy continued leading them through the maze of cubicles.

"You want to tell me you were expecting an operation this big?" Doyle whispered.

"No," Angel admitted. "Devin Matthews thought this was a four- or five-man operation, tops."

"Yeah, and I'll bet he didn't mention demons, either."

"No. I'm sure he didn't know about them." Devin

17

Matthews had come across to Angel as a young, intense guy who'd staked everything he had on the company he'd founded. Maurice Welker's theft of the game engine design could ruin him.

"I'm thinking maybe we should just deliver the pizzas and scurry away to make a new plan," Doyle suggested, trying to gaze around nonchalantly. "We're kind of at ground zero for Web-based Demon Central here. *And*, drastically outnumbered."

Angel started to agree, then they were through the cubicle maze. A stairway to the left led up to the second floor. More demons and humans were headed in both directions on the stairs. They barely gave Angel and Doyle cursory glances, but a svelte demon with snakes for hair grinned at Angel enticingly.

"You can put the pizzas in the break room," Randy said, waving toward one of the offices built into the back of the building.

Angel glanced through the window and saw a group of men seated on tables and chairs watching a hockey game on a television hanging from wall mounts.

Doyle set the pizzas on the table, his eyes glued to the screen. "Hey, the Kings are playing. Mind if we sit and watch for a minute? I've got a small wager on the game."

Angel was instantly aware of how he and Doyle

had become the objects of interest to the dozen men and women in the room. The break room was totally dark except for the soft glow of the television. He got a really bad feeling.

"Sure," Randy said. "Pull up a chair and watch the game." He started for the door. "I'll just go get—" Without warning, he sprinted through the door and slammed it shut behind him.

The men and women in the room got to their feet.

"You know," Doyle said quietly, "all of a sudden, I'm thinking maybe I'm not so keen on watching the game." He started backing away.

Angel backed with him, thinking if they could just put the wall to their backs they might have a chance.

Randy reappeared on the other side of the large window overlooking the cubicles in the middle of the warehouse. He slammed both palms against the window repeatedly and roared with laughter. "Come and get it! *Two* pizza guys for the price of one! Who says I don't deliver?" He fisted his hands and cabbage-patched on the other side of the glass.

The faces of the men and women approaching Angel and Doyle morphed, switching to savage, bestial features as their canines elongated. Without a word, the vampires launched themselves at their prey.

CHAPTER TWO

"Hey, Benito, you gonna help out, or are you gonna read comics all night?"

Benito Rodrigo glanced up at his older brother and grinned. "Just a few more pages, Ricardo. I've almost gotten to the end."

Ricardo dipped his mop back into the stained yellow mop bucket he used to clean the convenience store's scarred linoleum floor. He shook his head and wrung the mop out. "I'm gonna have to talk to Mama about me baby-sitting you while she's workin', you know. You're twelve years old, man. Plenty old enough to stay at the apartment by yourself."

Benito ignored his brother's comments. Ricardo was eighteen, barely old enough to work in the convenience store, and already he was acting like a man full-grown. Part of his brother's attitude, Benito knew, came from the way the girls were treating him now. They *oohed* and *aahed* enough to make Benito sick, but Ricardo told him that was because he was twelve. When Benito got to be older, Ricardo said, he'd appreciate such attention from girls. That, Benito thought frequently, would never happen.

"So what are you reading this time, *cabron?*"

Warily, Benito glanced up from where he sat beside the newsstand. Two piles of comics sat beside him. One pile he'd read, and the other pile he still wanted to read. With Ricardo working at the convenience store, he got to read comics free.

He checked the four round mirrors in the corners of the convenience store that let him look around and make sure no one else was in the store. A couple of times, Ricardo had tricked him, got him talking about comic books while Benito's school friends were around. He'd been razzed unmercifully at school the next day after those times. No one else was in the store with them.

"The new issue of *Hellboy*," Benito answered.

"That's the red monkey-looking guy, right?" Ricardo asked. "The one with the stumpy legs and the tail? Goes around fighting demons and stuff with that big glove thing?"

"That's the one," Benito replied.

"You got a shirt with him on it, don't you?"

"Yeah."

"Mama says if Father Carlos catches you wearing that shirt, he gonna make you sweep leaves around the church."

"Father Carlos wouldn't do that." At least, Benito didn't think the old priest would do that. The doorbell rang suddenly as a customer walked in. Benito was grateful for the distraction. It was only eleven twenty-five. Ricardo still had thirty-five minutes till the end of his shift, and if he remained irritable, each one of those minutes could be long and unpleasant.

"Damn," Ricardo enthused quietly.

A girl, Benito thought wearily. He turned the page in the comic and looked up at the mirrors.

It wasn't a girl, though; it was a woman. She was beautiful, like one of the girls in the magazines kept in plastic wrappers behind the counter. Long black hair ran down her shoulders and framed a pale face, but there was no doubting the Castilian ancestry that showed in the smooth planes of her features. Her eyebrows arched over dark eyes. She wore a black dress that hugged her body.

"Can I help you, *señorita?*" Ricardo offered as he slipped in behind the counter.

The woman in black turned to Ricardo and looked at him quietly for a moment. Ricardo smiled.

He's in love again, Benito thought disgustedly. Ricardo was always in love these days. Benito returned his attention to the comic in his lap. He was almost to the good part. Hellboy had already made his way through a creepy underground sewer and was about to face the monster in the pit. That was always the best part about a *Hellboy* comic, getting to see Hellboy and the monster fight.

"No," the woman said in a soft voice. "I just wanted to look."

Her voice sent a cold thrill down Benito's spine and for a moment he thought he was going to throw up.

"Sure," Ricardo said. "Look all you want. Plenty here to look at. Just let me know if there's something I can help you with."

The woman stepped closer to Ricardo, her eyes boring into his. "You're very young."

When he heard the woman speak again, Benito's stomach rolled threateningly once more. This time there was also a painful whistling in his ears. Even as the realization hit him, Benito scooted back into hiding between the newsstand and the video movie rental rack.

The woman reached out to stroke Ricardo's cheek.

Peering around the newsstand, Benito felt his breath lock in the back of his throat. *Get away, Ricardo!* He wanted to scream, but his voice didn't work either. His heart hammered in his chest. He couldn't remember ever having been so afraid.

"Your skin is so smooth," the woman crooned. "Like fresh-made butter."

Trembling, gasping the way he did some nights when his asthma flared up, Benito continued to watch. *Why is she so scary?* He had no idea. The woman wasn't as tall as Ricardo, and he could probably beat her in a fight if it came to that. But her words dragged through Benito's ears like fingernails on a chalkboard.

"Thanks," Ricardo said, stumbling over the word. His face flamed red.

The woman drew her hand back from Ricardo's cheek. "You're a young man, but you're not innocent anymore, are you?"

Ricardo shrugged his big-shot shrug. "I've been around. Why? You lookin' for a date?"

The woman smiled and turned away from him. "No. Youth is a wonderful thing, but innocence—" She sighed. "That is a much more precious thing."

Benito pushed himself against the wall, jamming himself tightly into the space. He wanted to get up and run for the entrance, but the woman stood closer to it than he did and he had the feeling that if he tried to escape she would stop him if she could. He had to wait.

The doorbell jangled again and six teenaged boys dressed in gang colors stepped into the store. One of the gang members caught the woman's eye. He was tall and thin, wearing gold chains, dark sunglasses, and a red hoodie. Gold teeth glinted when he smiled. "What's happenin', hot mama?"

The woman only smiled at him.

The gang member approached her boldly, his hands tucked into the hoodie's pockets. "I was talkin' to you, woman. It ain't polite to ignore a man what's talkin' to you."

"Hey," Ricardo said, his voice cracking. "I don't think she talks. Maybe she don't speak English. Maybe she don't talk at all."

The gang member stepped up to the counter and slammed a hand down. "You know what this is?"

Benito looked at the mirror in the corner behind Ricardo and saw the reflection of red raindrops dripping from a purple ace of hearts.

"I know what that is," Ricardo said.

"Say it, punk," the gang member demanded. "If you know what it is, then you give it a name."

"Bl-bl-bleeding Hearts," Ricardo said, staring hard at the gang tattoo.

The Bleeding Hearts were hardcore gangbangers who worked the neighborhood. Father Carlos had fought against them several times in the past, speaking out against their recruiting from any family that attended the church.

"That's right." The gang member smiled and took his hand back. "We're the Bleeding Hearts, an' I'm Thirteen. That's my lucky number, but it's unlucky for ever'body else. You know what I'm sayin'?"

Ricardo nodded.

Thirteen pulled his other hand from the hoodie,

flashing the chrome 9mm as he pointed it straight at Ricardo. "Empty the till, homes."

The other five gang members spread out. They pulled knives and pistols as well. One of them had a sawed-off shotgun.

"S-s-sure." Ricardo reached for the register with shaking hands.

Benito wrapped his arms around his knees, shaking so badly that he knew they were all going to hear his teeth rattling.

The woman's eyes narrowed as she studied the gang leader. "There isn't anything innocent about you," she told Thirteen. "How disappointing." She sighed, and immediately a chill ghosted through the room.

"I thought you said she couldn't talk," Thirteen told Ricardo.

"I thought she couldn't," Ricardo said, taking the money from the till with shaking hands.

The woman betrayed him, Benito thought. *The way evil women always betray heroes in the stories.* The thing that surprised him was that he'd never thought of Ricardo as a hero before.

"You know her?" Thirteen demanded.

"No. S-s-she just come in tonight."

The doorbell rang again and Benito glanced at the door like everyone else did. Officer Manny Hernandez stepped into the convenience store in his uniform. Officer Manny was from the neighborhood and had only made it into the Los Angeles Police Department a few months ago. Officer Manny was in his early twenties, a real man's age and not eighteen like Ricardo. Before he'd become Officer Manny, he'd been a basketball coach at the church. Most nights he checked in on Ricardo at the store before going on into work.

"Cop!" one of the gang members yelled. All of them spread out, taking cover in the aisles behind shelves filled with potato chips, canned goods, motor oil, and condiments.

Officer Manny drew his weapon and shouted, "Police!" just the way cops did in the comics Benito read for free at the store.

Thirteen uncoiled like a striking snake, throwing himself at the woman in black. The gang leader grabbed her by the hair with his empty hand and slid behind her.

Ricardo moved, although Benito never knew why he did, reaching out for Thirteen. The gang member pulled the woman to him, using her as a shield, and pointed the pistol at Ricardo and fired.

The 9mm round knocked Ricardo down behind the counter, filling the convenience store with the sound of breaking glass. Swallowing the scream that swelled up in his throat as tears filled his eyes, Benito almost pushed himself up, afraid that Ricardo had been killed. Then the woman began to laugh.

Her laughter overrode everything else in the convenience store, even drowned out the screaming siren of the ambulance that raced by on the street outside. The flashing red and blue lights reflected against the glass over the coolers and strobed through all four mirrors in the ceiling corners of the room.

Benito put his hands over his ears, but even that didn't stop the sound of the dreadful laughter. He knew then that the worst was yet to come.

Standing in the small lobby of the playhouse, Cordelia Chase gazed out at the parking lot through the windows. The banner proclaiming OPENING NIGHT tapped steadily against the glass above her line of sight.

She checked her reflection in the glass. She'd had her dark hair done late that afternoon, just in time for the play tonight. She'd also had her nails done. The red dress—to be worn before and after the performance—was new as well. It clung to her and had drawn more than a few glances from Doyle back at the office. Cordelia still wasn't sure how she was supposed to feel about that. *Doyle is a good—well, okay—friend, but guy material? Not hardly*. Doyle did have pretty eyes, but she was certain it was the color that attracted—*ewww*, no!—drew, *now that's the word*, her attention. The dress and nail appointments were unexpected bonuses from Angel that morning. *Even though vampires have dead hearts,*

they kind of understand the things a woman needs.
Who knew?

"Doesn't look like your guy is going to make it."

Irritably, Cordelia turned to face the speaker.

Jo Dean Hamilton peered through the window and folded her arms over her breasts. She was tall and lithe, a dancer at one of the upscale bars nearby who made good tips but wanted to be an actress. She wore her blond hair cropped short and had a heart-shaped face.

"He's not my guy," Cordelia corrected sharply. *If Angel's anybody's guy, he's Buffy's.* "And obviously you've got me confused with Watch-and-Wait-Frantically Girl, who would look out the window waiting for a guy to show up. Nope. Gave that up with sitting by the phone on Friday nights."

Jo Dean shot her an apologetic look. "Sorry. Didn't mean to scrape a nerve there."

"You didn't," Cordelia assured her, not to be polite, but to let Jo Dean know no one scored on Cordelia Chase that easily. "I was hoping to see my boss. That's not like pathetic guy-waiting. He promised he would be here if he could get away." *And in the business Angel's doing, you always have to wonder what he's getting away from.*

Two other female cast members walked up. Both of them were brunette, naturally perky and cute.

Cordelia despised perky and cute—except when they were being used as weapons. Under the right circumstances, say when she needed to get close enough to a vampire to kebob his heart, she could be as perky and cute as anyone. Tonight she didn't feel perky and cute. Checking out her reflection again, she decided, however, that she had definitely nailed devastatingly gorgeous.

"Fifteen minutes till showtime," Nikki said. "Aren't you excited?" She wiggled a little to show how excited she was.

Get a grip, Cordelia thought, watching the woman. *If a director were casting for 101 Nervous Pomeranians, you'd get the lead role.* The wiggle got even more pronounced whenever Nikki talked to the production staff or anyone who might be anyone.

"Hey, Cordy," Daphne asked, "is your friend going to be here?"

"Which friend?" Cordelia asked deliberately, letting Daphne know she didn't just have one friend in L.A. *After all, there's Angel and Doyle.*

"The tall, good-looking friend," Daphne said.

Oh, Angel. "Maybe later," Cordelia replied.

"Angelo is a private eye, isn't he?" Nikki asked. She leaned into the window and primped at her hair.

"Angel," Cordelia corrected. "And he's a private investigator."

"Eye, investigator." Nikki shrugged. "It's all the same thing."

"Not once you know the business," Cordelia said. "A private investigator is like, uh, really trained and stuff. Like in clue detecting and gathering. Twenty Questions. That kind of thing."

"I think private detectives are so intriguing," Daphne said. "Batman was always my favorite."

"Are you his secretary?" Nikki asked, still playing with her hair.

Cordelia hesitated for a moment. "No. I'm his partner." *Wow! Instant job promotion.*

"Really?" Nikki asked in apparent disbelief.

"Look," Nikki said to Daphne, "we'd better get back to the stage. If Erwin finds out none of us are where we're supposed to be, he'll have a coronary."

"Maybe it would improve his sense of humor," Cordelia suggested. "And who knows? After Erwin's dead this play could be really important."

Daphne and Nikki shot Cordelia confused glances and wandered back to the small stage area. A few more small groups drifted into the building and entered the small theater.

Jo Dean looked at Cordelia, her eyebrows knitted together pensively. "Is it true about you being a private investigator's partner?"

Cordelia dug in her purse and brought out one of the business cards she'd designed. She passed it over to Jo Dean. "Angel Investigations. We help the helpless. That's our motto. I made it up."

Cautiously, Jo Dean took the card and read it.

"Are you in some kind of trouble?" Cordelia asked.

Jo Dean started to shake her head.

"The only reason I ask," Cordelia told her, "is because I know the look."

"You do?"

Nodding, Cordelia confided, "Lots of experience." Everybody who came through the door of Angel Investigations wore that look.

"You didn't seem to notice earlier this week." Jo Dean's tone was almost playful, as if she were joking.

Cordelia looked at the woman. "I noticed the bruises on your right arm last Tuesday, *and* the trouble you had walking a couple days after that. I even noticed the way you put your makeup on a little more heavily. Don't mistake me not saying anything for me not being aware that something was going on."

Taking a step away, Jo Dean broke eye contact. "Maybe this was a mistake. I shouldn't have said anything."

"The mistake's already been made," Cordelia said. "And it was *his,* not yours."

Tears glimmered in Jo Dean's eyes. "This is stupid. I'll work it out with him." She turned to go.

"Jo Dean," Cordelia said. Then added, "Please."

The woman halted and put one hand over her face, her back to Cordelia as her shoulders shook slightly.

"One thing I learned a little about before I came here," Cordelia said, "and learned more about since I've been working with Angel, is that you can't help someone unless they ask for it and they're ready to take it."

Jo Dean was quiet for a time, then her shoulders gradually relaxed. She turned back to Cordelia with red-rimmed eyes. "I think I need help."

"We'll get you some help," Cordelia promised. *Where is Angel?*

CHAPTER THREE

As the first of the vampires launched into the air, Angel threw his arms out and twisted his wrists. Spring-loaded holsters shot wooden stakes out into his waiting hands. Angel struck without mercy, throwing the attack back into the face of the vampires.

The vampire in the air saw the stake coming but never had the chance to do anything about it. His eyes widened as Angel slammed one of the stakes through his dead heart. Immediately, the vampire turned to dust and rained down over Angel.

Doyle backed away, but not quickly enough. Two vampires landed on top of him and knocked him to the floor. They rolled on top of him and tried to lock him down as he punched and kicked.

Outside the large break room window, Randy continued slapping his hands on the glass and manically cheering the vampires on.

Angel shifted, dropping into a martial arts kata, centering his weight. He drove a snap kick into the face of the vampire in front of him and broke off a fang. The vampire reeled back into two more behind him, taking them all down on one of the conference tables. The table held for just a moment, then collapsed.

Still moving, Angel spun and threw the stake in his right hand. The stake only flipped once, then buried in the back of the vampire lying on top of Doyle. Once the wood pierced the vampire's heart, he turned to dust, pouring down over Doyle.

Doyle brought a knee up, driving it into the other vampire's rib cage with bone-breaking force. The vampire yelled in pain and rage, turning loose the half-demon's head for just a moment. Scrabbling in the now-vanishing dust of the other vampire, Doyle managed to pull out a stake he carried inside his jacket. He fisted it and attacked. The stake slid through the vampire's ribs and into his heart. He scrambled to his feet as the creature dusted over him.

Angel moved in a flurry of action, ripping the pointed end of his second stake across the vampire's face in front of him. Dark ichor welled up in the deep furrow that carved one cheek and across his nose.

"Get him!" one of the vampires yelled from the back of the crowd.

"Doyle," Angel called.

Doyle cursed. "Trust me, man, I'm not going to hold anything back here."

Instead of trying to hold his position, Angel morphed into full vampire mode and took the fight to his aggressors, using their numbers within the small room against them. His opponents sometimes got in Angel's way but he managed to strike one of them with every blow.

"He ain't human!" someone yelled.

A vampire lashed out with a roundhouse kick at Angel's head. Angel ducked beneath the kick, sweeping the vampire's foot forward faster with his empty hand. His opponent spun off-balance, tripping the small knot of vampires behind him. Angel charged into the gap and thrust the stake through the heart of the vampire on the right. Even as that vampire turned to dust, Angel whirled again, reversing the stake and shoving it through the next vampire's heart. While the other vampires retreated, totally blown away by the violence that had erupted from what they had considered easy prey, Angel knelt and staked the vampire that had fallen at his feet.

"He's that vampire we been hearin' about!" someone said. "The new guy in town that's killin' vampires!"

Angel rose, feeling the demon inside him feeding on the fear that most of the vampires around him exhibited now. The fear was warm and fuzzy, intoxicating. It was a feeling that a vampire could get used to. Angel could still remember the time that he'd lived for that feeling. And he could still remember the faces of the innocents he had killed and turned and done even worse to. The man that he was now took no satisfaction in those memories, but the demon writhed inside him, craving more.

"Well, he stops his killin' tonight!" a deep voice roared.

The crowd of vampires parted before Angel and a big man in scuffed, black biker leathers strode forward. His black hair hung to his shoulders in greasy dreadlocks. Hazel eyes tinted with orange lights stood out boldly from his demonic face. Scars marred the milk chocolate skin and piercings stood out at his eyebrows, nose, and cheeks. Jeweled rings glittered on the demon's hands. He stood a head taller than Angel and carried a short staff with a double-edged twelve-inch blade at either end.

"You know me?" the big man demanded. He moved the staff in front of him with deadly speed, whipping it across his body. The blades spun and gleamed.

"I know what you are," Angel said, standing his ground. "Torkoth demon."

The demon smiled. "That's right. There's not a more warlike demon race that's ever existed."

Angel was conscious of the vampires drawing

back. He heard Doyle panting behind him, but there weren't any violent expulsions of breath, indicating that Doyle wasn't currently engaged with an opponent.

Randy hooted on the other side of the big window. A glance at the window showed Angel that a larger crowd had collected.

"You know, I don't mind telling you," Doyle said, wiping blood from his face, "that I can remember being in some situations that never looked quite as dark as this one."

Angel looked back at the Torkoth demon and shrugged. "I don't know. I've been up against some pretty bad demons in the past." He smiled slightly. "I'm still here."

"My name's Darrel," the demon said. "It's going to be my pleasure to kill you."

"Darrel?" Doyle asked. "Darrel the Demon? Well hell, man, no wonder you got such a chip on your shoulder."

"Hey," Darrel said, obviously sensitive, "my name wasn't exactly my choice."

Doyle tried to keep his face straight. "You know, you're right. You ask everybody here, I'm probably the last guy should make fun of somebody's name."

"Don't worry about it," Darrel told him. He turned back to the vampires. "Nobody touch the runt. I got dibs on him—after I finish off his buddy." He glared at Doyle. "Last man I ever took my time to kill lasted forty-three days. You're going to be my new record."

"And you're thinking you've got a lock on this thing?" Doyle asked.

Darrel turned his attention back to Angel. The staff whirled in his hands like a perpetual motion machine. "Know what the rings on my hands are?"

"Soul gems," Angel said. He'd read about them, and even seen them a couple times.

"That's right," Darrel agreed. "I capture the souls of warriors I defeat in battle and put them into the rings. Person that has one of these rings can talk to the souls, borrow strength and skills, take money and things they've hidden away." He stopped the staff long enough to hold out a hand and showed the rings that covered all four fingers and his thumb. "I only keep the best of the lot. Sell the others for cash—a lot of it. You wouldn't believe what collectors will pay for one of these."

"Wouldn't be interested," Angel said.

"The stories I hear, you got your soul back somehow," Darrel said, smiling again. "Now a vampire's soul, that's something you don't see every day. You gotta wonder how much a collector would pay for something like that." He smiled and started spinning the staff again. "And I'll get to know all your secrets." He paused. "Maybe I'll look up some of your old friends, let you watch me slit their throats."

Angel steeled himself and didn't let the taunt

touch him. Once a soul was trapped in a Torkoth demon's ring, there were no more secrets. The demon would find out about Buffy. He shrugged out of the trenchcoat but kept his stake.

"You put that much faith in your toothpick?" Darrel asked.

"No," Angel said, "but it's what I've got." He watched the demon, spotting the slight shift of his opponent's left foot that announced the imminent charge.

The Torkoth demon came at Angel, the blades scything through the air, then darting out suddenly at Angel's neck. Angel threw up his right hand in a cross-body block, catching the shaft just behind the blade. Pain shot up Angel's arm, but he stopped the staff. Before he could move again, Darrel kicked him in the chest and knocked him off his feet.

Angel sailed backward and crashed into the wall. He pushed up at once and flipped over the staff as the Torkoth demon thrust it at him. The pointed staff blade dug into the side of the wall at the same time that Angel landed beside his opponent and slashed at the demon backhanded with the stake. The wooden tip gouged flesh from the demon's chin, leaving a flap hanging in its wake. Green blood dripped to Darrel's chest and he roared in pain.

Jerking the staff from the wall, the demon spun the blades again, backing away. "You're going to pay for that, bloodsucker." The staff whirled faster.

"Now far be it for me to interrupt your game plan there," Doyle said, standing with his back to a nearby wall on the other side of the room from the vampires, "but I'm thinking we're up to our eyeballs in hangers-on."

From the corner of his eye, Angel saw the men and women—human, demon, and vampire—gathered at the window. He didn't think about that at the moment, focusing on the big demon. The blade came at Angel's neck with all of the Torkoth demon's weight behind it.

Angel turned slightly, the razor-edge missing his throat by less than an inch. Leading with his left foot, he brought his empty right hand in against his chest and blocked Darrel's attempt to bring the staff crashing back into him. Angel slid up the staff quickly, torqued his body, then drove the stake in his left fist into the demon like a boxer unloading a short jab.

The stake buried in the demon's side till it reached his ribs. The torn muscles contracted immediately and tore the stake from Angel's grip. Without hesitation, Angel bunched his fist and slammed it into the demon's face, driving his opponent back a step with every blow. The demon's face mangled and pulped, and a part of Angel glowed in satisfaction.

Before the crowd of vampires in the room had realized the tide of the attack had truly turned, Angel gripped the staff with both hands and drove a foot of steel into the demon's heart. Darrel fell to his knees, a curse on his lips, and gazed up at Angel with hatred. Then the demon's eyes dimmed and his desperate hold on the staff went slack.

Struggling to control the bloodlust that fueled him now, Angel ripped the staff from the dead demon's chest. He twirled the staff in his hands, getting the heft and the balance of the weapon in a heartbeat.

"Get him!" one of the vampires roared.

Angel became a living scythe and death incarnate. He lopped off heads, which killed the vampires, and body parts, which slowed them down, then drove the blades at either end of the staff so far through their hearts that the wood pierced their hearts as well. A dust storm swelled inside the room and created a haze.

But even as he cut down the vampires' numbers, Angel knew they were seriously outmatched. Stepping back, he yelled to Doyle. "Smash the demon's rings."

"What?" Doyle pushed one of the vampires that had attacked him into the path of Angel's waiting staff.

"The rings." Angel speared the vampire through the heart with the staff. "Get the demon's rings." The vampire froze in shock, then turned to dust. "Smash them. Release the souls inside."

Quickly, Doyle knelt by the slain demon and pulled the rings from the corpse's fingers. He looked at the rings. "Okay, and how exactly am I supposed to smash them?"

Conscious of the group waiting with Randy on the other side of the big window, Angel stepped toward Doyle. He seized a ring set with a glittering emerald and threw it at the window.

The ring sailed through the air like a bullet. When the heavy gold band struck the window, glass shattered, leaving the ring trapped in the window. However, enough damage had been done to crack the precious stone as well. The soul trapped inside the gem poured out in a silvery rush, switching from a gaseous cloud to a primitive warrior dressed in ragged animal skins, wearing a beard down to his chest and carrying a stone ax. He blinked for a moment, then looked at Angel.

"Them," Angel said, pointing at the group nearest the warrior.

Without hesitation, the bearded warrior raised his stone ax and attacked. Bones shattered and brain matter flew.

"Hurry," Angel told Doyle. "When a soul is released from a Torkoth's gem, it has a thirst for vengeance. But that distraction only lasts for a few minutes."

In quick succession, Doyle smashed the remaining rings by throwing them against the walls and floor. Silvery souls drifted up from the rings. Most of them were ancient warriors, but there was a French swordsman with a plumed hat and a khaki-clad British explorer carrying an elephant gun in the mix as well. Only a few were human, and three of them were female. All of them stood momentarily confused.

"Instant army," Doyle said, smiling. "Gotta remember about them soul gems."

"Once the souls are freed," Angel said, "they want revenge on the person that trapped them. If they can't find that person, they'll turn on anyone else around them."

Doyle looked at the group and took a quick step back. "Oh."

Sparing the next vampire he confronted, Angel grabbed his opponent by the shirtfront and threw him toward the window. When the man hit the window, glass shattered, completing the mass exodus to get away from the warrior swinging his bloody stone ax and roaring like a tiger.

Angel charged through the empty window. "Let's go," he ordered his ragtag army. Although trapped in the rings, they'd maintained a transient association with the rest of the world. They had a limited knowledge of what was going on. Angel banked on the fact that they would remember he'd killed Darrel the demon so they could be freed.

The vampire that had broken through the window had also bowled Randy over.

A quick figure-eight with the staff decapitated two demons, then a sudden shove put it through the heart of the vampire Angel had flung through the window. Aware of the carnage the freed souls were causing throughout the warehouse, Angel turned his attention to Randy. He grabbed the man by the shirt collar and lifted him from the ground.

"Now," Angel growled, still in vamp-face, "now we talk, Randy."

The man cowered in fear, holding his hands up in front of his face. "Sure, man, sure! Whatever you say! Just don't eat me!"

Angel smiled coldly, then morphed his face back to human.

Doyle joined them, carrying a double-bladed short-hafted battleax he'd evidently picked up somewhere along the way.

"I want to find Maurice Welker," Angel said.

Randy stared at him for a moment, grimly aware that Angel still held him up off the floor. "Okay. He's in the back."

Angel glanced over his shoulder. The vengeful spirits still ran rampant through the warehouse. He pushed Randy ahead of him. "Let's go."

Hands over his ears to shut out the woman in black's horrible laughter, Benito Rodrigo pushed against the wall at his back. *Ricardo! Thirteen shot Ricardo! What's Mama gonna say!*

Thirteen stood partially in Benito's view. The gang leader still held the woman in front of him. "Shut up!" Thirteen growled. "What you laughing at, woman?"

"I'm just watching you play," the woman said.

"Play?" Thirteen looked offended. "You better watch what you sayin'. I go upside your head with the butt of this nine."

The woman turned effortlessly in Thirteen's arms. "I think I'd surprise you."

"Thirteen," Officer Manny said loudly. "You shot that boy behind the counter."

"That fool made a move on me," Thirteen replied.

"I don't think he's dead, Thirteen," Officer Manny said. "I've called for backup. This place is going to be crawling with police officers in less than a minute."

"You just killed a lot of people by doin' that."

"If the boy behind the counter dies—"

No! Benito thought, looking back at the counter. *Ricardo can't die!*

"—you're facing murder one," Office Manny said. "Maybe I can help him."

Thirteen was silent for a moment. His face knotted with indecision, and Benito knew then that the gang leader was as scared as anyone in the room. Thirteen checked the mirrors, too. "You go on and tend to him."

"Throw out your weapons," Officer Manny said.

"No." Thirteen glanced at one of the other gang members and nodded toward the back of the convenience store. The gang member Thirteen singled out slid back down the aisle and disappeared from Benito's view.

"You have to throw out your weapons," Officer Manny insisted.

"If you can save that peckerhead," Thirteen said, "you gotta do it. Otherwise, if he dies it's gonna be on your head. Gonna be you that kills him, not me."

Unable to sit back anymore, Benito sprang from cover and raced toward the counter. He had to do something for Ricardo. He had to know if his brother was even still alive. *Oh God, what if Ricardo is dead? Don't let him be dead!*

Officer Manny reached for Benito as he raced by, managing to hook his fingers in Benito's waistband. "Wait."

But Benito couldn't wait. He couldn't break Officer Manny's grip either, but his speed and weight did pull the officer from hiding and send them both sprawling across the open floor.

Instantly, Thirteen yelled, "Cap them!" He stood up from hiding, leveling his pistol. The other Bleeding Hearts members stood as well.

Lying facedown on the cold tile floor still lemon-scented from the soap Ricardo had been using, Benito knew he wasn't going home that night.

Officer Manny flailed for his weapon, which he had dropped in the unexpected tumble.

Before any of the Bleeding Hearts gang members could fire their weapons, the woman in black swept free of Thirteen's hold. "No!" she screamed in fiery anger. "You will not harm that boy! I will not allow it!"

"Fine," Thirteen said, "then you gonna die with him!" He thrust his weapon at her and fired, squeezing off rounds as fast as he could.

The convenience stored trapped the rolling sound of the detonations. Benito covered his head and prayed the way Father Oliveria had taught him. He wished he could close his eyes, but he stared at the woman in black hypnotically. Despite everything going on around him, despite the bullets flying through the air and the tile that shattered in front of his face, she still seemed the most fearsome thing in the convenience store.

Gale-force winds like the ones Benito had seen on the Discovery Channel blew up from nowhere. Electrical sparks suddenly leaped from light fixture to light fixture, shorting them out. Even as that set of lights failed, the battery-powered emergency lights over the entrance and under the four mirrors flared to life.

"*You will not harm my child!*" the woman shouted. The wind whipped at her clothing and pulled her hair loose in a flying mass. Then the woman was moving, fast as the Tasmanian Devil in a Bugs Bunny cartoon. She whirled and the wind pushed against Benito so hard he thought it was going to lift him from the cool tile floor.

Suddenly, the woman in black was among the gang members, twirling madly. Her long-nailed fingers flicked out.

At first Benito didn't know what the woman was doing, but then he saw that she was reaching inside the gang members' heads. Her finger glowed where it touched their foreheads, then it sank all the way to the first knuckle. When she drew her hand back, the gang members fell bonelessly.

Thirteen fired his pistol till it was empty. Bullets missed or passed through the woman in black and smashed into the chillers at the back of the store as she circled around to the gang leader. Carbonated beverages spewed caramel-colored foam all over the interior of the chillers.

"Stay away from me!" Thirteen yelled. He cursed frantically as he backed away.

"You would have killed my boy," the woman in black accused. Her forefinger stabbed deeply into the gang leader's left eye, sinking to the first knuckle. Thirteen struggled against her but couldn't manage to get free or to hit her. She lifted the struggling teen at the end of her finger effortlessly, holding him inches above the floor.

"Now," the woman said, "you die."

Benito watched in horror as Thirteen shriveled up like someone had hooked up a vacuum cleaner to his insides. In seconds, the Bleeding Hearts gang leader looked like one of the dried jalapeño peppers Benito's mother hung up around the apartment at Christmas.

The woman stepped back and her mocking laughter pealed again, filling the convenience store.

Benito found his legs and pushed against the floor.

The woman turned and unearthly red lights filled her eyes as she tracked Benito like a hawk. "Where are you going, my child?"

Heart hammering, Benito raced around the end of the counter and dropped to his knees by Ricardo. "Oh God, oh God, oh God!"

Ricardo lay on his back behind the counter, one leg doubled up behind him. Blood covered the front of Ricardo's shirt, but he was still breathing. Benito took his brother's hand. Ricardo's hand felt like ice and held no strength. "C'mon, Ricardo, stay alive. What are me and Mama gonna do if something happens to you?"

"Stay back," Officer Manny yelled.

Fearfully, certain he knew what was happening, Benito glanced up at the mirrors, spotting the woman in black at once. The wind still whipped through the convenience store and her dress and hair whipped with it. At first, Benito had hoped that the woman was going toward Officer Manny—although he felt a little guilty about that, but he saw now that she was headed straight for him, coming around to the end of the counter.

"Stay back!" Officer Manny got to his feet. He held his pistol in both hands before him like the police were supposed to do, not like the one-handed grip Thirteen and the Bleeding Hearts had used.

The heart! Benito thought wildly. *You're going to have to shoot her in the heart!*

"Come to me, child," the woman called in that soft, soothing voice. Her black eyes held Benito's.

Music tinkled in Benito's ears. Before he knew it, his legs quivered under him and he started to push himself to his feet. He moved toward her.

Ricardo's hand twitched in Benito's, then tightened, holding him back.

The spell broken, Benito gazed back down at his brother. "Ricardo!"

The older boy tried to speak, but blood trickled from the corner of his mouth. He shook his head weakly. His grip on Benito's hand was no stronger than old *Señora* Chavez's.

"My child," the woman called again.

Unable to stop himself, Benito looked back at her. Tears gleamed in her black eyes. Even as he watched, the tears spilled down the woman's cheeks.

Her mouth quivered spasmodically and grief

filled her face. "*Mi niño,*" she cried out. She held her arms out to Benito.

"No," Ricardo gasped hoarsely. He closed his hand more tightly around his little brother's. "*No!*"

But Benito knew he had no choice. The woman's call was too strong. Benito moved toward her, slipping free of Ricardo's hold on him. In two steps, Benito found tears in his eyes as well and they slid coolly across his hot cheeks as the wind pushed at him.

"Back away from the boy," Officer Manny said again. "*Señora,* I will shoot." He crossed the floor and grabbed Benito by the shoulder. "Stay with me, Benito. Stay with me."

Benito watched Officer Manny step in front of him as if everything happening was a dream. Officer Manny pointed his pistol point-blank at the madwoman's face. His arms shook.

The madwoman screeched in agony, then whipped a hand out, raking Officer Manny's face with her fingernails. The impact lifted him from his feet and knocked him into shelves of chips and picnic supplies.

Benito was hardly aware of the crash Officer Manny made as he tumbled to the floor. The madwoman's arms wrapped around Benito and it felt like a small electrical current raced through him. Her tears sizzled like acid against his skin as she embraced him.

"Benito!" Ricardo called weakly.

For a moment, Benito remembered that his brother had been shot and needed help badly.

"*Mi niño*," the madwoman said as she cried. She smoothed at his hair with a rough hand. "It has been so long since I last saw you." Despite her tears, the woman smiled gently, but the insanity never left her black eyes. "I never meant to hurt you. But love, you will understand as you grow older, love makes you crazy. I was crazy for a time, Benito, but no more. Now I am found, and I have found you."

Benito reached for her, unable to resist the warmth and security he now sensed that filled her. She had saved him from the Bleeding Hearts gang members, hadn't she? And she loved him. He embraced her, holding her tight.

Then a cold spear tore through Benito's heart and stole his breath away. Fear filled him instantly and he struggled to get away, struggled to breathe again.

"No," the madwoman said softly as she held him to her with that incredible strength, "you must not go. I need you."

Blackness filled Benito's mind.

CHAPTER FOUR

Angel followed Randy down the hallway. Behind him, he heard the vicious noise of the freed souls still wreaking havoc. Something blew up with an electric *bamf!* of detonation. "What's in the back rooms?" Angel asked.

Randy shrugged. "Computer equipment. Stuff like that."

"Sounds like the place I'm looking for." Angel spotted the door at the end of the hallway. The small offices on either side of the hallway were filled with trash and broken office furniture. Evidently only a few of the offices had been cleaned out for use.

"Welker will kill me if he finds out I brought you to him," Randy said.

"You think maybe I won't?"

Randy looked at him. "No. I don't think that."

"Good. Keep moving." Angel watched the doorway open at the end of the hall. A shaggy head poked out briefly, glancing at Angel, Doyle, and Randy, then moved on to survey the carnage in the warehouse.

At the same time Randy twisted, lunging at Angel with a switchblade knife. The knife slid deeply between Angel's ribs. Despite being a vampire, Angel still felt pain. He gripped the switchblade handle firmly and yanked it out. Grabbing the blade with his other hand, he snapped it off and threw the pieces to the floor.

Randy cursed in surprise and fear and tried to backpedal away.

Angel grabbed Randy, knocked him from his feet with a leg-sweep, and lifted him. Swinging his body, Angel threw the man at the door just as it banged shut. Randy slammed into the door, splintering wood and ripping the hinges from the jamb.

Moving faster than anything human that might have been inside, Angel entered the room, striding over Randy, the broken door, and the vampire beneath. Angel swept the room at a glance.

"Who the hell are you?" a tall, lanky man wearing a Britney Spears concert T-shirt asked. His stringy black hair hung down in front of his eyes and a curly goatee hid most of his mouth but blunted some of the effect of his hatchet face.

"Maurice Welker," Angel said, ignoring the question.

"I don't know you."

"That's okay. I know you. Devin Matthews sent me to get his software back."

Welker shook his head and grinned. "Don't know who you think you are, Klondike, but you aren't even going to leave this room alive."

"That's okay," Angel said, "I didn't exactly walk into the room in that condition." He reached for a jagged piece of wood at his feet. When the door had splintered, it had left shards scattered about the room. The piece Angel picked up was less than three feet long. The vampire still lying beneath Randy and the broken door reached out for Angel's foot. Before the vampire could close his hands around Angel's ankle, Angel staked him.

The vampire turned to dust. No longer held up by a body, the door and Randy dropped to the floor. Randy remained unconscious.

Welker waved to the other men and the woman backing him. The game designer morphed, taking on his vampire features. "Devin shouldn't have ever sent you. We get through with you, I'm going to have to pay old Devin a call. Should have killed him before I went into hiding."

Angel circled the room, stepping toward the wall to his left so none of the vampires could easily get behind him. Doyle took up another piece of wood and joined him.

A fat man wearing a yellow and white Hawaiian

shirt with parrots on it charged Angel, obviously not expecting Angel to be able to meet his superhuman speed.

Angel drew himself into an en garde position automatically. He'd spent a few lifetimes behind a blade in different cities in Europe and in taking part in one war or another. Before the fat vampire could break off the attack, Angel skewered him through the heart and he turned to dust.

"Way I figure it," Doyle said, glancing at the disappearing dust, "we're a Dustbuster short of really cleaning house with you guys." He brandished the wood he'd picked up before.

The vampires attacked en masse, rushing at Angel and Doyle and hoping to beat them down with sheer numbers. Hatred mixed with bloodlust in their eyes.

Angel thrust the broken piece of wood at the first demon, who managed to block it, breaking off the first foot of it. Moving swiftly, Angel countered the charge with a palm-heel strike that drove the vampire's nose up into his brain. His face turned into a bloody mask. The blow would have killed a normal man, but it only caused sudden agony for the vampire. The man stumbled back, holding his hands to his ruined face.

Stepping back, Angel caught the broken piece of wood before it fell. He shoved the biggest piece he held through the heart of the next vampire coming at him and the demon turned to dust. The next vampire smashed into Angel, driving him back against the wall. Angel brought a knee up into the vampire's crotch three times in quick succession, then head-butted the demon in the face, knocking him back. Before the vampire could recover, Angel sheathed the long piece of wood into the vampire's heart.

Doyle fought at Angel's side, barely staying out of reach of a vampire before getting into position to lop the demon's head off with the battleax. He blocked the next attack and waited for the next opening.

Moving forward again, Angel lashed out at the vampire whose nose he'd shattered. The vampire seized the piece of wood as it pierced his heart, managing to yank it from Angel's hand before he turned to dust. Splinters shot through Angel's palm and fingers, bringing instant, fiery pain.

Angel ducked and rammed a shoulder into a vampire wearing a T-shirt that said HONK IF YOU LOVE MUTANTS. Bringing the smaller wooden piece around in a tight arc, Angel slammed it home into the vampire's chest, shattering ribs and driving it through his heart. Even as the dusted vampire fell to the floor, Angel turned to confront Maurice Welker and the two remaining male and female vamps.

Without warning, Welker turned and grabbed the

woman beside him. She was slightly built, hardly more than half his size, with dishwater blond hair that ended at her jawline and a rose tattoo on her left cheek. Showing no remorse, Welker heaved the woman at Angel.

The woman flailed her arms and legs and kicked and screamed as she flew toward Angel.

Angel ducked and let her slam into the wall behind him. Before she could get to her feet, he staked and dusted her. By that time Welker was running toward the door at the back of the room.

Angel glanced at Doyle. "Take out the computers," Angel ordered. He ran after Welker.

The back door led out into a short hallway with another door at the end. Angel caught the door just before it closed and ran through. Another small delivery warehouse occupied that side of the vacant building. Broken pallets, cardboard boxes, and rats tumbling across concrete rubble barely made a dent in the warehouse's emptiness. Running feet echoed in the warehouse, sounding as sharp and as distinctive as gunshots.

Taking advantage of the precious lead he'd gotten, Welker reached the big cargo door and pushed it up. Metal screeched as the door's wheels ratcheted up the rails.

A small concrete loading dock extended out about twelve feet from the cargo door, four feet above street level. Concrete-filled steel posts that had once been painted caution-yellow with red tips stood up from the street like ground-out cigarette butts, only a foot in front of the loading dock.

Welker vaulted over the steel posts and tried to run, but stumbled in a pothole. Before he could get up again, Angel threw himself from the loading dock and slammed into the vampire from behind, knocking them both to the rough pavement.

Screaming almost incoherently, Welker drew a shiny revolver from his pants waistband. He fired point-blank at Angel, but Angel side-stepped and the bullet caromed off one of the posts in front of the loading dock. Angel fisted the short piece of wood he held and chopped it down against Welker's wrist. Bone snapped and the pistol fell to the pavement.

Welker started to reach for the pistol again, but Angel forearmed him in the throat and knocked him back. Mercilessly, Angel closed on the vampire.

"Wait," Welker said hoarsely.

Angel started to ignore the request. There wasn't anything the vampire could say that would keep him from dusting him. Still, he kept the stake against Welker's chest and didn't shove it through.

Welker blinked rapidly. "I want to trade."

"I don't do trades," Angel replied.

"I'll give you information," Welker promised, "and you let me live."

"What information?"

Welker glanced down at the stake pressed against his chest, then back up at Angel. "Word on the street is that you're against vampires preying on humans."

"You're wasting my time."

"There's a service," Welker went on hurriedly. "We use it. A lot of vampires who don't want to hunt use it."

"What service?"

"They deliver blood. I've got the number in my Palm." Welker moved slowly and took a small computer device from his pants pocket. "I'm going to call up the phone number." He punched buttons and numerals filled the color screen. "See? That's it. You just call that number and those guys bring a blood delivery."

"Where do they get it?"

"I don't know."

Angel thought furiously. His own needs were met through pigs' blood that he bought from a butcher he'd worked out a deal with. Pigs' blood wasn't even close to the real thing and never really took the edge off the demon's hunger that lived within him, but he managed. *Fresh blood only means one thing*, Angel thought. *Fresh victims.* "Who delivers the blood?"

"Vampires and demons," Welker answered.

Angel glanced at the number on the Palm and considered the situation. He didn't like any of it.

"Well?" Welker asked after a moment. "Do we have a deal? I told you about the blood delivery set-up, so I get to live."

"You can't live," Angel said. "You died a few months back when you went missing. I'm just making it official."

Welker's mouth made an *O* of shocked surprise. He started to say something.

Ramming the short stake through the vampire's heart, Angel watched Welker turn to dust. Streetlights glinted against the Palm's acrylic surface as it tumbled from the dust that had been Welker's hands and fell toward the hard pavement. Effortlessly, Angel caught the computer device. He checked the number again, committing it to memory. When he turned back to the warehouse, Angel spotted Doyle walking out onto the loading dock.

"You can scratch them computers," Doyle told him. "They've done and gone to cyber-hell. Not quite the same as staking vampires, but there'll be no resurrectin' them."

Angel nodded, not paying too much attention. He walked toward the alley that led to the street in front of the warehouse. He pressed the button on the Palm that brought up the number again.

Doyle stepped off the dock and dropped to the street. "So—we done here?"

"Not quite." Angel checked the Palm again.

Seven little numbers, and they held so much fear in them. "I found a loose end."

"You'll never guess who's here tonight!"

Drawn by the excitement in Nikki's voice, Cordelia turned to look at the woman.

Nikki, dressed in the black strapless dress the director and leading man had picked out for her to show off her rather considerable assets, stood in the doorway of the small space they'd set up as a dressing room.

Cordelia still hadn't figured Nikki's part out. Her character seemed to be added into the mix of mystery and sitcom. Nikki had no lines at all in the second act, but she'd been written in to hang on to the arm of the leading man as he attempted to pun and solve the murder that had occurred in the first act.

"Who?" one of the other women asked.

As she looked around the dressing room, Cordelia was struck again by the thought that there were far too many other women in the show. *If the director actually paid talent to show up for this, he'd go broke.* As it was, the stage had a really good chance of being more crowded than the chairs for the audience.

The impromptu dressing room contained a dozen secondhand folding chairs from a school sale years ago. The secondhand chairs were the only furniture in the room that had even been around a class.

"Adrian Heath," Nikki said excitedly. She fanned herself breathlessly—just as a true southern belle would, which was what she was portraying in the play.

"Who's Adrian Heath?" another woman asked.

"He's a television producer," Cordelia said, "and a millionaire."

"Right," Nikki said. "Adrian Heath produced *Malibu Mayhem,* the teen show about rich kids forced to take defensive driving classes after being in trouble with the law."

"Right," Daphne chimed in. "Heath also produced *Whose Potty Is This Anyway?,* the teen show about Beverly Hills girls forced to work as babysitters as part of community service handed down by Judge Binder."

"My favorite was *Daring High: The School for Spies,*" someone else said.

"Fine," Cordelia interrupted. "Maybe you all—*we* all—could just get a grip and look at the big picture for a moment."

All the actresses looked at her as if she'd just sprouted a second head.

"Hello," Cordelia said. "Big picture: as in, gee, what's Adrian Heath doing here, of all places?"

"Well," Nikki said archly, "it's obvious he's heard about the show tonight and decided to check it out."

Wrong, Cordelia thought. *If Adrian Heath is a television producer of any level and heard anything at all about this show, this is probably one of the last places he'd be tonight.*

"Right," Daphne said. "Adrian's probably casting for a new show."

And isn't it amazing how quickly you put yourself on a first-name basis? Cordelia turned her attention back to her makeup, glancing at it with a critical eye. If a television producer were in the audience, she definitely needed to be a little more attentive. She let out her breath and tried to calm herself.

At the moment nearly all of her financial support came from working for Angel. And she knew she did a good job for him, too. After all, where else could Angel have gotten a secre—*partner,* she told herself—who could file and bill and talk to helpless people on the phone as well as she could? Still, there was a part of her that knew she didn't want to rely on Angel for long.

She'd always thought she could rely on her parents. She'd figured they'd always be there with support and money and the truths that they were certain she wanted to hear. The IRS problem had blindsided her. She'd even had to work the last few months of high school, and wouldn't have had a prom dress if it hadn't been for Xander's unexpected generosity.

Relying on others was a bad thing to do. And Cordelia was determined not to have to do it. Her family had taught her that. She pushed the dark thoughts from her mind. Angel needed her as a touchstone to his humanity, and to his recent past. They didn't rely on each other, not really. It was a relationship that worked for both of them. Even Doyle had his supportive moments. Of course, he had to be part of Angel's redemption because of the whole vision thingy connection.

Still, if Adrian Heath was in the audience and there was any chance of scoring a part in a new television series, Cordelia was determined that she get that chance. No one deserved it—or needed it—more than she did. She turned her attention back to her makeup while the other women chattered animatedly around her.

Cordelia took in a deep breath and let it out. *You are a good actress. So you've had a little bad luck with commercials. Not everybody does commercials well. But you're a good actress. You're a professional. Well, almost.* Professionalism couldn't be more than two or three parts away. *There are no small parts, only small actresses.* Of course, whoever had said that hadn't seen the cast of thousands Carson Delaware had included in the play. *You are—*

"Cordelia Chase."

Startled, Cordelia turned and glanced at the entrance to the dressing room.

Carson Delaware entered the dressing room in

his period-piece double-breasted pinstripe suit. He was in his late twenties, broad-shouldered and good-looking enough, but he knew it, too, and that really spoiled the whole effect. "Cordelia Chase," Delaware repeated, glancing around the roomful of women. His brow wrinkled in perplexity.

"Here," Cordelia said, standing, not believing that Delaware had somehow forgotten who she was. *Not exactly the confidence-builder you'd hope for before an opening night.*

All heads turned to Cordelia as Delaware walked toward her. The director/playwright/leading man looked at her from head to toe and back again. His brow stayed wrinkled. "Is there something I don't know about you?" he asked.

"There's probably a lot you don't know about me," Cordelia admitted. *Let's start with what I look like, for openers.*

"I just don't see it," Delaware said bluntly.

Cordelia looked down at the tight jeans and crop top she was wearing. "See what?"

"Why Adrian Heath is asking about you."

"He is?" Cordelia was shocked, but quickly tried to recover. All the other actresses were gawking at her now and she didn't want to pass up the opportunity to be the center of attention—the calm, cool, collected center of attention. For a moment, it almost felt like walking through the halls of Sunnydale High. The experience was near intoxicating.

"Yes," Delaware replied, "and I was wondering why."

Me too, Cordelia thought, but she said, "Perhaps you should ask him."

"I thought I would ask you."

"Well," Cordelia said, sweeping her hair off one shoulder with a hand, "there is that *thing.*" *It has to be some*thing, *right?*

"Thing?" Delaware's eyes rose.

"Right," Cordelia said. "The *thing* Adrian and I were talking about."

"And what *thing* would that be?"

"I'm sorry, Mr. Delaware, but I can't go into it." *Mysterious is always good.*

Delaware considered that as the other actresses hung on every word around him. "Opening night is not a good night to invite someone like Adrian Heath to see the play. There are still a lot of bugs we need to work out in the performances, and it takes time to do that. I'd like you to remember that in the future."

"Oh, don't worry about that," Cordelia said in the velvet claw voice that used to send sophomore wannabe fashion plates scurrying for cover, "I can always go out there and ask Adrian to leave and tell him we're really not ready for him tonight."

To his credit, Delaware didn't seem to miss a beat. "That's all right. I'm sure the play will be wonderful. We'll all be wonderful."

"That's us," Cordelia said. "Wonderful."

Delaware turned and walked to the door. "Adrian asked me to give you a message."

Cordelia waited.

"As soon as you're done with your performance in tonight's play, he'd like you to join him in the audience." Delaware turned to gaze at her hopefully. "I'm also expecting a full report on what he thinks of the play."

"Sure," Cordelia agreed. As soon as the director/writer/leading man stepped from the dressing room, the other actresses mobbed her. All of them wanted to know what Adrian Heath was like, how she'd met him, and a thousand other things that Cordelia simply had no answer to or was unwilling to say.

It felt great.

However, the question remained: What did Adrian Heath really want from her?

CHAPTER FIVE

Angel and Doyle sat in the convertible in an alley across the street from the warehouse they'd invaded. Most of the workforce had left the building, but there were enough demon and human bodies left behind to garner a small headline on the morning news or hit the television news channels. *Unless something weirder happens tonight,* Angel amended. It was L.A., after all. His newly adopted city had more than its share of craziness.

He took his cell phone from his trenchcoat pocket and punched in the number from the Palm. The phone rang twice before it was answered.

"Speak," a rough male voice growled.

Speak? Angel hesitated only a moment. "I need a delivery."

"Gimme a name."

"Maurice Welker." Angel listened intently.

"You're not Maurice Welker."

"Maurice had me call," Angel said. "I'm new. Maurice has probably talked about me. You know, the new guy."

"Yeah, yeah, right, right. What do you want?"

"Maurice didn't tell me," Angel said. "I guess you can send the usual."

"The usual, right. One from type A, one from type B, plenty of type O with positive and negative chasers." The guy snickered at his own joke.

Angel turned his head, hearing the music in the background now. The twangy noise couldn't be anything except country-and-western music. *A bar?* Angel wondered. The number he'd dialed could be to a cell phone, which would leave the blood suppliers totally mobile and harder to track. "Maurice said to make sure it was fresh."

"Hey, we're always fresh, new guy. We only pump on demand. You want the delivery at the same place?"

"I guess," Angel said. "At the warehouse, right?"

"Have someone out front to meet us." The phone clicked dead.

Angel punched the phone off.

"Well?" Doyle prompted.

"We wait," Angel said.

Doyle sighed. "You see, now that's the part of your job I really hate. All the waiting. I mean, do you know how *aware* you get of time passing? It's enough to drive you blarney, I'm telling you."

Angel didn't say anything. He'd learned how to wait centuries ago. That was one of the first lessons every predator learned.

The tricky part to pretending to be Adrian Heath's friend, Cordelia decided as she left the dressing room and stage area by a side door, was knowing what he'd look like. She'd seen Heath's picture a couple of times in the trades, but few people really looked the way they did in those posed publicity shots.

However, with an audience of only sixteen—most of them friends of the other actresses Cordelia had met during rehearsals—it got easier.

Adrian Heath sat in the back, sandwiched between two large men who'd given up having necks years ago. Adrian was in his early thirties and dressed in a black Italian suit that also set him apart from the rest of the audience. Instead of a dress shirt, he'd opted for a dark green turtleneck.

"Miss Chase," Adrian invited, sweeping an arm to one of the folding chairs beside him. The bodyguard there quickly moved over two seats.

"Mr. Heath." Cordelia gave him her brightest I'm-ready-to-be-a-star-right-now smile and offered her hand.

"Call me Adrian." Adrian took her hand briefly and offered the chair again.

Cordelia sat.

Adrian sat as well. He was six feet tall with a medium build. He wore his blond hair short and carefully styled. His eyes were hazel-green. A scar along the left side of his chin only added to the ruggedly handsome features.

The small room—Cordelia hadn't ever once thought of it as a theater—filled with light again as the third act began. Silence fell over the audience as Carson Delaware strode onto the stage and stared down at the sheet-draped body in front of a cardboard fireplace with twinkling Christmas lights for embers. The sheet-draped body also had chalk-lines drawn around it.

"That sheet-draped body?" Cordelia whispered, pointing. "That's supposed to be me." Her character had been killed in the second act.

"I know," Adrian whispered back. "I watched you get strangled and shot and stabbed."

"My character wasn't very nice."

"So I gathered. Though I must admit I didn't have a clue about that until you were killed."

"I suggested that Carson make my part a little stronger," Cordelia said defensively. "I don't think the audience really gets the time to understand her motivations."

"Probably not. However, the dismemberment scene isn't something I think I'm going to forget anytime soon."

"One of the other actresses is seeing a guy who does special effects for slasher movies."

"He must be very good at what he does."

"It was the head thing that got you, right?" Cordelia asked.

"Miss Chase—" Adrian said.

"Call me Cordelia. All my friends do."

Adrian smiled graciously. "Thank you, Cordelia. I know you must be wondering why I came here asking for you."

"Yes." Cordelia acted calm. It was more acting than she'd been required to do in Carson Delaware's production of *Dead Men in Plaid Skirts Don't Do Windows*.

"Would you mind if we skipped the rest of the play?"

"You don't want to see it?"

Adrian shook his head. "Not really. It's not going to meander in any direction that I'm really interested in anytime soon."

"That's okay. That's my stunt double up there working. We can go."

One of the bodyguards led the way, talking rapidly into a headset. When Cordelia glanced back during an unexpected lull in the play, she saw Carson Delaware standing center stage and looking like he was going to have a nervous breakdown.

Outside, the air held a chill. Cordelia started to

pull her coat on. Adrian quickly stepped around and helped her.

"Thank you," Cordelia said, feeling really good about the care he showed her.

"You're quite welcome." Streetlights flashed on Adrian's platinum wedding band.

A black limousine glided to a stop in the parking lot. The chauffeur hopped out and opened the door. Cordelia allowed Adrian to shepherd her into the luxurious backseat. Adrian joined her and one of the bodyguards sat up front with the chauffeur while the other sat in the back on the seat across from Cordelia and Adrian.

"So how did you find out about the play?" Cordelia asked as the limousine rolled sedately out into the street.

"I was looking for you," Adrian replied.

"You were?" *Wow!* Cordelia struggled to remain calm. "What made you come looking for me? I mean, I've done a couple of commercials and read for some parts, but I didn't think those were anything you'd be aware of."

"I wasn't aware of them," Adrian admitted.

"You weren't?"

"But I'll want to check them out now that I know about them."

"If you weren't looking for me because I'm an actress," Cordelia said, "then why were you looking for me?"

Adrian reached inside his jacket and took out a business card.

Cordelia glanced at the card, recognizing the angel-like shape on one side that she'd drawn. The phone number was also listed. "Where did you get that?"

"A friend suggested I look into it concerning a problem I have. I tried to reach you at the office earlier. I kept getting the answering machine."

"That's because no one is there." *Duh! Now that was stupid, Cordelia.* She tried to recover. "Because everybody's out on a big case."

Adrian looked at her.

"I'm not there," Cordelia said quickly, "only because the people Angel and Doyle are following know me by sight." She shrugged. "So we agreed that I should probably do the play."

"I see. What kind of case?"

"They're recovering stolen software." Cordelia paused, thinking how that might sound. "I'm not talking about video games off the shelf or something like that. It's software that's probably worth millions of dollars. The FBI might even have to be brought in. And maybe the CIA." *There. That sounds impressive, doesn't it?*

"I didn't know you people handled operations like that," Adrian said.

The limousine churned steadily through the downtown area. Street performers were out on the pedestrian traffic–only streets, and hucksters worked the street corners. Sidewalk cafés and restaurants had dozens of people sitting around cutting deals and trying to impress the hell out of each other.

"That's our motto. No case is too big. Actually, our *second* motto. We help the helpless is our first."

"You may not even be interested in my problem," Adrian said. "It's very pedestrian by comparison."

"We're thinking of adopting a third motto," Cordelia said. "No problem is too pedestrian. That could be an interesting third motto. But more to the point: how can we help you?"

"It's my wife," Adrian said, twisting the ring on his finger. "She's missing."

"If I was a betting man, and I am, I'd say that's got to be them."

Angel quietly agreed with Doyle as they watched the eighteen-wheeler roll through the deserted street in front of the warehouse where Maurice Welker had set up his Internet operations. The flat-black tractor and trailer came to a stop at the curb. Air brakes hissed as it shuddered to a stop.

"There's no name on the truck," Doyle said quietly.

"See if you can read the tag if you get the chance." Angel slid over to the convertible's door. He reached into the backseat and retrieved the morning star, which he'd refitted with wood spikes instead of its usual steel points. He'd also put fresh stakes in his wrist launchers.

"Where are you going?"

"Thought I'd say hello." Angel stepped from the alley. He headed behind the truck, moving into the gray smoke hissing from the air brakes.

The eighteen-wheeler rumbled loudly out on the street and the sound echoed between the buildings. A man opened the passenger door and climbed down.

Taking up a position at the back of the truck, Angel watched as the passenger dropped to the street. The way the guy moved let Angel know at once that he wasn't human. A blood smell also lingered on the truck in spite of the diesel stink.

The driver got out on the other side. "Thought Maurice was going to have someone meet us." He walked toward the back of the truck.

"Was supposed to," the other guy said, yelling over the roar of the truck as well.

"I don't like it when they change things."

"Maurice is a big customer. You don't want to blow him off."

"Go knock on the door. See if Randy's around."

While the passenger from the eighteen-wheeler walked to the front of the building, Angel slid around to the passenger side of the trailer. He bent his knees and leaped straight up, managing to catch the edge of the trailer easily. Without making a sound, he pulled himself to the top of the trailer and stayed low.

The driver opened the double back doors on the trailer and stepped back.

Lying on top of the trailer, Angel felt the cold air inside rush out, even more chill than the night around them. The blood smell grew stronger and Molly Hatchet's "Flirtin' With Disaster" boomed from within.

"Hey," the guy who'd been in the passenger seat called. He banged his fist on the warehouse doors. "Open up! Got a delivery for Maurice."

At that moment, Angel's cell phone rang. Even though it was in his trenchcoat pocket, the sound was loud enough to be heard over the truck's rumbling engine.

The man's eyes widened and Angel knew he'd been overheard. Instantly, wanting to take advantage of whatever surprise remained on his side, Angel caught the edge of the trailer in his free hand and flipped over, landing on his feet just inside the trailer. He stayed focused on the driver but listened to the sudden movement behind him in the trailer as well. Judging from the speed he heard, Angel knew there were vampires in the truck as well.

The driver's face morphed into a vampire's.

Angel struck immediately, burying the morning

star's wooden spikes into the vampire's heart and dusting him. Dodging to one side as footsteps slapped against the metal trailer floor, Angel tripped the vampire that tried to attack him. The vampire fell onto the street, sprawling against the rough pavement with a flesh-shredding impact.

The cell phone continued to ring.

Turning, Angel swept the trailer with his gaze. Humans—males and females of all ages, most of them looking like homeless people—struggled weakly against the arm and leg chains that held them to the trailer walls.

Plastic tubing ran from each of the victims inside the trailer, tapping every person and turning him or her into human blood kegs. Brightly colored tags hung from each victim's neck and it was immediately apparent that the tags were color-coded. Plastic garbage bags partially held and covered drained corpses that were white and dove-gray.

"Don't know who you are, buddy," a big vampire wearing biker leathers snarled, "but you just stepped into a whole lotta T-R-O-U-B-L-E." He grinned maniacally and morphed into his vampire face. He pulled a sawed-off shotgun from motorcycle saddlebags on the trailer floor nearby.

Angel crossed the distance separating him from the vampire at a dead run. He grabbed the shotgun's abbreviated barrels in one hand and swung the morning star with the other. The wooden spikes sank deeply into the vampire's head, eliciting a squalling bleat of enraged pain.

Unable to free the morning star, Angel kept his grip on the shotgun and whirled inside the man's arm. He brought his elbow back in three quick blows that snapped the vampire's head back with each impact. Then Angel grabbed the vampire's arm, dropped to one knee, and pulled hard, levering his opponent over his shoulder. As the vampire fell, he released the hold on the shotgun.

Angel brought the shotgun up in both hands as the big biker vampire rose again. The morning star stuck to the vampire's head like a growth.

The eighteen-wheeler started forward without warning, lurching into movement so fiercely it almost knocked Angel and the biker vampire from their feet. Angel looked past the vampire and saw the street moving behind him.

The biker vampire rushed forward, screaming obscenities.

Angel fired the shotgun's first barrel directly at the big vampire's chest. The detonation hammered the inside of the trailer, drawing frantic cries from the survivors who were strong enough to voice them.

The vampire stumbled backward from the impact, but halted a foot short of the trailer's end. A big grin stretched tight over his fangs.

Angel moved to the second trigger inside the shotgun's guard and squeezed it as well. The double-aught buckshot turned the vampire's smile into a bloody mess and blew him through the trailer's swinging back doors. He hit the street and bounced.

"Look out!" someone wheezed.

Angel turned as another vampire surged from the shadows. Caught by surprise, Angel went back and down, losing the empty shotgun. He triggered the quick-release strapped to his wrist and grabbed the wooden stake that filled his hand. The cell phone rang again as Angel rammed the stake into the vampire's heart.

Forcing himself to his feet despite the motion of the truck hurtling through the deserted streets, Angel set himself aright just as two more vampires rushed from the front of the trailer. Judging from the blood on their hands and faces, they'd been sampling the wares.

Both of the newcomers were dressed in biker leathers as well. One of them swung a sword at Angel's midsection. Angel dodged back out of the way, but didn't completely escape the blade. Fiery agony trailed across his abdomen just below his navel.

The sword-wielding vampire grinned in blood-thirsty enthusiasm. He stepped forward again, feinting.

Pushing the pain from his mind, Angel lifted his other arm and triggered the hidden spring device.

The wooden stake leaped across the distance and embedded in the swordsman's heart. The vampire managed one short, surprised expression before turning to dust. His partner gave Angel no quarter.

"Do you know who you're messin' with, man?" the bearded vampire demanded. His eyes blazed with unholy light. "We're Diablos, man."

The cell phone continued to trill.

The vampire lifted Angel from his feet and flung him down against the trailer bed. The vampire fell on top of Angel with bruising force, then levered a forearm under Angel's chin and forced his head back. Pushing with his knees and toes, the vampire drove Angel back to the end of the trailer so that his head hung over. Then the Diablo vampire rose up and pushed more heavily against the underside of Angel's jaw.

"Gonna break your neck, man," the vampire threatened. "Gonna snap it off and watch you blow away. Nobody steps up onto Diablo territory."

Head hanging over the end of the trailer bed, Angel watched as the vampire he'd blasted with the shotgun got to his feet. The vampire shook his head as if to clear it, then took off in pursuit of the eighteen-wheeler. With his vampire's speed, he was actually closing on the truck.

The big convertible shot from the alley with the lights off, fishtailed for a moment, slid threateningly close to a dimmed streetlight, then straightened out and roared forward as the tires grabbed the pavement.

The cell phone rang again as Doyle drove over the vampire in front of him. The convertible wobbled for a moment, lost traction, then shot forward again, leaving the vampire behind as pothole filler. Maybe the impact and being run down wouldn't kill the vampire, but Angel knew the guy wouldn't feel like jumping back into the fight immediately.

"You got a friend?" the vampire asked Angel. "Guess we'll chill him, too."

"No," Angel grated hoarsely. "You won't." He brought a knee up into the big man's crotch with bone-crunching force. The vampire screamed and loosened his hold. The truck hit a bad patch of street and shook violently, lifting Angel and his attacker inches above the trailer bed and sliding them threateningly toward the edge. Taking advantage of the situation, Angel pulled and pushed the vampire up and over, managing to shove him out the back of the truck.

The vampire dropped across the front of the convertible, skidded for a second, and came to a rest against the windshield.

Doyle's going to be really happy about that, Angel thought. He got to his feet, holding on to the side of the trailer, and glanced back into the shadows. "Are there any more?"

"Not this time," someone answered weakly.

The cell phone rang again.

Only Cordelia has the number, Angel realized. Looking at the people strapped to the walls, he also realized that she might be in trouble. He took the phone out as he watched Doyle take evasive action against the vampire pressed up tight against the convertible's windshield.

Angel punched the TALK button. "Hello."

CHAPTER SIX

"Hello," Cordelia said brightly into the telephone as she accepted a glass of wine from Adrian Heath. "Angel?"

"Yes, Cordelia."

Angel sounded all broody and short-tempered, but Cordelia ignored that. On his good days Angel tended to sound broody and short-tempered, unless he had a case to occupy his attention. *Preferably a case that didn't make him remember something about his past when he'd been Angelus. Of course, you live two hundred and fifty years, like there's going to be something you've never done before, right? Fat chance.*

"Look," Cordelia said, "we need to talk." She was aware of Adrian's constant attention, and she liked the way the guy seemed to hang on her every word.

"We are talking. Are you okay?"

"I'm fine," Cordelia said. *Finer than fine, actually.* But she didn't want Adrian to know that. She acted like dealing with millionaires with missing wives was something she did every day. "I've decided the agency is taking on a case." *One that could pay out extremely well,* she wanted to say but didn't. She would later.

"I'm kind of busy right now."

Cordelia ignored that. Angel always thought he was busy. "We need to meet."

"Cordelia, I'm trying to rescue a truck full of victims from a blood-dealing biker vampire gang. At the moment, the driver is speeding down the street and could end up killing everyone trapped in here. Doyle's fighting a vampire wrapped around his windshield."

Okay, Cordelia thought reluctantly, *those are so not your run-of-the-mill excuses for not talking.* "Call me when you can."

Angel made no reply, just broke the connection.

Cordelia glanced up at Adrian and handed the limo phone back to the bodyguard. "Angel's really busy. Crime-fighting gets really tense sometimes."

"Will he be able to join us?" Adrian asked.

"Sure," Cordelia replied. "He just has to wrap things up out there and said he'd get back with me as soon as he could. He's a conscientious kind of guy."

"I'd heard that once he gets involved with something he tends to stick even when things get . . . messy."

"Nope. Messes don't bother him." Cordelia sipped her wine and glanced at the streets. The limousine was still heading west. "Where are we going?"

"San Pedro," Adrian answered. "You don't think Angel will be too long?"

Remembering the situation Angel had said he was in, Cordelia replied, "No."

"Good. I'm sure Captain Thomsen won't mind holding the yacht."

A *yacht?* Cordelia's heart sped up a little in anticipation. Things were just getting better and better. Maybe her ship *had* come in—finally.

Doyle swerved to the left as the vampire plastered against the convertible's windshield swiped at him over the top. The GTX's tires squealed as they briefly rubbed against the curb. *Now that, that I'm going to hear about. Angel's not going to care for that at all.*

"C'mere, skinny," the vampire growled. He flailed at the half-demon again.

Then again, Doyle amended, *there's always the possibility that I won't survive the little party favor Angel dropped on me.* He swerved to the right this time. The vampire slid a precious few inches but didn't even come close to sliding off the convertible's front.

The vampire caught the edge of the windshield and pulled up. He grinned maliciously.

Over the vampire's shoulder, Doyle could still see the fleeing eighteen-wheeler as it drew farther and farther away. *Okay, now this isn't working out at all.* He cursed at the vampire and jammed on the brakes.

Rubber shrilled as the GTX tried to stand on its nose. Then Doyle shifted the transmission into reverse and floored the accelerator. The vampire slid backward as the seatbelt closed in tightly over Doyle. Flailing with his free hand, the vampire missed his hold on the windshield and clung by one hand as the convertible hurtled backward.

Gazing back over his shoulder, his scalp prickling because he couldn't drive backward and keep watch on the vampire at the same time, Doyle cut the steering wheel hard to the right. The GTX floated in a tight turn as it came around in a complete one-eighty. Centrifugal force pulled at Doyle just as he knew it would pull at the vampire clinging to the windshield. Then Doyle dropped the transmission into a forward gear and floored the accelerator again, shooting the car forward in a bootlegger's reverse.

The new direction caught the vampire unaware, slamming him back into the windshield, then sliding him up and over to one side. Unable to hold on to the windshield, the vampire skidded free and dropped into the street.

Doyle drove a hundred yards away, then brought the GTX around in a tire-eating one-eighty again. This time he was facing the vampire, who rose to his feet looking much the worse for wear. The half-demon reached into the backseat and took out the crossbow Angel had deposited there.

Placing the crossbow's stock against his chest, Doyle grabbed the bowstring and slid it into a cocked position. He loaded a quarrel from the quiver in the backseat.

Blocks ahead, the eighteen-wheeler rounded a corner and disappeared.

The vampire ran at Doyle.

I am not, Doyle told himself, *a bloody hero*. But there was something about hanging with Angel that brought out the best in him. He knew that now. It was a side of him that he hadn't seen in a long time.

Still, Doyle pinned the accelerator to the floorboard. The tires screeched in a banshee wail as they shoved the convertible forward. Doyle laid the crossbow on top of the windshield at the ready, his finger curled loosely over the trigger. He released the seatbelt and pushed himself up so he could see over the windshield and aim down the crossbow's length. Everything depended on timing. With his power and speed, the vampire had every chance of leaping into the speeding car with Doyle and killing him.

Overcoming his reluctance at the transition,

Doyle forced his change into Brachen demon form. The Brachen demon blood came from his father's side, but what had hurt him most of all was that his mother—the person he'd trusted most in his life—had never told him of his demonic nature.

When the change took him, Doyle felt the spikes shove out from his face and felt a little pride when the vampire's eyes widened. *Okay, now there's a surprised look.*

Less than twenty feet away, the vampire made his move and tried to leap into the air.

Stronger and faster now in demon form, Doyle lifted the crossbow one-handed and fired. The quarrel leaped from the crossbow channel and zipped through the vampire's heart. Doyle dropped back into the seat and tossed the spent crossbow into the backseat once more as the convertible shot through the swirling dust that had been the vampire.

Doyle kept both hands on the steering wheel as he changed back to his human appearance. He sped down the street, hoping he'd remember where the eighteen-wheeler had turned. *You just hang on, Angel. The cavalry's coming.*

Angel searched the survivors on the wall for the two who looked the strongest. One of them was a man who looked like he was in his early seventies and wore ragged clothing that made it plain that he'd been living on the streets. The other was a woman in her late twenties in designer workout wear.

"I need you to free the others," Angel told the man as he broke the shackles that bound him. "Do you understand?"

"Yeah, I understand." The homeless man ripped the IV needle from his arm. "Some of 'em ain't gonna make it."

"I know. We're here for the ones who will." Angel turned to the woman and ripped her shackles apart as well. "Can you help him?"

"I'm not strong enough to rip these handcuffs apart."

"It's okay," the homeless man replied. "There's keys here." He'd hunkered down and picked up the keys the vampires had dropped. He tossed one of the sets to the woman.

The woman's hands shook as she held the keys. "I can't. I'm afraid."

Swaying with the runaway truck, Angel took the woman by the shoulders and looked her in the eyes. "Some of these people here can be saved. They *need* to be saved."

"I don't know any of these people. I just want to get out of here."

"It's okay," Angel insisted, hearing the homeless man already working on the first victim's restraints. "There's no one here who can hurt you. I've got to go stop the truck before anyone else gets hurt."

The woman nodded. "Okay. I . . . I just want to go home."

"We'll all go home," Angel said. "Just help whoever you can." He let her go and glanced at the old man.

The old man waved at Angel. "You go on, son. Me an' the lady here will take care of these folks."

Angel trotted to the back of the trailer, grabbed the top edge of the doors, and swung up on top. He got to his feet and ran along the trailer. They were still in the old neighborhood, but the truck was streaking back toward the downtown area.

Sparing a backward glance, Angel saw the convertible's twin headlights streak around a corner in the distance and start closing the gap. He felt a little better knowing Doyle had made it, too. At the front of the trailer, Angel leaped across to the tractor cab. He landed on his feet and quickly bent down toward the driver's side.

Bullets erupted through the thin metal cover of the tractor cab.

Angel felt one of them core through his leg and groaned with the pain. He leaned down again and smashed his fist into the driver's side of the windshield, spraying broken glass into the cab.

The driver responded immediately by yanking the steering wheel hard right.

Angel slid over the left side of the cab and headed face first toward the street. At the last moment, he caught hold of the huge mirror beside the driver's door and stopped his fall. His feet swung down and briefly touched the pavement before he pulled them up and put them on the vehicle's running board. For a moment, the truck's lumbering movement smashed him against the door, then the driver's door window blew out suddenly, torn to pieces by a hail of bullets.

Angel yanked his hand back and swung over the street while hanging from one arm for just a moment. He caught sight of the two sets of huge truck tires humming across the pavement, just waiting for him to drop. He'd survive it because of his vampire nature, but it wouldn't be a fun experience.

The driver shoved the pistol through the broken window and took aim.

Angel grabbed the pistol and ripped it from the vampire's grip. He dropped the weapon to the street and reached for the door handle. Once he had the door, he released the mirror and punched the vampire driver full in the face, knocking the man to the other side of the cab.

Angel stood on the running board and opened the door, watching as the big truck pulled to the right and headed for a line of buildings. Sliding into the seat, Angel straightened the wheels just as the passenger side went up on the curb. He wiped out a small rust-eaten Pinto sitting up on concrete blocks before he could dodge. The derelict car tumbled over and over in front of the eighteen-wheeler, knocked about as easily as a child's toy.

The vampire launched himself from the other side of the truck cab at Angel. "You ain't gonna save them, man," the vampire said. "Me an' you, we'll live through the crash, but those people back there are gonna *die*."

Angel tried to fight his opponent off but couldn't do that and steer the truck at the same time. The vampire in the cab with him was the only one left in the group. Angel wanted to keep one of them for questioning, but having no choice, he grabbed the wooden stake from his trenchcoat pocket where he'd shoved it and staked the vampire.

Hurting from the bullet wound and the slash across his belly, Angel brought the huge vehicle to a halt in the middle of the street. Then he noticed the CB radio blasting.

"Blackhawk, are you there?"

Thinking that he might still have a chance to find out who was behind the blood-delivery operation, Angel picked up the handset and keyed it. "This is Blackhawk."

There was a pause.

In the mirrors, Angel watched Doyle pull up alongside the eighteen-wheeler. Prisoners left the trailer on trembling legs. Some of them fell before they could make it across the street and others helped them back to their feet.

"Who is this?" the voice on the CB radio demanded.

"Blackhawk," Angel said, trying again. "There's been some trouble." He watched the victims stumbling erratically across the street, fleeing as fast as they could from the horror they'd been put through. Whoever was behind the blood-delivery scheme couldn't be allowed to stay in business. There was no reply, and after only a moment more, Angel knew there wasn't going to be. Sirens screamed in the distance.

Frustrated, Angel ripped the handset from the CB and threw it outside. He climbed down from the cab of the eighteen-wheeler and joined Doyle.

"We've got a first-aid kit in the trunk," Doyle said.

"Get it," Angel said, walking toward the victims.

"It's not going to be enough."

"It's a start." Angel strode up to the old homeless man he'd freed. "Sounds like more help is coming."

Shoulders shaking with silent grief, the old man knelt on the ground beside a small, slim man. The other old man was dressed as shabbily as the first, and his eyes stared sightlessly up at the sky. The homeless man looked up at Angel's approach. Tears fell from the old man's rheumy eyes. "This here's Jimbo. We made it through the Korean War together, looking out for one another."

Angel felt the old man's sorrow and wanted to walk away from it because it was too rich, too raw.

"We thought we was gonna die at the Chosin Reservoir, but we didn't." The homeless man tenderly closed Jimbo's eyes. "Young fella like you, you probably never even heard of the Chosin Reservoir."

"Yeah," Angel said quietly, feeling the weight of the old man's pain. "Yeah, I have. It was seventy miles and four days of a hellish retreat for the First Marine Division. They had to fight against eight Chinese Communist divisions, in sub-zero weather."

The homeless man nodded. "That's something you don't forget. It was that what made me and Jimbo family. We lived through divorces and kids that didn't want nothing to do with us when we got old, and we lived out on these streets here 'cause we didn't ever have no place else to go. But we had each other."

Angel remained silent, respecting the man's grief.

"You ever lost family?" the old man asked without warning.

Guilt slammed into Angel and he heard the demon inside him laughing maniacally. Back in Ireland, he'd had a family: a younger sister hardly more than a girl, a mother who worried constantly about her husband and son, and a father whose frustration with his eldest child seemed to know no bounds. When he'd grown into a young man, Angel had turned from them all, sought out the taverns and drink, enjoying the stories of men who told of journeying out across the seas and all the fine adventures they'd had while doing it.

Then, one night while he was deep in his cups and feeling sorry for his lot in life as he so often did back in those days, Angel had found Darla. She'd been a proper temptress, blond and darkly radiant. She'd been the kind of woman who made men write songs and fight wars for honor as well as recognition. He'd lost his life to her crimson kisses that night, as well as his soul.

When he'd returned from the grave, spent and hungry and filled with the demon, Angel had returned home. He'd gone to confront his father, hoping to see the man finally bend before the power Angel now held in unlife. Instead, the black rage had gathered upon Angel like a flock of ravens. In minutes, he'd slain his family and drank their blood. Nearly one hundred years had passed before his soul was returned to him and he felt the guilt and agony of what he'd done to his own blood.

"Yeah," Angel answered, having to force the words through his dry throat.

"Then you know how I'm feeling now," the old man said.

"I know," Angel said. "Maybe I can help."

"How?"

"If I can find the ones behind them, I promise you I'll put them out of business."

"You?" The old man looked at him in disbelief.

Angel nodded.

"If anyone can get it done, you see," Doyle said, walking up beside Angel, "Angel is the guy to do it."

The old man glanced at Doyle. "You help him?"

"We're partners," Doyle answered. "Mostly."

"You ain't quite human either, are you?" the old man asked.

Doyle hesitated.

"No," Angel said, deciding that if they were going to be honest with the old man, they were going to be fully honest. "He's not."

The old man nodded. "I didn't think so. You live in the underbelly of this city long enough, you develop a sixth sense about things like this." He studied Doyle for a moment longer. "You know about losing people, too. I can see it in them green eyes of yours. And there's a darkness that clings to you that ain't entirely of your makin'."

Doyle glanced away.

"You make peace with yourself, boy," the old man said. "We don't ever know exactly when we're gonna leave this world for whatever comes next."

"I'm not one for looking on the bleak side of things," Doyle said. "I ain't leavin' till I'm good and ready."

"Maybe so," the old man admitted.

The sirens sounded again, still not drawing any closer that Angel could tell. He took a business card from his pants pocket. "We're running out of time."

He offered the card to the old man. "I could use help."

The old man shook his head and moonlight silvered the tears on his face. "I ain't no warrior no more. Done more killin' than would have pleased me a long time ago."

"An extra pair of eyes on the street," Angel said. "That's all I'm asking. If you see something, hear something, give me a call."

Hesitantly, the old man took the card. "Maybe. I ain't gonna promise nothin'."

"No problem," Angel said. "I just need to ask you a couple questions."

The old man nodded.

"How did you get taken?"

"Them vampires come for us," the old man said, a haunted expression on his face. "They swept through the alleys where homeless live. Most of them in the trucks, they're homeless just like me an' Jimbo was. They got a few other folks here an' there, too."

"How many of them?"

"The vampires? A lot more than you killed tonight."

"Do the Diablos, the biker gang, run all of this?" Angel asked.

"I saw a lot of Diablo jackets," the old man replied, "but I seen others, too."

"Do you have any idea where they're headquartered?"

"No. They herded us up last night, me an' Jimbo an' some of the others that lived where we lived. The vampires that took us held us on the street, then divided us up into three trucks. Maybe there was four or five trucks. I couldn't tell you. Me an' Jimbo, we was on the third truck." The old man shook his head apologetically. "That ain't much, an' I know it, but that's all I know."

"We'll find them," Angel promised.

"Maybe not soon enough for them other folks that got took when me an' Jimbo did. They sucked people dry tonight makin' deliveries. They got a funeral home workin' with them, too, that disposes of the bodies. That truck stopped twice tonight an' offloaded bodies for crematin'."

"Thanks for the help," Angel said. "If you find out anything—"

"Maybe," the old man said again. "I ain't promisin' nothin'."

Angel nodded, then turned and walked away.

"God keep you, Angel," the old man called, "because there's a lot of evil out there that'll tear you down if it can."

"I know," Angel said quietly. His redemption wasn't going to be easy, and he'd known that when he came to L.A. He headed for the eighteen-wheeler, unhooked the trailer that still held the corpses, then climbed up into the tractor cab. After pulling the tractor ahead, he pushed the cigarette lighter in, waited for it to pop out cherry-red, took it out and shoved it down into the passenger seat.

The cigarette lighter smoldered immediately, then a cheery little blaze spread across the seat cushion and climbed swiftly into a blaze.

By the time Angel dropped back to the street and headed for the convertible, the flames inside the truck roiled hungrily. When he slid behind the steering wheel, the flames crawled out of the truck windows and spread quickly. Before he made it to the end of the block, the flames managed to get hot enough to detonate the slow-burning diesel in the big tanks. Angel watched as the resulting explosion ripped the truck cab to pieces.

The cell phone rang and Angel took it from his trenchcoat pocket. "Yeah?"

"Well?" Cordelia asked impatiently. "Have we got an ETA on that arrival? Adrian's holding the yacht for you, but the guests are getting restless."

"Yacht?" Angel asked.

That caught Doyle's attention.

"It's his yacht," Cordelia explained, "but it's more like camouflage while he talks to you. *Us.* When can you be here?"

"Where are you?"

"San Pedro. Los Angeles Harbor."

"Not long," Angel said. "Doyle and I need a change of clothing and there's one other stop I need to make." He broke the connection before Cordelia could say anything.

"A yacht?" Doyle asked, looking hopeful. "Now and there's a sign that things might be pickin' up just a little for Angel Investigations."

"Something I learned about rich people and their problems, Doyle. Whenever money doesn't solve whatever's wreaking havoc in their world, you can bet it's really nasty."

CHAPTER SEVEN

"This is a crime scene. You can't go beyond this point," a young policeman said.

Angel stopped on the other side of the cordoned-off area surrounding the convenience store only a few blocks from the warehouse area where he and Doyle had put Maurice Welker out of business. Four marked LAPD units and two detectives' unmarked sedans were parked in the street behind red-and-white striped sawhorses that kept the media and the neighbors out of the area. An ambulance parked near the door sat idle and waiting, the lights whirling around. The coroner's wagon seemed to be doing all the business.

"I'm here to see Detective Lockley," Angel said. "I called the PD and they told me I could find her here."

"Yeah," the young officer said. "She's catching on

homicide tonight. What's your name? I'll let her know you're here."

"Angel."

The officer left his post and trotted into the convenience store.

"Now this, this isn't good," Doyle said quietly at Angel's side. "I'm gettin' a weird vibe here. How about you?"

"Yeah," Angel replied. "Me too." He could feel it in the air, almost strong enough to make his skin prickle and the hair on the nape of his neck stand up. Whatever had caused it was old and strong, and not even remotely human.

A few minutes later, Kate Lockley strode from inside the convenience store. She was tall and blond, wearing jeans and a black leather coat over a plaid shirt. Her detective's badge hung on a chain around her neck. She let herself through the cordon.

Immediately, a small contingent of reporters hustled toward her with camcorders and microphones.

"My car," Kate said to Angel. Then looked meaningfully at Doyle. "Me and you."

"Tell you what," Doyle said brightly, "why don't I just go wait in the car?"

Kate opened the door to one of the unmarked sedans and slid in behind the wheel. A lighted cherry on a magnetic base swirled on the roof. She reached across and unlocked the passenger door.

Angel slid into the car and shut the door just ahead of the media crowd.

"Lock the door," Kate instructed, "or they'll try to open it."

Angel locked the door and ignored the media washing up against the side of the car like a wave swarming a tide pool. "I—"

"Wait," Kate interrupted. "Those jerks can tape you, get somebody to lip read it later. Whatever we talk about, it's got to be private."

After two minutes of getting nothing but the two of them sitting in the car and being ignored, the media group was drawn away by the emergence of yet another body bag being brought out of the convenience store.

Kate turned to Angel. "Are you involved in this?"

"I don't even know what *this* is, Kate," Angel responded. "I called the detective's division and they told me I could find you here. I've got a favor to ask."

Taking a deep breath, Kate raised a hand to the side of her face and let her lungs empty slowly as she returned her attention to the convenience store. In a more controlled tone, she said, "I got a convenience store full of dead kids. Some of them are members of a youth gang. The Bleeding Hearts. For the most part, they're no loss. They've been hell on wheels down in this community for years; dealing, drive-bys, homicide, and armed robbery. It was only a matter of time till all of them were taken off the street."

Angel listened.

"But there were two kids in there," Kate continued, "who look like innocents. There's an eighteen-year-old who was working behind the counter. He's in critical condition and not talking much. They already shipped him to the ER. His brother was twelve years old. He's in the smallest body bag over there."

Glancing over at the body bags, Angel remembered how small his sister had been when he'd killed her. "That's too young to die."

"From what the neighbors tell me," Kate said, "he was a good kid. Just happened to be in the wrong place at the wrong time. His mom was working late-shift at the factory and he was there at the store with his brother. The Bleeding Hearts came in and tried to rob the place. I got that from the off-duty police officer who arrived on the scene. He's in bad shape, too. He has a fractured skull, a concussion, and some disorientation." She paused. "The convenience store is shot to hell. The kid behind the counter was shot once in the chest. But the other kids—" She looked at Angel again. "—they look like prunes. Totally desiccated, the coroner tells me. He can't explain it and neither can I."

"Are there any puncture wounds?" Angel touched his neck.

"No." Kate blew out her breath. "I've worked deaths like that. No one's ever figured those out either, but these aren't like that."

Okay, so maybe we can rule out vampires, Angel thought. But that wasn't much. There were a lot of other things in the city that were as bad as vampires.

"The police officer told me that a woman killed the Bleeding Hearts and the little boy in the store," Kate said. "He gave her description as Hispanic. Late twenties, maybe early thirties. Dressed all in black. Good-looking. Dark hair and dark eyes."

"Strong woman," Angel commented.

"The uniforms rolled on the area at once," Kate said. "The boy behind the counter tripped a silent alarm, and the police officer called the robbery in as soon as it went down. When they arrived, they found no sign of a woman in black. I want you to check around in all your haunts that I don't have access to, see if you can find out who this woman is."

"A favor for a favor," Angel said.

Kate nodded. "The police officer said the woman had to have been mentally unbalanced. She was crying—shrieking, is the word he used—the whole time she was killing the gangbangers. And the little boy. The Bleeding Hearts threatened her, took her hostage at gunpoint when the robbery went down. But the boy, he didn't do anything to her, Angel, and she killed him anyway." Tears glimmered in her eyes, but she held them back. "Kid cases are the hardest. My dad always told me that. Told me that's when a police officer really finds out if he or she has the stomach for the work. A kid case can tear you apart."

Angel watched the activity at the convenience store, wondering about the electrical sensation he'd felt.

"What favor are you looking for?" Kate finally asked.

"There's a truck that caught fire a while ago," Angel said. "If you haven't heard about it, you will. If anything turns up in police files as to who owns the truck, I'd appreciate knowing who it is."

She was silent for a moment. "You're not going to tell me any more?"

"I can't," Angel replied.

"Can't or won't?"

Angel didn't reply.

Kate shook her head. "You've been a help in the past, but I don't much care for the way you operate. If you didn't get results or I could accomplish the same thing through the PD, I wouldn't work with you at all."

"I know," Angel said. He opened the unmarked sedan's door and stepped out. "I'll see what I can find out about the woman who did this and get back to you."

"Do that." Kate got out on her side of the sedan,

thwarted the media people who raced for her again, and stepped back into the safety of the cordoned area.

Angel watched her go and felt bad for her. Kate took her job seriously and it constantly brushed her up against things she didn't understand and probably never would. The shadows around the city stayed dangerous. He felt the electrical tingle at the back of his neck again.

"Been an active little neighborhood," Doyle commented when Angel joined him in the car.

Angel put the convertible in reverse and backed out into the street. "How's that?"

"All the excitement at the convenience store," Doyle said. "And I heard some of the people standing near the car say that the local priest, Father Oliveria, was attacked in the church only about an hour before this happened."

"That's the way it is with bad luck," Angel said. "Some days it keeps on coming."

"I'm thinking as how *this* is a yacht," Doyle said as they neared the big ship.

Angel surveyed the yacht's running lights as it sat at anchorage off the Ports O'Call Village pier in San Pedro, and estimated the vessel as a sixty-five-footer. He admired the Old World craftsmanship. Polished wood and brass held a buttery gleam under the port's security lights. Rigging pinged against the three tall masts and yardarms rigged Marconi-style. The triangular canvas sails were furled and neatly stowed.

A young, uniformed security guard escorted them through the checkpoints in the private sector. The rush of the incoming tide and the conversations of the other boat and ship crews calling to each other from their decks blocked most of the city sounds out.

The leaning Angel's Gate Lighthouse stood tall in the water out by the Federal Breakwater. The breakwater was over a mile and a half long and made up of nearly three million tons of rock that had been brought over from Santa Catalina Island. The lighthouse's trademark rotating green light spun around the harbor, marking the entrance to the port. The two-note blast of the foghorn rolled over the surrounding area every thirty seconds. Tugboats and other vessels moved out on the dark water.

"This is Mr. Heath's craft," the security guard said, pointing to the yacht. "Have you been out here before?"

"No," Angel said. "First time."

"She's *League Strider,*" the security guard said. "She's a good ship. Besides the sails, she's powered by a hundred and fifty horsepower engine. Mr. Heath entertains on her often. You'll enjoy cruising on her. Have a good night."

"Thanks." Angel followed Doyle toward the yacht, but didn't feel very happy about the coming experience. Even from the pier boardwalk leading to the slip, Angel could see that a party had started aboard the vessel. He usually avoided scenes like this when he could. His leg and his stomach still throbbed from his wounds. He'd be more or less healed by morning, but he was still uncomfortable at the moment. He scanned the yacht for Cordelia, but he didn't see her.

A security team dressed in Hollywood chic on board *League Strider* checked the invitation Adrian had left waiting for Angel and Doyle at the private entrance, then radioed ahead for Adrian to meet his guests. The security team, a guy and girl, wore jackets that had been expertly tapered to conceal their weapons from anyone who didn't know enough to look.

"And this," Doyle said enthusiastically as he watched the people mingling on the deck, "this is what I call a proper bash."

"We're working," Angel reminded him. "Usually when we're working, that involves someone trying to kill us. You might want to keep that in mind before you go home tonight with your head in a basket."

"You see, now there's where maybe you should reconsider a little. See, your cases and my visions involve someone tryin' to kill us," Doyle coun-

tered. "Now this here is one of Cordelia's cases.
I'm thinkin' this is going to involve food, drink, and
a chance to get recognized for the Oscar-winning
actress she wants the rest of the world to recognize
her as. We get the opportunity to play the supporting cast. I see no danger there. However, I intend
to avail myself of those buffet tables I see on
deck."

A moment later, Cordelia appeared behind the
yacht security team. She grinned from ear to ear as
she invited them onto the vessel like she'd been
doing it all her life. "Tell me," she said. "Is this not
fabu?"

Angel nodded. "Fabu. The very word I was going
to use. Where's this prospective client of yours?"

"Belowdecks in his private cabin," Cordelia said,
waving the security guards away as she took Angel's
arm in a conspicuously appropriate manner befit-
ting the Hollywood atmosphere. "Belowdecks is
what we say when the area is . . . well, below the
decks."

As soon as they stepped onto the deck, the security guards signaled the yacht crew. Immediately the
mooring lines were cast off and the vessel rocked
away from the pier.

"What's Adrian's problem?" Angel asked as
Cordelia guided him through the buffet area. She
also provided a running commentary on the dozen
television stars who were in attendance, recogniz-

ing most of them from current and past series work.

"His wife is missing."

"Cordelia, I don't do that kind of work."

"I took on this client. He could be good for the agency. He could be good for me. He produces teen dramas and sitcoms."

Angel hesitated.

"C'mon, where's your sense of adventure? Don't be disappointed yet. She could have been kidnapped by a demon white slavery ring or brainwashed into some evil-worshiping cult."

"And she could have run away because she didn't want to stay with her husband. In which case, I'm out."

"It's not like that. He loves his wife, and he's worried."

"That doesn't mean she loves him back."

"Angel, please. All I'm asking you to do is listen to him. I mean, I work with you, traipsing around in sewers—which, by the way, ranks as positively *ewww!*—and I've helped fight vampires and demons that would have killed and eaten me. It's not going to hurt you to rub shoulders with the rich and famous for a few hours with me."

"Okay," Angel admitted.

Cordelia stopped beside Angel and struck a pose as a cameraman shooting the festivities turned toward them. "Smile. *Entertainment Tonight* is shooting footage here. They'll pass me over if they see me hanging on the arm of guy who has bitter-beer face."

The cameraman turned and found a new subject.

"Man," Cordelia complained, "he didn't even get my best side."

"Has Adrian gone to the police?" Angel guided Cordelia through the crowd.

"No. He doesn't want to. He'll explain." Cordelia glanced around covertly, still holding on to Angel's arm. "I wish you'd worn a tux. A tux would have made a much better impression. You do have one, don't you?"

Angel ignored the question, taking care to keep Cordelia moving. Being around so many people was slightly unnerving, and it sharpened the demon's hunger within him. Two hundred years ago in Europe, he'd strode into rooms with parties not too unlike this one, and he'd left a trail of bloody, mangled bodies in his wake. Not having to worry about crowds was one of the things he'd most liked about Sunnydale.

The yacht gave a warning blast of its whistle. Gently, the engine engaged and the big vessel came around and rolled sedately out into Los Angeles Harbor.

After what Angel was sure was the long way around, Cordelia took him to the yacht's stern, then led him down into the hold. Overhead, sails rose into the air and captured the wind with whip-cracking force.

The stairs let out into a spacious great room with an accompanying galley. People and buffet trays filled that area as well. The guests swayed a little as the ship moved with the wind and the throbbing basso of the engine died. Music videos played in the two forward corners of the great room, but nobody seemed interested. *Most of them are here for appearances*, Angel guessed. It was Hollywood. The town was like that.

"Not that way." Cordelia led him back to the aft cabin. "The captain's quarters." She knocked on the door just as Doyle joined them.

"There you are," Doyle said. "Thought I'd lost you for a moment." He held an overflowing plate in one hand and a champagne glass in the other.

"Terrific," Cordelia said. "Adrian's first impression of you will be that you're a walking famine. I'm so sure he'll want to hire starving detectives."

The door to the aft cabin opened.

Cordelia turned, breaking off her remonstration at once, her scowl morphing into a charming smile by the time she faced the man in the doorway.

"Angel?" the man asked, offering his hand. "I'm Adrian Heath. Thanks for coming on such short notice." He stepped back into the roomy cabin. "Come on in. We'll have a little more privacy here."

Every piece of furniture had been carefully

chosen due to space considerations and look. Hand-worked wood and hand-tooled leather finished out the bed, built-in dressers, the small built-in executive desk supporting a notebook computer and two phones, and the entertainment center. A small ceiling fan pushed the air around inside the room.

With the bed pushed up into the aft wall, two benches on the port and starboard sides of the cabin faced each other. Cordelia sat with Adrian on one side and Angel took the other side. Doyle remained standing after briefly shaking Adrian's hand.

"There's plenty of room," Adrian said. "Or I can have a chair brought in if you'd prefer."

"No, I'm good," Doyle said. "You see, I might make another trip out to the buffet and there's no sense in bothering anybody."

Out of Adrian's sight, Cordelia shot Doyle a warning glance.

"Cordelia tells me you were out on business when she first called to arrange this meeting. Everything went well?"

"So far," Angel answered. An uncomfortable silence dragged out.

"Cordelia also told you that I wanted to retain your services."

"She said your wife is missing."

117

"She is." Adrian stood and opened a small wet bar built into the wall. "Would you like a drink?"

Angel shook his head. "Why don't you tell me about your wife."

"What do you want to know?" Adrian responded.

Angel locked eyes with the man. "If your wife is missing, why are you throwing a party?"

CHAPTER EIGHT

Cordelia watched in angry frustration as Adrian Heath's face blanched at Angel's question. She couldn't believe that Angel had been so . . . so . . . so blunt and tactless. But mostly she couldn't believe that she hadn't already wondered that about Adrian to begin with.

Laughter from the galley outside the aft cabin's closed door drifted into the room, underscoring the incongruity.

"The party," Adrian answered slowly, "was scheduled months ago. I couldn't let my wife's disappearance stop this."

"Why not?" Angel asked.

"Because Hollywood is a town built on image," Adrian replied. "No one outside my immediate staff knows Marisa has disappeared. I can't afford to let anyone know. There are several deals in the works that I've worked months and years on to pull together."

"What kind of deals?" Cordelia asked before Angel could say anything. Angel gave her a look. "I mean, maybe some of your business rivals abducted your wife. As a hostage so they could use her against you."

Adrian shook his head. "Marisa disappeared two days ago. If it had been one of them, wouldn't I have heard from them by now?"

"Probably," Doyle said. "And then there's the downside of a kidnapping. The longer a kidnapper has a victim, the less likely it is that they're coming back."

Now that's a big help, Cordelia thought sourly.

Suddenly, Doyle must have realized what he'd said. "I mean," he added, "that's what the Discovery Channel special said. Now me, I wouldn't say that's how it's going to work in this case."

"Oh God." Adrian dropped the champagne from his trembling hand. The glass shattered against the hardwood deck. The liquid followed the pitch and yaw of the yacht as it sailed through the harbor. In the distance, the lighthouse foghorn roared again, sounding mournful and hollow. "Marisa can't be dead. I haven't thought of her as dead. Not once."

"What have you thought of her as?" Angel asked quietly.

"Angry, mostly. I've been putting these business deals together for the last few months. After she disappeared, I realized I hadn't been spending very much time with her lately. Her parents are dead, as are mine. There's no one else but us."

"I don't know much about your business," Angel said, "but I don't think this was the first time you had to devote that kind of energy to a project. So why think that was the cause this time?"

"Because," Adrian answered hoarsely, "I can't think of another damn reason why she'd leave. It doesn't make sense." Some of his anxiety was overshadowed by the anger that burned within him. "It's been two years since there's been an Adrian Heath produced show in syndication. If you're not careful, that can be a lifetime in this business. People forget you. Marisa knows that. We met through this business."

"Where did you meet her?" Angel asked.

"She got a part on a series I did eight years ago. A thing called *Daring High: The School for Spies.* At first she was just going to be a walk-on, but she has this look, you know?"

Angel shook his head.

"Do you have a picture?" Cordelia asked.

"Sure. I should have already gotten one for you. I'm not thinking very clearly." Adrian used a key to unlock the desk drawer and drew out an 8 x 10 glossy.

Cordelia took the black-and-white picture and glanced at it. The woman's name was written in practiced, flowing script in silver in the lower right corner: *All my love, Marisa.* She was pretty, Cordelia had to give her that. She wore a spaghetti-strap blouse and had a petite build. The gleam in her eye was challenging, but the smile on her lips was inviting. She had the sultry look of a younger Jennifer Lopez, only Marisa's hair had been daringly short and frosted platinum blond. She looked all of eighteen or nineteen.

"She's twenty-seven," Adrian said. "I know she doesn't look it in that picture. That's what makes her so good in the teen shows. She just kind of holds that look." He took a towel from the wet bar and cleaned up the champagne spill and the broken glass.

"What happened between you and Marisa on the last day that you saw her?" Angel asked, looking at the picture.

"The normal routine," Adrian said. "We got up, I made a few phone calls. We had brunch together, talked over the trades, talked over the new show, potential ideas for scripts and story arcs. Then I went to the office."

"Have you already cast the new show?" Cordelia asked. She ignored Angel's reproachful glance. It was all information they might use; some more so than others.

"Some of it. Marisa even has a major part."

"What did Marisa do that day?" Angel asked.

"She stayed home."

"Is that what she usually does?"

"Stay home? Yeah. Unless I need her at the office. Marisa is really good at handling people. It never hurts to be good-looking and female in this business." Adrian glanced at Cordelia. "You're an actress. You know what I'm talking about."

Cordelia nodded and tried to keep the excitement from her face. Adrian had noticed that she was an actress *and* good-looking *and* a woman. It was a hat trick.

"Did Marisa have anything planned that day?" Angel asked.

Adrian shook his head. "I checked her agenda. Nothing was written there."

"She left her agenda behind?" Angel asked.

"Marisa left *everything* behind," Adrian said. "Her wallet. Her purse. Her charge cards and checkbook. When she left our house, the only thing she took with her was the clothes on her back."

"Did she have a car?"

"Yes. It's still at the house, too."

"She *walked* away from your home?" Cordelia asked in disbelief.

"Yes."

"She may have taken a cab," Angel put in.

Cordelia could tell by the distracted look in

Angel's eyes that he was giving the mystery serious consideration. *Okay, that's a good sign. Now we're up to at least a consultation fee, and I have a reason to stay in touch with Adrian.* Even as she thought that, though, she couldn't help but glance at the picture of the young woman that Angel held and feel concerned. *Why would anyone walk away from all the things Adrian has to offer?*

"Did Marisa ever take a cab from your house?" Angel asked.

"No. If she needed the limo, she just called for it and we worked out the scheduling. She's independent, and she likes having her own car."

"Cordelia, we'll need to call the cab services around the neighborhood and see if any of them made a pickup at the Adrian home."

Cordelia opened her purse and took out a pen and notepad. She wrote *taxis* on the first clean sheet. *Okay. We're on the job.*

"If you don't mind me sayin', there's another scenario," Doyle spoke up. "You see, Marisa could have left with someone."

"That would explain why her car had been left," Angel said, "but not why she left all her personal effects behind."

Adrian gazed imploringly at Angel. "Look. People who've been around the things that you do say that you're good and you're discreet. With all the business dealings I've currently got hanging, those are qualities that I need. They're qualities that I think Marisa needs."

"What she needs," Angel said quietly, "is the Los Angeles Police Department. They've got more manpower and they're more experienced than I am in this sort of thing."

Cordelia held her breath, hoping Angel didn't talk them out of a job.

"The LAPD has a standard seventy-two hour window that a person has to be missing before they'll investigate," Adrian said. "Unless there's some sign of physical abduction. In Marisa's case, there isn't any. Forty-three hours have already passed. I don't want to wait another twenty-nine hours for Marisa to be missing before I can tell the police department."

"If I can't find her in that time," Angel said, "it would be better if you went to the police."

Adrian shook his head. "What if something is medically wrong with her? Say she had some kind of aneurysm that left her amnesiac. If she left the house not knowing who she was and the wrong kind of people recognized her from television reports or flyers, I'd be putting her in jeopardy."

"Does your wife have a history of mental illness?" Angel asked.

"No."

"Anything happen lately that might lead you to believe that had happened?"

"No, dammit! I've got a creative mind. Comes with the territory. Sometimes I'm my own worst enemy." Adrian looked at Cordelia for support. "It's gotten to the point that I can't sleep at night. Every time I close my eyes, all I can think about is Marisa."

"It's okay," Cordelia replied. "Angel understands. He's just covering the bases. People wig out in this town. Sometimes you can see it coming."

"No. If that's what happened with Marisa, I didn't. If Marisa wigged out, she did it without leaving me anything." Adrian forced himself to breathe out. "If there was one clue, I'd have followed it. There's nothing. One morning my wife was there, and when I got home that evening she was gone. At this point I'm ready to consider alien abduction."

Angel stood, and when he did Cordelia felt him fill the room. *That's what I like about Angel,* she thought. *When he's there, you know he's really there.*

"I want her back, Angel. I want my wife back, and I want to know that she's all right." Adrian crossed his arms over his chest, standing alone and uncertain. "She's all the family I have. My parents died in a car wreck when I was a kid. My grandparents raised me, but they're gone, too. We got married four years ago. See? We even waited till we knew for sure what we both wanted. I was scared. She was scared. Neither one of us was exactly an angel before we got married, but since we've been married there's only been us. What we have between us is real. You know what I'm talking about?"

"Yeah," Angel said.

Cordelia saw sadness flicker in Angel's eyes for just a moment, then it was gone.

"How long before we put into port?" Angel asked.

"An hour, hour and a half tops," Adrian replied. "I wanted to talk here because the house is too empty. And because I knew that under the cover of the party, no one would really question whom I saw. They'll probably think you're an actor trying to get a part."

Angel glanced around the aft cabin. "You spent time here with Marisa?"

"Every chance we got. *League Strider* was our home away from home. We'd come out here and go for a run down to Mexico or up to Vancouver. Take a sanity break."

"You mind if I take a look around the room?"

"You're welcome to join the party first," Adrian said.

"I'm not much of a partygoer."

"Feel free," Adrian offered. "But I've got people to meet and an appearance to maintain. A lot of those people out there are going to be asking where Marisa is."

Angel nodded. "We'll put the time here to good use. Is it okay if we borrow the computer?"

"Sure. With the ship-to-shore sat-com link you've got access to the Internet." Adrian headed to the door. "If you need anything, let me know." He let himself through the door and closed it.

"So what do you think?" Doyle asked Angel as soon as they were alone.

"For now," Angel replied, turning his attention to the closet, "I choose to believe him."

"Well *of course* you believe him," Cordelia said. "Surely you of all people can see the pain that man is in. He loves his wife and he's scared because he doesn't know where she is. He's got that same look in his eyes that you do when you think about Buffy."

Angel didn't say anything; he focused on going through the clothing in the closet.

Cordelia focused on Doyle. "And what has you playing Suspicious Guy?"

"Well," Doyle said hesitantly, "Adrian Heath talks about his wife just walking out of the house and leaving everything behind like that."

"So?"

"Okay," Doyle said, "so picture this. Your husband's got money, lots of it. We're talking scads here, if I'm any judge of this boat."

"Not a great leap of imagination," Cordelia said. "I've gotten kind of used to thinking along the lines of having a husband and lots of money. Only it might not have to be his money; it could be mine."

"Bear with me. For now it's your husband's."

"Not exactly comfortable with that thought," Cordelia said.

"An' that's exactly what I'm talkin' about," Doyle said. "I'm thinkin' if you had a shot at takin' some of that money with you before you left, especially your own clothing and jewelry and car, you'd take it. Am I right?"

Cordelia thought about the scenario for a moment. "Marisa leaving like that doesn't make sense."

"Right." Doyle nodded and smiled. "Now Adrian, he's probably thinkin' to himself how it don't look so good for him now. If he brings the police in, he's going to have them lookin' at stuff like that, too. And if there's a staff at the house, which I'm betting there is, they're going to know nothing's missing. If there's really nothing missing."

"Still not getting clued in as to what the police will think," Cordelia admitted.

"If nothing is missing from the house except for Marisa Heath," Angel said quietly, "police investigators might come to the conclusion that she never left the house."

"You mean she might still be there? Why would Adrian hire us to look for his wife? That doesn't make sense."

"They might," Doyle said, "find Adrian's poured a new floor in the basement."

"To hide her body?" Cordelia asked incredulously. "That's sick."

"It's been done," Doyle pointed out. "Ever read *The Telltale Heart*?"

Cordelia thought about the possibility, but she was reluctant to give Adrian Heath up as the guy who could jumpstart her acting career. "No, it has to be something else. Some weird kind of reason that only we can find out."

"If he did anything to harm her," Angel warned, "I'll turn it over to the police."

"He didn't do anything to her," Cordelia insisted.

"Why don't you try calling the cab companies," Angel suggested. "Ask them to check their drivers' logbooks to see if they picked up any fares at Adrian's address. If we find a cab that took her out of there, Adrian's in the clear."

Cordelia sat at the small executive desk and lifted one of the phones while Angel started to pull clothing from the tiny closet.

Vinnie Stefano watched the woman dressed in black walking down the street and thought she must be in some kind of trouble. The wind held a chilling bite to it, whipping at the black dress and tangling her hair. She wouldn't be outside in the cold weather unless she was in some kind of trouble.

Or unless she was looking for trouble.

Usually there were other women on the street. Women who would rush out to the cars that stopped at the lights in the downtown area not far from the hotel district. They wore outfits a lot like the one the woman in black wore, but they were talkative, either joking with each other or being mad with each other. And they sold dates—lots of dates.

Tonight with it being so cold and windy, the women had retreated to public places, to restaurants and hotels, or just worked out of cars in parking areas.

Vinnie liked looking at the women. There was something mystical about them. That was a word he'd picked up from watching the Psychic Hotline channel. *Mystical.* He liked the way the word rolled off his tongue. The woman in black was mystical.

Without warning, the woman in black turned her head and looked directly at him.

Vinnie wished he'd known she was going to do that, because if he'd known he could have looked away and not been caught looking. He hated being caught looking. The women always griped at him and called him filthy names, and after he finished his job he'd go home in a bad mood and his mother would notice. His mother would ask him, as she always did, what was wrong. And he'd tell her, as he always did, that the women had caught him looking at them—again. Then his mother would be upset and tell him that women were the root of all evil and were to blame for the world getting kicked out of the Garden of Eden.

When he was little and his mother had told him all the stories about the Garden of Eden and how God created the world and all the animals, Vinnie had thought that he'd like to see the Garden of Eden. It would be kind of like going to the zoo— only there wouldn't be any bars. He'd always wanted to pet a bear or a lion or a dolphin. He didn't get to do those things at the zoo.

The woman stopped in front of Vinnie and stared at him. Her eyes were darker than anything Vinnie had ever seen. Remembering himself and his mother and his manners, Vinnie snatched the woolen beret from his head. "Sorry," he apologized. *A gentleman always takes his hat off to a lady.* It was one of the rules his mother had taught him.

"Who are you?" the woman asked.

"Vincent," Vinnie said. "Vincent Stefano." He paused, feeling his knees trembling for no reason that he could think of. Sometimes they did that when he forgot to eat. But he only forgot to eat when his mother was too sick every now and then to tell him to go feed himself. He'd had soup and two ham and cheese sandwiches before he had left home.

"What are you doing out here?" the woman asked.

When she spoke again, Vinnie realized it was something about the woman's voice that made his knees weak. It was like he was scared of her. "I'm working," he said.

"Doing what?"

"Delivering papers." Vinnie expected the woman in black to start making fun of him at any moment. He almost wished she did, because then he'd know everything was going to be all right, that she was just like the other women who usually worked the corners. "I got a walking route. I fill coin boxes and stores with newspapers. That's my job."

The woman smiled, but no warmth ever quite touched her eyes. "I don't see any papers."

"They'll be here soon," Vinnie said, nervously working his beret between his big hands. "The truck brings them and kicks them out. I always get here really early because I don't want to oversleep and miss my delivery time." And he liked to look at the girls.

"Have you seen my children pass by?" the woman asked.

"No." Vinnie shook his head. Sometimes when he got nervous like this he knew he didn't talk so good and it helped to nod or shake his head.

"I've lost my children." Abruptly, the woman laughed.

The sudden sound scared Vinnie and he took a step back, wondering how somebody laughing could scare him so much. Then he realized it wasn't just the sound of laughter in the woman in black's voice. There was a lot of pain, too. "I'm sorry," Vinnie said. "I could help you look for them. I like little kids, but I haven't seen any little kids walk down this street. It's too cold for little kids to be out. And it's too late, too."

Tears glinted in the woman's eyes. "I believe you. You're something of a child yourself, aren't you?" She raised a hand and tenderly stroked his cheek.

Despite his best intentions and everything his mother had said about respecting others, Vinnie drew back from her touch. Her fingers made his skin feel all crawly.

"Are you afraid of me?" the woman demanded.

Vinnie looked at her and saw the tears in her eyes pool up then spill down her cheeks. He felt guilty, thinking he'd made her cry. He tried to say no. He even wanted to say no. Except that his tongue knew he wouldn't be telling the truth, so it wouldn't let him speak.

"Don't be afraid of me." The woman brushed Vinnie's hair out of his eyes.

Vinnie trembled at her touch.

"You never did anything to harm me." The woman in black continued fussing with his hair. "You are so childlike, so like my own children. Did you know that?"

"No, ma'am," Vinnie answered. As frightened as

he was, he grew even more scared when he saw the
police cruiser roll to a stop at the curb behind the
woman. Two policemen rode inside, and Vinnie
knew them both. Despite what his mother said
about policemen being his friends, Vinnie knew the
two policemen in that car were bad men. They hassled the women who worked the corners. *Hassle*
was another neat-sounding word. He'd picked it up
from the women as they talked about and to the police.

Both the policemen stared at the woman in black.

"Hey," Vinnie said to the woman in black, "you
gotta get out of here. If those policemen think
you're talking to me, you're going to get in all kinds
of trouble." The other women who had talked to
him while he'd waited for his papers had gotten in
trouble. Griggs and Daniels, the policemen, had
made fun of the women for trying to get the "mental cripple's" paper money. They'd acted like it was a
joke, only they hadn't been laughing.

The woman in black turned and looked at the police car.

"No," Vinnie said, panicking, "don't look at
them!"

The woman in black smiled. "It is they who
should fear me."

"Why? You got a big-time lawyer?" The women
who worked the corners sometimes talked about
big-time lawyers.

135

"No," the woman in black answered.

"They'll hurt you," Vinnie said. "They've hurt other women working the corners." Griggs and Daniels hassled the women into getting what they wanted. Sometimes it was money, but sometimes it was business they conducted in the alleys between the buildings.

"I haven't been hurt," the woman in black said, "in a long, long time."

Vinnie figured that was kind of puzzling because she'd been crying just a second ago. "You need to get out of here." He turned away from her, thinking if the two policemen didn't see her talking to him that everything would be better.

Abruptly, Griggs opened his door and stepped out of the police car. He was short and compact, his Kevlar armor making him seem thicker across the chest. He held his nightstick in his hand. The moonlight glinted in his spiky blond hair.

Daniels was tall and quiet. He shaved his skull and wore a gunfighter mustache. He sat behind the police car's steering wheel and watched.

"Hey," Griggs called. "Get over here."

"Me?" the woman asked.

"Yeah, you. I ain't talking to the gimp."

At the name, Vinnie's face turned red. Griggs and Daniels didn't talk to him much, but when they did they always called him names.

"Perhaps," the woman said, "I don't wish to talk

to you." The tears had dried from her face and a wild glint filled her dark eyes.

"Lady, I don't give a rat's—"

Abruptly, the woman turned and walked down the street.

Griggs slammed the door shut and slapped the police car on the roof. While Griggs pursued the woman on foot, Daniels followed in the cruiser.

Vinnie knotted his woolen beret between his hands. *She's in for it now! She's really in for it now!* Griggs and Daniels were bad enough as they were normally, but when they got mad things got even worse. Sometimes they put the women in the hospital. Vinnie had seen ambulances have to pick them up out of the alleys. Once, one of the women had been forced into the cruiser and she'd never been seen again.

The woman in black walked without looking back. When she reached the alley by the small theater where Vinnie sometimes went to see black-and-white movies of Frankenstein and Dracula on Saturday mornings, she turned and went inside.

Vinnie wanted to yell at her and tell her she was making a mistake. But he didn't because he was afraid. He knotted his beret and watched as Griggs trailed her into the alley; Daniels followed in the police car. Despite his fear and knowing the two policemen would hurt him if they caught him watching because they didn't like witnesses, Vinnie stopped at the theater's corner and peered into the alley.

The alley ended after only a short distance, butting up into the brick wall of the building facing the street on the other side of the block. Garbage cans and refuse heaps lined the walls and filled the alley with a sour stench.

Griggs walked toward the woman without hesitation, slapping his nightstick into his empty hand. Daniels followed behind him, keeping the woman in the police car's lights.

The woman in black turned around and faced her pursuers.

For a second, Vinnie thought about going to try to get some help. In spite of the way she scared him, he didn't want to see her hurt by Griggs and Daniels. But he knew by the time he actually found someone to tell, let alone someone who would call the police on the police or come to the alley, it would be too late.

Daniels got out of the car carrying his nightstick as well. "Looks like we got us a feisty one tonight, partner," he said in his deep voice.

Griggs snorted. "That's okay. Fiesty's the way I like 'em."

The two police officers advanced on the woman. The cruiser's headlights seemed to deepen the shadows behind her and Vinnie would have sworn they moved like living things.

"Don't try to stop me from finding my children," the woman warned. "I will not be stopped again. They belong to me. I paid for them."

Vinnie didn't understand everything the woman was talking about, but he knew from what his own mother told him that children weren't cheap. *They take a lot of money and patience and care to rear properly*. He didn't know how many times he'd heard that speech.

"Do you know what she's talking about?" Daniels asked, hesitating for a moment.

"No. Does it matter?" Griggs countered. "Hey lady, you got two choices here. You can go down hard or harder, but either way you're going down."

Without warning, the woman started to laugh and cry at the same time, and the combination of noises paralyzed Vinnie. He clung to the theater wall in wordless terror, more afraid than Frankenstein's monster or Dracula had ever made him.

Then the wind picked up, rushing through the alley and moaning, mixing with the woman in black's howling laughter.

CHAPTER NINE

"You're goofing off."

Spotting the accusation in Cordelia's eye when she made the harsh pronouncement, Doyle quailed inwardly for a moment, then quickly recovered. *If I didn't really care what she thinks about me, I'd be in much better shape dealing with her.*

"Keep your voice down," he pleaded. They were in *League Strider*'s great room and the party was still in swing. Adrian Heath talked to people, introducing them to each other, then moving on to stroke the egos of more attendees.

"I will not keep my voice down," Cordelia objected.

Doyle grabbed a fresh bottle of Guinness stout from the galley serving table, took hold of Cordelia's elbow, and muscled her to a corner. "What are you all in a twist about?"

"Angel and I have been working ourselves stupid in that little room trying to find out all we can about Marisa Heath's disappearance," Cordelia said, "and you've been out here swilling beer, eating junk food—really expensive junk food—and hitting on women."

"It's not what it appears, Cordelia." Doyle glanced around, swaying slightly as the yacht continued its tour around the harbor. The foghorn droned again, somehow penetrating the loud music streaming from Bose speakers.

"What's not what it appears?" Cordelia crossed her arms.

"I'm not just swilling and eating and hitting," Doyle said. "I'm also getting information from these people."

Cordelia raised her eyebrows, showing serious doubt.

"I'm checking out Adrian's story. About him and his wife being so close."

"And?"

Doyle sighed. "Disappointing as it is, they seem to be quite the couple. Everyone has nothing but good to say about both of them. It's getting so I can barely stomach it."

"I didn't expect anything different." Cordelia helped herself to some of the popcorn shrimp on Doyle's plate.

Doyle watched her take the shrimp and bit his

tongue to keep from saying anything. Everyone he'd talked to tonight, and there had been quite a lot of them, seemed to zero in on the popcorn shrimp. There was none left on the buffet now, and he'd scarcely had more than a couple bites himself. "The broccoli's good," he said, though he hadn't tried it and had only put it on his plate to disguise how much of the shrimp he'd made off with.

"Broccoli leaves those little seed things between your teeth," Cordelia said.

"Right, right. What was I thinking?"

"Adrian called Angel and told him we'd be docking in fifteen or twenty minutes."

"He *called* Angel? We're on the same boat."

"It was easier to go through the cell phone than to try to come back from topside," Cordelia said in a patronizing tone. "Topside is what we call the top side of the boat."

"Upper deck."

"No, those are baseball cards."

Two women, both blond and lovely with toothpaste-fresh smiles, joined them. "Hey, Doyle," the woman on the left said, "I wanted to straighten Tori out."

Doyle vaguely remembered talking to the women earlier, but didn't know if he'd talked to them together or singly.

"No," Tori said, "I wanted to straighten Dani out."

Doyle smiled at them and waited, trying not to look anxious. After Adrian Heath had made it plain to the bartender working the galley that Doyle was a special friend of his, all of Adrian's other special friends who had upwardly mobile written up as part of their game plan had decided to get to know him. It had made talking about Adrian much easier, because everyone wanted to tell their own *how-I-met-Adrian-and-Marisa* stories and impress Doyle with how great a friend they were, too.

"Tori obviously wasn't listening to you when you were talking," Dani said. "She thinks that you're not a producer but you're one of the staff writers on *Palisades Cove.*"

"He's the guy who writes most of the steamy love scenes," Tori insisted. "And he tweaks the ones he doesn't write when he's hired to script-doctor Bruce Willis movies."

Doyle looked back at the women as they looked at him. Cordelia was surprisingly silent beside him. *Now you've gone and really stepped in it.*

"Hey, Doyle," a debonair man called out as he passed by. "I've got to take off, but congratulations again on that Boys R Toys case. Man, I can't believe no one knows those guys had been kidnapped earlier this year. You'd think their PR person would have spun that back into more exposure."

Doyle shrugged helplessly and counted his lucky stars that the man kept moving.

"Boys R Toys was kidnapped?" Tori asked incredulously.

"And you helped get them out of that?" Dani asked.

"What are you really?" Tori asked.

"Well . . ." Doyle looked at Cordelia. *I'm going to have to fess up. God, I hate that.*

Cordelia took a step forward. "Actually, Doyle can't tell you what he really does. Otherwise he'd have to kill you."

Dani and Tori looked at each other, perplexity turning to radiant smiles. "He's a spy!" they said at the same time.

"I've never talked to a spy before," Dani said.

"I've talked to a couple guys who said they were spies," Tori admitted, "but they weren't. You could tell." She looked at Doyle. "Are you a good spy or a bad spy?"

"He's a spy who has to be going," Cordelia said, taking Doyle by the arm.

"Must be some kind of code," Dani said.

Doyle watched the two women reluctantly turn and walk away. He glanced back at Cordelia. "I told so many stories I forgot who I was telling what. Thanks for the save."

"Don't mention it," Cordelia said, threading through the crowd with him in tow. "And I *really* mean that: don't *ever* mention it."

"Actually, it felt kind of good having you stick up

for me that way," Doyle admitted. No one had done that for him in a long, long time. "I might could get used to that."

"I wasn't sticking up for you. I was sticking up for us. I don't want anyone to think that Angel Investigations is anywhere as lame as—"

The rest of Cordelia's statement sounded like it was coming from underwater. The words reached Doyle's ears, but they made no sense. Pain split his skull, filling his eyes with black spots, and the vision swept over him like a tidal wave.

Vinnie Stefano cowered by the corner of the theater and peered into the alley. The strange wind swept litter into swirling dust devils that skittered through the dark alley. It also got so cold that Vinnie felt his teeth chattering.

The woman in black cackled even worse than Cruella de Ville in *101 Dalmatians*, Vinnie thought. He realized that his teeth weren't just chattering from the weird cold snap, but also from the sound of the woman's voice. *How can she laugh at them?* Vinnie didn't know, then thought that it was probably because the woman in black hadn't seen what Griggs and Daniels had done to the other women who had tried to fight them.

The two policemen stepped toward the woman in black and raised their nightsticks. Before they could swing the sticks, the woman in black kicked Griggs's nightstick away and spun on into Daniels, hitting him along the side of the head hard enough to lift him from the ground and knock him a dozen feet away.

Griggs cursed loudly and threw the nightstick at her. The woman in black continued laughing and wailing at the same time.

"I will have the children this time!" the woman in black snarled. "I will have them all! I will pay for my sins with their blood!"

Griggs yanked his pistol from its holster and brought it up in front of him. He fired three times, the muzzle flashes spitting out foot-long flames and filling the alley with thunder. Before Griggs could fire again, the woman in black was on him. She grabbed him by the shirtfront and yanked him to her. At the same time, she punched Griggs in the face so hard that her fist drove completely through the policeman's head. Pulverized bone and brain matter poured from her hand. Her arm had gone through Griggs's head to her elbow. She gazed at the blood for a moment, then withdrew her hand.

Griggs's nearly decapitated body fell heavily to the ground, jerking spasmodically.

Daniels got up and sprinted for the police car. He slid behind the steering wheel, locked all the doors, and keyed the ignition. The engine turned over immediately. Inside the cruiser, Daniels screamed curses and looked back over his shoulder, racing for the other end of the alley. He talked over the radio handset, screaming so loud that Vinnie could hear his muffled voice. "Officer down! Officer down, dammit!"

The woman in black waved at the car. A tremendous howl of wind tore through the alley and caught the police car, slamming it into the wall on the passenger side, closest to Vinnie. The airbags deployed, filling the interior of the police car as the engine died.

Walking slowly, the woman in black closed on the police car.

Without warning, shots punctured the airbags and ripped through the windshield from inside the police car. Still laughing and crying at the same time, the woman in black shattered the driver's window. She reached in and pulled the door from its hinges with one hand, and yanked Daniels out with the other.

Daniels pointed his weapon at her. The woman in black caught both of his hands with one of hers and twisted sharply. The popping crunch of bones breaking filled the alley. Daniels screamed in pain and fear, dropping to his knees in front of the woman. He probably would have fallen all the way except that she held his mangled hand. She reached for him. "No!" Daniels shouted. He cursed and tried to pull away.

The woman in black was relentless. She held the police officer easily, then touched him between the eyes with her other hand.

A white-hot spark leaped from her finger to Daniels's head. The policeman acted as if he'd been hit with a shotgun blast. Knocked from the woman's hold, Daniels's corpse fell backward and rolled over, coming to a stop like a puppet with the strings cut.

Slowly, the horrible wind died away and the litter dropped back to the cracked pavement.

The woman in black stopped laughing and crying, but her tears still gleamed silver in the moonlight as they threaded down her beautiful face. She turned and looked at Vinnie. Without a word, she headed straight for him.

"Come here, boy," she called. "Come here and see what I have for you."

Vinnie didn't want to go over to her, but he was too scared to run away.

"Doyle. Hey, Doyle."

Pain still filled Doyle's head as he tried to crack his eyelids open and look at whoever was talking to him. His vision was blurry at first, caused, no doubt, by the agony that ripped into his brain through his temples. "Angel?"

"Yeah," Angel replied. He knelt beside Doyle and held his arm.

Behind Angel, Doyle saw a large group of interested observers. "I'm all right," he told Angel. "Just got one of those . . . damned headaches."

A well-dressed young man in an Italian suit and L.A. Kings cap leaned down and spoke with Doyle. "It's the microwaves the Russians are shooting at us every day. You get enough of them, your brain gets scrambled. That's why I wear this." He showed Doyle the shiny material inside his hat. "Aluminum foil. It blocks out the Russian microwaves."

"Now, that's good to know," Doyle said weakly.

"Yeah," the young man replied, clearly offended. "Well, I was just trying to warn you. You'll be sorry when you people are reduced to the IQs of baboons."

Angel helped Doyle to his feet. "Are you okay?"

Even with his eyes wide open, Doyle could still see the image burned into his mind by the vision he'd been given. "I will be as soon as we get to talk. *Alone.*"

"It's okay, people," Cordelia said to the crowd. "He's just seasick. No big deal."

With Angel's help, Doyle stumbled down to the aft cabin and sat on one of the chairs. The pain was almost blinding. "I could really use something for this headache."

"Headache?" Cordelia said after she shut the door to give them privacy. "Aren't you supposed to pass out before you have a hangover?"

"Cordelia," Angel said. "Do you have any pain reliever?"

"For him or me?" Cordelia sighed, then took her purse up from the desk.

"It was a vision." Doyle leaned forward, resting his elbows on his knees and holding his head in his hands. The slight rocking motion of the yacht on the water made his stomach writhe uncomfortably.

"A vision?" Cordelia shook her head. "No way. We don't have time for a vision right now. We're looking for Adrian Heath's missing wife."

"It was a vision," Doyle insisted.

Angel took the pain reliever from Cordelia and handed two tablets to Doyle. "Who was in the vision?" Angel asked, pouring a glass of water from a pitcher on the desk.

"A young woman and a small child," Doyle answered. "She looked twenty-something. I think the kid looked four, five, maybe."

"Did you get a name?" Angel asked.

Doyle shook his head and instantly regretted it. He closed his eyes to block out the light and to rebuild the image in his mind. "What I got, she's twenty-something, with short, spiky blond hair. Blue eyes. Kid looks a lot like her, got a sweatshirt with a patch on the breast, a cartoon character, something like that. She's wearing khaki shorts and an orange halter."

"Does she work at this place?"

"I don't know."

"Are there any distinguishing marks?" Angel asked.

Doyle studied the young woman in his mind again. She was laughing and talking with a big man behind the counter at the bait and tackle shop. "Nothing that I could see. She's in a bait and tackle shop. I can smell the fish in the tank behind the counter, and there's a sign on the wall advertising them. Guy behind the counter knows the woman. He's a big mountain of a man. Huge. I'm thinking the guy must be nearly seven feet tall. Shoulder-length auburn hair, beard and mustache. When we get ready, we're not going to have any problems finding him." Straining, trying to make the vision more clear in spite of the pain, the half-demon focused on the big man's work apron. Embroidered blue letters held a name trapped on the olive green fabric. "His name's . . . Mark, Marty, something like that. Mirror at the back of the counter has Rudy's Fishing Tours on it."

"Is it day or night?"

Doyle tried to see, but the vision had been focused on the woman and the man at the counter. Even the mirror didn't reflect doors or windows, only shelves of food and gear and an ancient red cola machine. "I don't know. I couldn't see."

"Is there anything else?"

Doyle opened his eyes and regretted it when the

light in the room made his head ache again. "No. That's it. That's all I got."

"Guys, listen to me," Cordelia insisted. "We really don't need to get deflected from the Adrian Heath case."

"We don't have a choice," Angel said. "Those people in Doyle's vision are in trouble—"

"Marisa Heath could be in trouble, too."

"We're not going to ignore that," Angel promised. "You work on digging up all that you can on the Heaths. We can't make a move there till we know more." He cut his gaze to Doyle. "See if you can track down Rudy's Fishing Tours and this bait and tackle shop."

Doyle nodded. Even that hurt.

League Strider's engine came back on with a vibrating blast. It was located below and beneath the aft cabin. Someone knocked on the door. Adrian Heath peered in. "We're docking. Thought you'd want to know."

"Thanks," Angel replied.

"So?" Adrian appeared uncomfortable.

"We're still checking the cabs," Angel said. "That will take a while."

"You'll let me know?"

"As soon as we know anything," Angel promised.

"I'm counting on you to bring her back to me."

"I can't promise you that," Angel said.

Adrian looked troubled. "You're saying that you don't think you can find her?"

"What I'm saying is that when we find your wife—"

"*When,* not *if,*" Cordelia put in.

"—we're not going to bring her back if she doesn't want to come back," Angel finished.

"She'll want to come back," Adrian said. His voice held anger and frustration now. But Doyle thought there was also a trace of uncertainty, too.

"Just so you know," Angel said.

"She'll want to come back," Adrian repeated. When no one said anything, he turned and led them from the cabin.

Vinnie stopped just in front of the woman in black and gazed fearfully into her eyes. He was so scared he thought he was going to throw up. Whimpering, he closed his eyes tightly so he wouldn't see whatever it was she was going to do to him.

"Are you afraid of me?" the woman asked.

"Yes," Vinnie answered immediately, but it took a while to get out because he was shaking so badly his teeth chattered.

"Why?" she asked.

Vinnie felt her playing with his hair, brushing it back from his face. "Because I don't want to die," Vinnie said. He squeezed his woolen beret between his fingertips.

"Everybody dies," she said.

"Vinnie! Vinnie!" a woman's voice called out behind him.

The voice sounded familiar to Vinnie. He thought maybe it belonged to one of the women who regularly worked the street corners. He hadn't even been sure they would remember his name, much less care what happened to him. Sometimes he ran errands for them while he waited on his papers, getting them coffee from Starbucks down the street, or maybe sandwiches from the Neighborhood Dogs and Grill.

"Get away from her!" someone else shouted.

I can't! Vinnie thought, keeping his eyes shut tight. *I can't get away!*

"You have a child's innocence," the woman in black said. "I like that."

Trembling, unable to wait any longer, Vinnie opened his eyes. "Are—are you going to kill me? The way you killed Griggs and Daniels?"

The woman locked eyes with him for a moment. She drew her hand back and he noticed how it looked like a bird's claw, all folded up and ready to strike.

Vinnie wondered if he'd feel her shove her hand and arm through his head, or if it would be like he'd just fallen asleep without knowing it, the way he did sometimes.

"Get away from him!" one of the women behind Vinnie yelled.

"The police are on their way! We know your face!" another yelled.

The woman in black shook her head and smiled slightly. "No, Vinnie. You have the beautiful innocence of a child about you, but you're not a child. To me, you're nothing."

Vinnie didn't know what she was talking about. He heard her words, but all he knew was that she said she wasn't going to kill him. "Thank you for not killing me."

"You do whet my appetite for more children, though, Vinnie." Drawing her hand back from his face, the woman in black smiled again. "This world owes their children for taking mine. And I will have them." She turned and walked away without making a sound.

As he watched the woman walk away, Vinnie realized that she took the cold and the wind with her, leaving only the dead men behind. By the time some of the women reached him and started pulling him back toward the theater as the sound of a police siren suddenly rent the air, the woman in black disappeared among the shadows.

"You're going to be okay, Vinnie," one of the women said.

"I know," Vinnie said, trying to hide the tears that still streamed from his eyes. "She hurts children. She's going to keep hurting the children until someone stops her!"

The women tried to console him, but it was no use. Vinnie knew the woman was looking for children and when she found them she was going to treat them just like she'd treated Griggs and Daniels.

No one could stop her.

CHAPTER TEN

"Contrary to your nasty suspicions and Doyle's, Adrian Heath is in no way financially destitute."

Angel glanced up from the book he'd been reading and looked at Cordelia. She stood in the doorway between the outer office and his private office. "What?"

"Adrian Heath," Cordelia said, arms crossed and looking very smug. "Rich. *Very* rich. He wouldn't need to kill his wife and bury her in the flower garden to keep his yacht afloat and develop television shows. He also provides major funding to seven charities."

Angel placed the heavy book on his desk next to the piles of other books he'd been going through during the night. Late morning sunlight limned the window blinds. Even if the blinds fell, his desk was positioned safely out of harm's way. As long as he avoided the direct rays of the sun he could walk around in daylight without bursting into flames.

"This is California," Angel pointed out. "Maybe he was afraid she'd divorce him and take half of everything."

"Personally," Cordelia said, "I could live on half of everything Adrian Heath makes and never miss a single extravagance."

"You could." Angel was intrigued and impressed. The idea of Cordelia unleashed with a world of extravagance at her fingertips was mind-boggling.

"Adrian Heath is worth upward of one hundred million dollars."

"I thought he hadn't made a television show in years."

"He hasn't," Cordelia agreed. "Television shows aren't how Adrian makes his money." She paused. "Well, it's how he makes his money, but not *all* his money."

"Where does it come from?"

"His great-grandfather, Bertram Heath, was big business in Los Angeles in the 1880s. He bought up a lot of real estate around L.A. that was later used by the Hollywood people and city development. At the time, no one wanted that land or thought they would have a use for it. Besides that, he started up a lot of businesses in the Huntington Park area south of L.A. and in other places. Reading about him, about all the wheeling and dealing he did back in the day, I get the feeling he could have been the little bald Monopoly game guy. Bertram Heath was college buddies with William Randolph Hearst and other tycoons."

Angel nodded.

"So you still suspect him?" Cordelia asked.

"Maybe he didn't like the idea of being the guy who lost the family fortune."

"Adrian wouldn't have lost it," Cordelia said proudly. "Marisa Smith signed a pre-nuptial agreement stating that she wasn't entitled to any of Adrian's inherited money or any profits generated by those holdings and investments in the event of a divorce."

"Smith?" Angel asked.

"That was her maiden name."

"Ah. Where did she come from?"

"I haven't dug into her past too far," Cordelia admitted. "I've been concentrating on Adrian. Like you asked me to do."

"Okay," Angel agreed, "maybe we can rule out a motive based on financial problems. There are still other reasons Adrian Heath might have murdered his wife."

"Such as?"

Angel glanced at Cordelia, surprised that he had to point out the obvious. Of course, Cordelia was only realistic and tactless; she hadn't managed to accumulate his penchant for cynicism yet. "Maybe she had a thing for pool guys and Adrian didn't like it."

"Then she had it coming."

Angel shifted, leaning forward slightly. "Look, Cordelia, you're not here to defend him and I'm not here to hang him. We're trying to find his missing wife."

"Then why aren't you out there pounding the pavement or beating up snitches for information? That's what you'd do if this was one of those Powers-That-Be vision quests."

"I could pound the pavement if I knew what direction to pound it in," Angel said wearily. He hadn't slept at all last night with everything that was going on. Cordelia had gone home and to bed and had been back at the office bright and early. "As for beating up snitches, find me one. I'm in the mood to beat up someone." He shook his head because though the thought was spoken to placate Cordelia's fault finding, he knew it was true. Sometimes he wondered if his willingness to rely on violence wasn't a throwback to his days as Angelus. Most days he didn't care.

"I'm just getting the impression that you're not giving this case everything you could," Cordelia said. "I'm going through the Internet as fast as my fingers will let me, and you're in here reading—" She strode over to the desk and flipped the front cover of the massive book so she could read it. "—*Hudein's Childprey: A Narrative Compendium of Those Foul Things that Devour the Young?*" She blinked. "Ugh. Okay, definitely not light reading, but I don't see that it would offer anything up concerning tracking missing wives."

"This relates to something else I'm working on." The homeless old man's words had been reverberating in his brain. *You ever lost family?* Angel had been haunted by the memory of his family all night, and thoughts of them still lingered this morning. He'd thought about the two homeless men, all the other victims of the blood-supply ring, the families of the dead teens and small boy in the convenience store, and Adrian Heath.

"And you're reading about that *why?*"

"Something Kate is working on," Angel answered.

"Okay, let me explain something." Cordelia tried to look patient, but condescending was usually as close as she got to it. She perched on the edge of his desk. "Kate already has a job as detective for the city of Los Angeles. She's getting paid to protect and serve the interests of the community—*and* she gets benefits. *We*, however, have been selected to look for Adrian Heath's missing wife."

"Kate asked me to help her out with a case."

"Loan her the book. That's helping."

Angel didn't bother to reply. Both of them knew that Kate Lockley might have brushed up against the demon world a few times since Angel had known her, but she wasn't aware of all the things that were found there. "Does Adrian have any family?"

161

"Distant cousins, I think. There was a rift in the family when Adrian's parents died. Adrian's grandfather didn't want to see his father's empire broken up—that is, Bertram's empire—so when Adrian's parents were both killed in the car wreck, the grandfather figured he'd groom Adrian to keep the companies together."

"Has he?"

"Yes. Of course, it helps that most of those companies have board members who have been in place for years."

"Okay, let's dig into Marisa Smith for a background search."

"*Let's?* As in, you're joining me?"

Angel glanced at the book on his desk, a growing sense of ill ease filling him. In the books, there had been plenty of demons that preyed on children. Children were victims of choice for a lot of demons because they were smaller and weaker and didn't know all the precautions to take without proper training. The material was revolting. "Yes. I'm finding too many possibilities for Kate's problem. I'm going to have to narrow the search."

Cordelia nodded toward the couch in the outer office where Doyle had sacked out earlier. "Where's Doyle?"

"He's looking for the woman he saw in his vision. The location is down at the beach, and at this time of day I couldn't go."

Cordelia smiled.

"What?" Angel asked.

"Thinking of Doyle," she said, "out in the bright morning sunlight and smelling the ocean air. With a hangover."

Doyle winced as he walked across the beach. Even the sunglasses he wore didn't cut the harsh, glaring sunlight enough to keep it from stabbing into his eyes. Sand crunched underfoot and filled his shoes.

Small children yelped as they played in the water under the watchful gazes of mothers and a few fathers. Gulls screeched, diving into the rolling green water after bits of flotsam that caught their eyes. The basso *chug-chug-chug* of diesel engines hammered the air from the fishing boats working along the ocean horizon, but Doyle knew they'd be finishing up their day before long. Even a few sport sailboats crossed the water.

Thankfully, Rudy's Fishing Tours and Supply Shack was only a brief walk from where Doyle had left the cab. The high-peaked, single-story building gave the appearance of sprawling. The weathered wooden exterior showed years of hard abuse from the elements as well as halfhearted attempts at upkeep. Fishing nets, grayed from exposure to salt water as well as the sun, draped the building, festooned with huge red-and-white floats and improbably colored plastic fish and seahorses. Doyle had found the San Pedro address in the phone book.

The half-demon stepped up onto the rolling wooden boardwalk in front of the building and followed it past the ice freezer to the front door. The interior was small and cluttered, filled with shelves of fishing supplies and snack foods. Coolers in the back held soda, juices, and beer. Long-bladed ceiling fans swept the cool air over the room, causing Doyle's skin to prickle. The bait tank behind the counter bubbled happily and reeked enough to turn his stomach. He sipped air for a moment till he got acclimated and his stomach stopped trying to tie itself into knots.

Doyle spotted the mirror he'd seen in his vision behind the counter and breathed a sigh of relief. Since this was the place he'd seen, finding the location meant he didn't have to wander up and down the beach all day. Or go to other beaches.

He approached the counter and spotted the racetrack form lying open between a cash register and a fishbowl filled with multicolored balls of hard candy. A dulled pencil held the horseracing form open and childlike writing was scrawled in the margins. Doyle scanned the names of the horses to see if any of them held any appeal for him.

"Can I help you with something?" a deep voice asked.

Doyle looked up and saw the huge man from his vision coming from a doorway behind the counter.

The man wore a shirt similar to the one he had worn in the vision, only now Doyle could see the name embroidered there. "You're Mortie?"

The big man placed a heavy box on the floor and opened it with a knife. "If I ain't, Mortie's missing one of his shirts now, ain't he?"

Despite the headache pounding between his temples, Doyle grinned.

Mortie took rolls of fishing line from the box and placed them on the shelf. "You need something, or did you just show up to read shirts?"

"I'm thinking maybe you could help me. I'm looking for someone."

"You got any ID or paper that says I got to help you?"

"No. I'm not a cop. I'm looking for a friend."

Mortie finished with the fishing line spools and stood up behind the counter. "Fishing line I got. Bait I got. Magazines and motor oil I got. Looks like I'm fresh out of friends." He smiled, but the humor never showed in his muddy eyes.

Doyle reached into his pocket and brought out a twenty-dollar bill. He smoothed it onto the counter top.

"I look like a guy that would take a bribe?" Mortie shoved his big face halfway across the counter and tightened his jaw.

"I'm just looking for a friend," Doyle said, taking a half-step back.

"Usually friends know each other's names. And they tend to leave each other phone numbers and addresses."

"Must have left all that in my other shirt."

Mortie glanced at the twenty. "If that don't get you home, it's a start. You can pick up your other shirt and come back."

"Look, you ever been in love?" Doyle asked.

Mortie gave him a cold stare. "Is this some kind of come-on? 'Cause if it is, you're going to have *Louisville Slugger* stamped across your butt when you walk out of this store." He reached below the counter and brought up a wooden baseball bat.

"No," Doyle said quickly, stepping back again. "I'm not coming on to you. Not that you're not a fine physical specimen, because you are. And big, too. There's this girl I saw a couple days ago. Ever since I saw her, I can't get her out of my mind. Me, I'm thinking it must be love, right?"

"What makes you think she's been in here?" Mortie didn't put the bat away.

"Because this is where I saw her."

"I've got a good mind for faces. If I'd seen you before, I'd remember you."

"I didn't come in the store," Doyle said. "I was outside. I saw her come in here."

Somewhat relaxed, Mortie slid the bat back under the counter. "You don't get past your hormones, you ain't never going to have a future."

Doyle tried a smile. "The way I look at it, I ever outgrow my hormones, who cares about the future?"

A smile flickered on Mortie's face. "I understand where you're coming from, Mac, but this ain't the *Love Connection.*"

"I got twenty bucks says you can point me in the direction of this girl."

"You're sure she came in here?"

"Yeah."

Mortie took a piece of hard candy from the fishbowl, unwrapped it, and popped it into his mouth. "I see a lot of people come through here in a day."

"You'd remember this woman. If it'd been a guy, I wouldn't have asked. Guys who hang around the beach, they all look alike, right?"

"Most of them. That's why you stand out so much. When was the last time you tried getting a tan?"

"Tanning cuts into my night life too much," Doyle said. "Let me tell you about this girl. I'll bet you remember her."

"Sure." Mortie went back to stocking the shelves, putting up magazines and cigarette packs in individual sliding holders about the counter. "I remember her or not, the twenty's mine." He plucked the bill from the counter.

"Deal." Doyle watched the big man in the mirror on the wall behind the counter as he described the woman he'd seen in his vision.

When Doyle finished, Mortie shook his head. "Never seen her."

"A girl pretty as that, you never noticed?" Doyle sounded incredulous. "Maybe I should check you for a pulse."

Mortie cut his eyes to the mirror, staring back at Doyle. "That's what I said."

Doyle knew the man was lying, but there wasn't a way to press the issue. "Sure. How about I get a beer and hang around for a little while."

"Suit yourself. Beer's three bucks."

Doyle started to complain, thinking about asking the guy if he thought he was made out of money, then thought better of it. The guy was almost seven feet tall. Mortie made most demons look like cream puffs by comparison. *You know the girl,* Doyle couldn't help thinking, *why are you protecting her?* The half-demon laid three singles on the counter top and headed back through the rows to the coolers.

He took a beer from the cooler and turned around. Frustration chafed at him. He knew Angel would want to move on the blood delivery operation as soon as they had more information, and he'd want to try to find Adrian Heath's wife, and now there was this vision thing bouncing around. *Why does it have to happen all at once?*

And that wasn't even taking into consideration the mysterious woman in black Angel had promised to help Detective Lockley search for. Judging from the books Angel had started looking at last night and had still been looking at this morning, Angel believed the solution to Lockley's mass murderer to be more part of their work than the detective's.

Oh, boyo, Doyle told himself, *you really didn't know what you were getting into when you let the Powers That Be talk you into this gig, did you?* Of course, there'd been no real talking to be done. The Powers That Be had sent Doyle to help Angel.

Doyle gazed around the store, then his eyes lit on a large corkboard display covering the wall between the bathrooms. Photographs, index cards, and business cards created a montage of advertising.

The pictures all seemed to be of tour guides and boats operating out of the San Pedro area. The business and index cards all offered names, numbers, hours, and rates of boats and captains. Some of the photographs showed fish customers had caught, and others showed whales in the ocean. Whale tours were conducted between December and February.

Doyle took a sip of his beer, hoping that it would help with the headache still pounding at his temples. Then he saw the blond-haired woman who had been in his vision.

She stood in the stern of one of the fishing boats, holding up a tuna that looked as big as she was. She wore frayed jean cutoffs that fit her like a second skin, a red-and-white-striped T-shirt under a gray vinyl jacket, and a white captain's hat cocked at a jaunty angle. Her smile was huge and carefree. The sun had warmed her skin to a burnished bronze.

"Hey," Doyle said, turning, "this is the—" He halted, suddenly aware that Mortie had come up beside him without making a sound.

The big man held the baseball bat in both hands, one hand on the grip and the other on the barrel. Mortie punched Doyle in the face with his fist around the bat's grip.

Doyle's head snapped back, rebounding from the wall. Pain exploded inside his head as he dropped to his knees. His beer shattered into a foaming mess on the floor.

Mortie plucked the picture from the corkboard and shoved it into his shirt pocket. Anger darkened his big features. "You're out of here, little man. You want to do it on your own, or do you want me to drag you out by your heels for the gulls to fight over?"

Doyle wrapped his hands over his head. "Slow down. If it's all the same to you, I'll just show myself out." He got up cautiously, thinking Mortie was probably waiting till he got good and level before swinging the bat off his shoulder.

"Next time I see you around here, I'm going to break something." Mortie paced him, following him to the door.

"I don't want to hurt her," Doyle said, thinking

maybe Mortie would wait till he stepped outside to hammer him with the bat. Maybe the big man had a thing about somebody bleeding on his floor. "I want to help her."

"Help her what?"

And yeah, that was the question, wasn't it? The Powers That Be had given Doyle the vision ability, but he was pretty much in the same boat as Cassandra from Greek mythology. It was in his power to see danger, but no one believed it. He backed into the door.

"Hannah's had enough grief," Mortie said. "I'll be damned if I let her go through any more." The big man stepped forward suddenly and rammed the barrel of the bat into Doyle's stomach, driving him through the doors and off the edge of the boardwalk.

The blow knocked the breath from Doyle and filled the back of his throat with bile. The half-demon was airborne for just a moment, then he fell heavily to the sand in front of the boardwalk. He clawed his way back to his knees, his ears ringing with pain. His stomach rolled restlessly, then emptied in a gush. He held himself on shaking arms till his stomach stopped rebelling, feeling the sun beat down on the back of his neck. "I'm . . . just trying . . . to help her."

"Help her what?" Mortie demanded.

Aware of the small crowd watching the encounter

171

and knowing he couldn't exactly start explaining the whole vision thing, Doyle slowly pushed himself to his feet. *There have been more embarrassing moments,* he told himself. *There must have been.* But he couldn't think of any as he stood on trembling legs. "Just try and take care of her."

Mortie took the baseball bat up in both hands. "Is that some kind of threat?"

"No," Doyle said. Knowing he was better off just cutting his losses, he kept his arm wrapped protectively over his stomach and stumbled away.

Angel stared over Cordelia's shoulder at the computer screen where they'd been working for the last hour. Screen after screen of information had popped up regarding Marisa Smith, or Marisa Smith and Adrian Heath, or Marisa Heath. None of the information went back any further than eight years ago when Marisa had gotten a part on *Daring High*.

"It's like Marisa just stepped off a cloud in downtown L.A. eight years ago," Cordelia said disgustedly.

"Like Venus." Angel straightened with a few twinges of pain. His wounds from last night's encounter had almost healed.

"Venus?" Cordelia looked up at him.

"Sandro Botticelli's *The Birth of Venus.* It's a painting. About the birth of Venus, the Greek goddess of love. She was supposed to have sprung full-born from the sea."

"If you had a television set down in your lair, I'd accuse you of watching too much Discovery Channel." Cordelia sipped her Starbucks latte. "People don't just appear."

"Adrian said she was twenty-seven," Angel pointed out. "Eight years ago, she'd have been nineteen. She probably lived with her parents until she got out on her own."

"There's no credit history before she was a cast member on *Daring High*."

"She was nineteen. It's kind of hard to have a credit history at nineteen."

"My dad gave me my own charge card at fourteen," Cordelia objected. "My car was registered in my name at sixteen."

Angel looked at Cordelia.

"Okay, so maybe I didn't have the typical teen life." Cordelia stared at the screen, then tapped keys. She shifted through the news stories written about Adrian Heath, stopping when she reached the ones concerning his marriage to Marisa Smith. The local papers had only mentioned the event briefly, but the trade papers and media had covered the wedding in more depth. "There's something else that bothers me. Where was Marisa's family during the wedding?"

"Adrian said that Marisa had lost her parents."

"You'd think they'd have at least mentioned their names. You know, Marisa Smith, daughter of Mom and Pop Smith."

"What about the marriage license?"

Cordelia tapped the keys again. In a digitized flicker, an electronic copy of the marriage license appeared on the screen. "John and Mary Smith."

"Okay, she had parents."

Cordelia glanced at him, raising her eyes in disbelief. "John and Mary Smith? C'mon, that's really weak."

"People really are named John and Mary, you know."

"I want to find one or both of these parents," Cordelia declared.

"Why?"

"It's a hunch. You know, one of those intuitive things we detectives get from time to time. When the facts don't add up or they add up too easily, you get a hunch." Cordelia frowned at Angel. "I've been in this business long enough to develop instincts, you know."

Angel decided not to argue or point out that a couple months as a part-time detective, *not* specializing in traditional cases, hardly qualified as *long enough*. Cordelia had a tendency to be . . . well, *Cordelia*. And as Cordelia she sometimes saw things that others didn't see. Of course, sometimes those things that she saw were completely in her mind.

"She's hiding her parents," Cordelia said. "It's pretty convenient that her father and mother are both dead, don't you think?"

"How do you figure that?"

"Well," Cordelia said, "they're both gone. Not in the way. Not being embarrassing. Not trying to manage her or tell her what to do."

"Oh," Angel said. "You do realize that people who become successes in Hollywood or political office sometimes . . . have relatives creep out of the woodwork. If her parents were interested in her career . . . or alive, I think they'd have put in an appearance."

"Unless they didn't know."

Angel folded his arms. "I'm lost."

"Suppose Marisa's parents are both in prison—"

"Both?"

"Sure," Cordelia insisted. "Stranger things have happened. Or maybe there's some other reason she would have been embarrassed to mention them." She smiled suddenly. "What if they're in the Witness Protection Program?"

"Cordelia," Angel said calmly, "are you doing readings for the soaps again?"

Cordelia smiled more broadly. "Maybe her parents are blackmailing her. They could have threatened to go on some talk show and spill the beans."

"About what?"

Cordelia sighed in exasperation. "I don't know. Whatever secrets Marisa is hiding."

"What makes you think she's hiding anything?"

"The way she went into hiding. Unless you want to vote for alien abduction."

Angel reluctantly nodded. There was no arguing that. Something had made Marisa Heath disappear from her life, husband, and home.

"I kind of like the Witness Protection Program idea," Cordelia said.

"Let's hope it's something else." Angel worked his stiff neck. "Let's keep working the information on Marisa. If the problem didn't come from her husband, then it came from her. Maybe she has other problems we haven't turned over yet."

"There is one other thing that looks promising." Cordelia tapped the keyboard. "Some of Adrian's businesses are located down in the Huntington Park area. A lot of complaints have been filed, and there have been a number of protests over the years."

Angel watched the computer screen fill with newspaper pages. Groups carrying signs stood in front of factories on desolate streets, kept at bay by uniformed security guards with dogs and a tall fence topped with razor wire. "Is this one of Adrian's factories?"

"This one isn't, but the article names Adrian Heath's companies on a list of those that are causing serious pollution in the area."

Angel studied the picture. "How violent have the protests been?"

Before Cordelia could answer, the phone rang. "Angel Investigations," she answered smoothly. "We help the helpless." She listened for a moment, made a gag-me face, and handed the phone over to Angel. "It's for you. Police Woman."

Taking the phone, Angel stepped back toward his office. Neither Detective Kate Lockley nor Cordelia seemed to like each other for reasons that Angel couldn't understand. He'd stopped trying to figure out women's reactions to each other over a hundred years ago. It was all still fascinating to watch, but he watched from a safe distance these days.

"Hello, Kate," Angel answered.

"I've only got a minute," Kate said. "Have you turned up anything on the woman in black?"

"No."

"If there's any way you can turn the heat up on that, I need it."

"What's wrong?"

"Two police officers were killed last night," Kate said.

"I remember hearing something about it over the radio this morning. It was some kind of gang activity or something like that?"

"That's the way the press is getting it," Kate replied. "But that's not what went down. It was the woman in black again. Witnesses gave us descriptions that matched the one the officer at the convenience store gave us."

Angel listened silently, knowing Kate would tell the rest of the story when she was ready.

"According to the witnesses, the woman shoved her hand completely through one of the officers' heads. The coroner said it was the kind of damage you'd expect from a tornado throwing a two-by-four through a man's body."

"What about the other officer?"

"He'd been manhandled. The woman even reached into the car and yanked him through the glass. But he died from aneurysms. According to the coroner's reports, the Bleeding Hearts gang members died the same way."

"Where'd the woman go?"

"She walked away. The witnesses were a mentally challenged newspaper guy and a few working girls. I interviewed the newspaper guy myself. He said the woman was looking for her children."

"Her children?" Something stirred restlessly in the back of Angel's mind.

"That's what she told the witness. She said that her children were taken from her and the world owed her its children. Does that make any sense to you?"

"No," Angel replied. "Not yet."

A voice called Kate's name in the background at her end of the connection. "I've got to go. You know I don't like asking, and I wouldn't if I had another choice. But I've got the feeling if we don't find out who this woman is quickly and shut her down, the body count is going to go a lot higher."

"I'll be in touch," Angel promised. "Did you get a chance to find out anything on that eighteen-wheeler?"

The story about the kidnapped victims had broken over the news that morning as well. Speculation through the media was that the clandestine organization behind the kidnappings was doing everything from selling their victims' blood to cultists to providing DNA for illegal research labs. No one was talking about vampires.

"It was a gypsy rig," Kate said. "The plates on it were stolen and the paperwork all dummied. Forensics is still checking out what was left of it. What's your interest in it?"

Angel didn't answer. He didn't intend to tell her the truth and he didn't intend to lie to her.

The voice in the background called Kate's name again.

"I've got to go," Kate said. "Find out what you can about the woman in black and get back to me." The phone line clicked dead.

The woman was looking for her children. Kate's remembered words sent a chill down Angel's spine, which was very unusual since his body normally matched the room temperature. Something yammered in the back of his mind but he couldn't quite get a grip on it. *You ever lost family?* the homeless man had asked. For a moment, the images Angel had seen in the books during last night's research session blurred in his mind, overlapping the images of his family lying dead in the house that they had shared.

The demon writhed within Angel, and he could feel the glad hunger of the beast in that part of him that remained anchored in darkness. Was he any better than whatever thing the woman in black turned out to be?

"Angel."

Drawn back to the present by Cordelia's voice, Angel looked at her.

"Reality break," Cordelia said. "I wanted to make sure you were still with me."

"The pollution," Angel said.

"Right." Cordelia tapped the keys, shifting stories around as she spoke. "Primarily, that section of the city is concerned with toxicity levels. Some of those areas were zoned as waste dumps before the Environmental Protection Act redefined different levels of pollution. The companies responsible for the dumping have either gone out of business or decided to declare hardship so they could take their time cleaning up after themselves."

"But the toxic sites are still a problem for the people who live there," Angel said.

Cordelia nodded. "The neighborhood is primarily low-income. The housing is cheap and the people there really don't have a place to go. The people who own the apartment buildings keep the rent low enough so tenants don't want to move out."

"Because they know no one else would rent those apartments."

"Yes. If they did go out of business, one of the environmental impact studies says a lot of those people living there now would become homeless. Families would be broken up."

You ever lost family? Angel tried to clear the old man's voice from his mind but only succeeded in muting it. "The toxicity levels are harmful?"

"Not necessarily so," Cordelia said. "According to another report referenced in these articles, the main problems facing the community are concrete dust from the brickworks and air pollution. Things have gotten so bad there a lot of the people have renamed the neighborhood Asthmatown. The incidence of asthma in the neighborhood is a lot higher than anywhere else in the area."

"Asthma?"

"It's a respiratory disorder," Cordelia said. "Not something *you'll* have to worry about. Concrete dust, smoke, and other foreign particles breathed in by an asthmatic person irritate the lungs. As a result, capillaries used to transfer oxygen get sealed up. The person feels like they can't breathe in, but the actual problem is that the air gets trapped in the lungs and they can't breathe out. Primarily children and the elderly are affected."

"How bad is it?"

"People die every year from asthma attacks there." Cordelia tapped the keys again. "Protest groups track the numbers of deaths as well as hospital emergency room visits. The last fatality from an asthma attack was only five days ago; an eight-year-old boy named Cristofer Segura." She paused and brought up a newspaper article showing a small, grinning boy. The small headline beside him read: *Protesters in Huntington Park Claim Pollution Responsible in Death of 8-Year-Old.* "That's really sad, you know?"

"Yes," Angel said. "That's the same area that Kate's convenience store is in." *The woman was looking for her children.* Had the woman in black lost children to the disease? But demons didn't have the same weaknesses to most human diseases and illnesses.

"Maybe some of the protesters decided to kidnap Marisa Heath."

"Why her? Why not someone else?"

"Maybe she was just the first. Also, Adrian is known throughout the Hollywood sector. Maybe he's not a big deal in some people's books, but the media would definitely carry the story about his missing wife."

"Then why not deliver a ransom note? Shut down your factories or else."

Cordelia shrugged. "I don't know."

"Have the protesters ever acted violently before? Or done property damage?"

"Not in anything I've found."

"It's hard to imagine that they would move from nonviolent protesting to kidnapping." Angel shook his head. "It's something else, Cordelia. If there's been no contact with Adrian, maybe it was a revenge thing solely against Marisa."

"Revenge for what?"

"We'll have to find out." Angel's thoughts twisted and squirmed in his mind like an overturned basket of snakes. Nothing was adding up and none of the things he was involved with seemed to lead anywhere. The phone rang, breaking his limited concentration.

"Angel Investigations," Cordelia said. "We help the helpless." She smiled sweetly. "Oh, it's you. How about that sunshine? Isn't it great to be alive and out in the California morning?" She passed the phone off to Angel. "Doyle."

"Yeah," Angel said, hoping Doyle had something to go on. Staying in the office wasn't working out for him. "Have you found the woman?"

"No," Doyle replied, "but I found a guy who seems to think highly of her. Nearly stove my ribs in with a baseball bat."

Angel listened as Doyle described his morning. *Nothing's going to be easy.* "The only thing you can do," Angel said when the half-demon finished, "is stay with the bait shop."

"I'm thinking maybe Mortie needs to be hung up by his toenails—"

"Then do it," Angel said.

"Me?" Doyle cursed. "You ain't seen how big Mortie is. I'd need a winch."

Angel spotted an elderly woman walking slowly through the hallway outside the front office. She looked at every office number, then stopped at the office door. "Stay with it, Doyle. I've got to go."

"Go where?"

"Looks like we're getting a new client," Angel said.

At that, Cordelia looked up from the computer monitor and shock filled her face. She turned to Angel and pointed at the elderly woman.

"Tell whoever it is that we're up to our ears," Doyle suggested. "You stay this busy, we're going to have to open up a branch office. Hey, two guys are headed my way. What do you think I should—"

"I'll talk to you later." Angel broke the connection and cradled the phone. *It's daylight,* he told himself. *Doyle can't get into that much trouble.*

"She has to be lost," Cordelia whispered as the elderly woman stepped into the office.

Angel didn't think so. The woman was dressed in a severe and voluminous black-and-white nun's habit, and the only thing she seemed unsure about was answered in a moment.

"I'm looking for Angel Investigations," the elderly woman said.

"Do you think Angel Investigations has done something bad?" Cordelia asked. "Because if that's what you're thinking, you're wrong. And we resent the whole implication. See, you entered the office and lightning didn't strike anyone, did it?"

The nun looked at Cordelia and pursed her lips in disapproval. She held her rosary in her hands.

"I'm Angel," Angel said, a little nervously.

With a brief, practiced glance, Angel sized her up. She was eighty years old if she was a day, and her flesh had started to sag from the bones. Her eyes remained level, muddy green and intense. Her Spanish ancestry showed in the planes of her face and her skin coloration. "I'm Sister Juanita Canales, and I need help. It's a matter of life and death."

Angel nodded.

"There are many children in danger," the old woman said.

CHAPTER ELEVEN

Eleadora Longoria massaged her aching back and watched her second-grade class at recess. Normally a small woman, she felt like she was incredibly huge with her pregnancy. And no matter what she did with her feet, they always swelled terribly after only an hour of class even when she tried to remain at her desk.

She glanced out at the street on the other side of the chain-link fence. Traffic moved slowly out there, and every now and again a car or truck would pass by and the driver would honk and wave at the children playing in the schoolyard.

When she spotted the woman in black coming down the street, passing through the shadows of the sheet metal factory on the other side, Eleadora envied the woman her figure. *Once,* she told herself, *I was that slim and pretty.* It seemed hard to believe now.

The woman in black kept walking, and for a moment Eleadora wondered why such a pretty woman would walk. Surely she had a car or had a man who had a car. Or had family. Even though most of the families that attended the school were within walking distance, this woman didn't look like a pedestrian. But her stride was calm and measured, as if she'd done this every day of her life.

A squeal attracted Eleadora's attention. "Gabriel," she admonished a young boy who had been chasing one of the girls, "if I see that again, you'll go inside and spend your recess in the principal's office."

Gabriel didn't look her way, but he stopped his pursuit.

The children often played hard, running after each other even though they knew the rules forbade them to chase each other or even race. Too many injuries happened in the crowded playground now that the paved areas had started to crack. There was never enough money in the school funding to make repairs. Some days Eleadora felt like the land was trying to absorb the old school back into the ground.

Despite the cool weather, she still perspired heavily and that embarrassed her as well. It seemed her body was out to betray her in her final trimester. Everything she'd thought she'd known about herself now seemed to be a distant memory.

"Is your back aching, Mrs. Longoria?"

Eleadora looked over to Mrs. Nunez, the fifth-grade teacher who had taught her when she'd been a little girl at the elementary school. Eleadora was certain Mrs. Nunez was past retirement age, but her husband had passed on ten years ago and she had nothing else she wanted to do with her time except teach and nurture children. The school board had evidently chosen to let her stay. Good teachers were hard to come by.

Mrs. Nunez was just the way Eleadora remembered her. The woman was wrinkled as a prune, but still walked straight and could whip an entire classroom into shape with a single word. She wore a shapeless navy-blue-and-white dress and a red scarf that held her flat-brimmed straw hat to her head. Gloves hid her liver-spotted hands these days.

"My back is aching terribly, Mrs. Nunez," Eleadora replied. As teachers, they were required to call each other by their surnames to teach the children respect.

"You shouldn't be taking on playground duties," Mrs. Nunez said. "There are other women who can fill in for you."

"No," Eleadora replied. "I will do until I'm no longer able to do." She glanced at the older woman. "I once had a great teacher who taught me to extend my limitations."

Mrs. Nunez smiled slightly. "I'm quite sure she wasn't referring to having a teacher stand duty so close to term. How far away are you now? Two weeks?"

"Sixteen days. Fifteen and a half. It is noon, after all." Eleadora rubbed her back again, but it still didn't help. Only Juan's hands seemed able to massage the ache away.

"The baby could come at any day," Mrs. Nunez warned.

"I know. But I don't want to use my sick leave until after the baby arrives."

"I understand. You have spoken to Father Carlos about christening the baby?"

"Yes, but I heard there was an accident at the church last night."

"I had not heard."

"There was a break-in after they had poor Cristofer's eulogy last evening."

"God forbid that such things await any of His children," Mrs. Nunez said. "I was at the eulogy. I had thought surely his mother would come."

"She may not know. Maria left Cristofer just after he was born."

"That one was always wanting more from life. She was such a sad child." Mrs. Nunez sighed. "I do not know how mothers can leave their children these days. It was bad enough when the fathers started doing such things."

"I could never leave this baby. He or she will only know the love of Juan and me."

Mrs. Nunez smiled reassuringly. "You married well. Juan will be a good father, and you will be a good mother. I may not have been so blessed, but trust my wisdom in this matter, anyway."

"I will. And thank you." Eleadora knew that Mrs. Nunez had never had children of her own, but she'd loved every child who had come through her classes. That was not, Eleadora had learned in the past three years, an easy thing to do.

"Who is that woman?" Mrs. Nunez asked.

Glancing across the street, Eleadora saw that the woman in black had stopped. She stood on the other side of the street and stared at the playground. *At the children,* Eleadora realized. A chill passed through her and her unborn child twisted inside her belly.

"I don't know," Eleadora answered.

The traffic remained heavy for a moment. Then, when it lessened, the woman in black stepped from the curb and approached the school.

"There is something . . . *wrong* about her," Mrs. Nunez said quietly.

Eleadora felt it as well. Panic welled up within her, slamming into her with the intensity of a wave coming up from the beach. Her baby fought inside her belly, twisting and turning as if trying to escape. Unconsciously, she cupped her arm around her stomach, rubbing lightly, knowing from experience that she could calm her baby most of the time. *You feel it, too, don't you, little one? How wrong this woman is.*

The children nearest the chain-link fence glanced up at the woman in black's approach. They stared at her the way the mice in the apartment hallways stared at the cats an instant before they were pounced on. More of the children quieted in turn, like ripples spreading out from a pool, watching the woman in frozen fascination.

"She's after the children," Eleadora whispered hoarsely. Her heart pounded as the fear spilled over her. Her baby continued moving frantically. She couldn't name what prompted her to make such a declaration, but she knew it was true.

The woman in black stepped in close to the chain-link fence. The slight breeze whipped her dark hair. A bloodless smile twisted her lips. "Children," she said happily. "How nice to see you."

Before she knew she was in motion, Eleadora was lifting her whistle to her lips. "Mrs. Nunez, get the children inside the school." She glanced down at the curly-haired fifth-grader at her side. Esteban had been sent to her class for in-school suspension. Spending the day in a second-grade class was big punishment for a fifth-grader. "Esteban."

The boy glanced up at her. "Yes, Mrs. Longoria."

"Go get Mr. Vasquez. Hurry!"

Esteban was up and gone like a shot, probably grateful for the chance to get out from under her scrutiny, but maybe he sensed the danger the woman in black presented as well. Mr. Vasquez was part janitor and part security guard for the school.

Eleadora put the whistle to her lips and blew fiercely. The piercing blast drew the attention of every child on the playground. "Recess is over! Everyone line up and follow Mrs. Nunez into the building! Now!"

Normally, some of the children lagged even though it might mean writing sentences later. However, today they all hurried.

Mrs. Nunez picked a leader and started the children into the building in a quick, orderly fashion.

Legs trembling, Eleadora stepped toward the center of the playground, not knowing what she could do against the woman in black, but not wanting to leave the children's flank unprotected as they withdrew.

"What are you doing?" the woman in black demanded.

"You need to go away," Eleadora commanded fiercely. "No one can talk to the children while they're on the playground."

"Bring them back," the woman in black said. "You can't just take them away."

Looking at the woman's face, Eleadora suddenly realized the woman in black was crying. Tears flowed down her cheeks. Maybe she was mentally or emotionally disturbed. "Go away," Eleadora ordered, "or I will call the police."

"You can't take the children from me. I won't let you. They are mine." The woman in black thrust her hands into the spaces in the chain-link fence and pulled. Metal strands popped with harsh pings, and—incredibly—the fence tore like tissue paper.

Taking a hesitant step back, Eleadora peered over her shoulder and saw that not all of the children had made it into the building. She turned back to the woman in black, not knowing what kind of creature she faced.

When the tear in the fence was big enough, the woman in black stepped through gracefully. She stared at Eleadora, then opened her mouth and laughed maniacally as tears trickled over her lips and into her mouth. "You can't stop me, foolish woman. Those children are mine. I paid the blood price for them. They are all mine."

Trembling, Eleadora managed to hold her ground. "No."

"I will kill you," the woman in black threatened. "And I will take your child from you as well." She held up one hand, the nails gleaming, edged and sharp.

"Leave the schoolyard!" a fierce voice ordered.

Eleadora stared at the woman in black as her attention switched to Ernesto Vasquez. The man stepped toward the trespasser. Vasquez was in his forties, a solidly built man with gray, cottony hair and a pencil mustache. He wore a khaki janitor's uniform. His wife, Clementina, worked in the cafeteria.

Tears continued to run down the woman in black's face as she laughed. The sound was lyrical and haunted, dredged from the pits of painful despair.

"I'm only going to ask you once to leave on your own feet," Vasquez threatened. "Then I'm going to throw you over the fence myself. The police are already on their way."

"They will come," the woman in black said, "but they will hasten only to their deaths." She stepped forward again.

Vasquez grabbed her by the shoulders. The woman in black moved so fast that Eleadora almost couldn't see the motions. The woman's hands exploded up between Vasquez's at the same time a cold wind raked across the playground. The wind swept litter and dust up from the playground and peppered Eleadora with stinging grit.

Grunting in surprise, Vasquez doubled a fist and punched at the woman in black's head. She grabbed his fist effortlessly, then twisted it and squeezed. The sound of splintering bone almost made Eleadora throw up. Vasquez dropped to his knees, screaming in pain. Still, he tried to rope the woman in black's legs with his free arm. The woman slammed her free palm against Vasquez's face. He stopped screaming and dropped to the ground, bright blood bubbling from his mouth and nose as his eyes froze in a death gaze.

The woman stepped over the man's dead body. She was still crying and laughing, her shoulders shaking with the effort. "Step aside," she demanded.

More than anything else in the world, Eleadora wanted to step aside, but she couldn't leave the children inside the building unprotected. "N-n-no," she said in a trembling voice.

The woman stopped laughing, but the tears continued to fall. "You would seek to stop me even if it means the life of your unborn daughter?"

Daughter? Eleadora didn't know how the woman could be so certain about such a thing. Eleadora and Juan had deliberately chosen not to know the sex of their child. "I can't let you pass."

"You can't stop me," the woman in black said. She took a step forward.

The baby twisted and turned inside Eleadora, jerking frantically as if trying to get free of the flesh and blood prison that held it—*her?*—there. Eleadora stood frozen, not knowing for a moment if she was standing up to the woman or was simply too scared to move.

The woman in black moved within arm's reach. Her dark eyes held Eleadora's. "You would die, then?" the woman in black demanded.

Raw, primitive fear fed adrenaline through Eleadora's system. "You will not harm my child. You will not harm any child at this school." The strange wind whipped around her, pulling at her big dress and her hair, causing goosebumps to cover her.

The woman in black drew her hand back to strike. Her face was etched marble, pitiless.

"Will you kill yet another innocent, *bruja?*" Eleadora demanded. She didn't know where the words came from, hadn't even known she had the strength to speak. "There is no evil in my child, nothing you can seek out or touch or corrupt. My child is sacrosanct. My love for my child is pure."

"Are you so sure?" the woman in black asked.

Eleadora stood there, unable to move, not knowing why she'd spoken as she had. But it had seemed so right.

The woman in black lowered her hand. "You've only delayed the inevitable, teacher. No one may stay my hand if I wish it. I will walk the earth as long as I want this time, and even God will hide His face at the things I will do." She turned and walked away, stepping over Vasquez again without looking at the man she'd killed.

Eleadora heard screaming sirens down the street as the woman in black stepped back into the shadows of the city.

"Mrs. Longoria!" Esteban cried, coming up to her. "Who was that woman?"

Trembling, suddenly weak, Eleadora placed her arm over the small boy's shoulders. "She is a *bruja*, Esteban."

"A witch? But I thought they weren't real."

"Most are not," Eleadora told the boy. "Until today, I had never met one. But that woman . . . she was a *bruja*." When she noticed Esteban staring down at Vasquez, she took him by the hand and led him back to the school.

On the way, her water broke and she knew her baby was coming. Only a little earlier, such a thing would have made her glad and feel relieved. She had waited so long for the baby to come, and been so uncomfortable these past weeks.

Now she cried, wishing that she could keep the baby within her where it would be safe. Once it was born, the evil of the world would touch her child and it would be prey for the *bruja* as well. She would not be able to keep the woman in black from taking her child then.

Nothing, she felt certain, could stop the woman in black.

CHAPTER TWELVE

"Angel?" Doyle listened to the empty white noise that filled the phone receiver. *I can't believe he just hung up on me.* He continued hanging on to the receiver as if he were still talking to someone, watching as the two big men bore down on him. *Oh yeah. There is no doubt they're headed for you, Doyle. The big question is: Why?*

He stood in the shade of the awning in front of Cap'n Buy Krikey's Souvenir Shop and Sailboat Rentals. The pay phone was mounted on the front of the building. The paved boardwalk was partially buried under sand.

Down the beach, half the distance to the rolling curlers marking the water from the tide and the boats, a group of twenty-somethings of both sexes played loud, raucous volleyball. A guy only slightly older but showing three or four days' growth of beard watched the action behind a pair of amber-tinted Oakleys.

Doyle looked past the two men approaching him as if they weren't there.

The bigger guy was broad as a football player and looked like he worked out on a regular basis. If he hadn't hit thirty yet, it wasn't far away. Sandy blond hair streaked with blue highlights framed his chiseled face, and it was easy to read the anger there. He wore green windbreaker pants and a black tank with TUFF ENUF in red letters.

The other guy was about the same age and was built along the same lines. He wore a short-cropped beard, mirrored sunglasses, camou pants that showed salt scars from frequent encounters with brine and a red shirt bearing a Betty Page Jungle Girl print.

Both men stopped in front of Doyle.

"Need to talk to you," the bigger guy said.

"I'll be just a minute," Doyle said. "I'm talking to my sergeant at the precinct." He made a show of turning back to continue the conversation with the phone. "Yeah, sarge, I know I'm supposed to be handing out more tickets at the beach, but this whole undercover thing isn't working out for me. I mean, everybody I talk to makes me for a cop. Guess I've just got that look, you know."

"Please hang up and try your call again," the recorded operator's voice said.

Doyle cursed, trying to pull the earpiece tighter.

The big guy took another step forward, plucked the phone from Doyle's hand, and hung it up.

"Hey, you can't do that," Doyle protested. "You're interfering in police business."

"Show me some ID," the big guy suggested.

"You're asking *me* for ID?" Doyle asked, feigning exasperation. "Man, I can't believe that. I draw this detail, everybody on this beach makes me for an undercover cop without a second look, and you want to see ID."

"You've been asking questions about people," the bigger man said. "Mortie busted you up a little a few minutes ago and you didn't arrest him."

Doyle tried to make his voice fierce, borrowing cop inflections he'd heard over the last few years when they'd rousted him. "You see, I'm setting that up now. Maybe you want to ride along with Mortie when they take him downtown to the big house." *There; that sounds like cop-talk, doesn't it?*

"This is San Pedro," the big guy said. "You get popped for a beef here, you go to San Pedro lockup. I've been there a time or two."

Doyle searched his pants. "Man, somebody nicked my wallet. But you can bet when I find out who did it they'll be taken down hard."

Without warning, the big guy grabbed Doyle by the shirt lapels and yanked him from the building. Keeping hold of Doyle with one hand, he backhanded him with the other.

Doyle's head popped around to the side and black spots flooded his vision.

"Do I have your attention?" the big guy asked.

"Yeah. You got my attention." Doyle tasted blood inside his mouth.

The man in sunglasses quickly frisked Doyle and went through his pockets. "Got no wallet. Little bit of folding cash." Surprisingly, he put the money back into Doyle's pocket.

"I don't know who you are," the bigger guy said, "and I don't want to get to know you. I never want to see you again after we talk." He brought a knee up into Doyle's crotch.

Doyle crumpled to his knees, folding up in a fetal position. Before he fell, the big guy punched him in the face, driving him down into the sandy ground.

"You stay away from her," the big guy threatened.

"Who?" Doyle asked, hoping to get a name.

The big guy fisted Doyle's shirt and yanked him to his knees again. Before Doyle had a chance to block, the man drove his fist into his stomach three times. Gasping for his lost breath and filled with red-hot agony as the pain in his ribs flared to new heights, Doyle slid bonelessly to the ground.

"Any more questions?" the big guy asked.

Doyle shook his head and waved the guy off, surrendering. He kept his eyes averted, knowing from experience that sometimes even looking at an aggressor could instigate a continuation of the beating.

A minute stretched out long and hard and thin. *Surely somebody has called the police by now,* Doyle hoped.

"Terry," a new voice said calmly, "looks to me like he's had enough."

"This isn't any of your affair, Harper."

"If this guy ends up in the hospital," Harper said evenly, "I'll be a witness. He didn't even try to fight you. Do you think your sister's going to like hearing about this?"

"Mind your own business, Harper."

"I will, as long as you know you're done here."

The big guy cursed the newcomer out for a moment with a fisherman's expertise, and briefly turned his attention to heaping more abuse and threats on Doyle. Then, as quickly as they'd come, the two men turned and walked away.

Hardly daring to look, Doyle watched them go between his splayed fingers. He glanced up at the man who'd stepped in, noticing that it was the man who had been watching the volleyball game earlier. "Man, it's a good thing you came along," Doyle groaned.

"Because you were about to kick his ass, right?" Harper grinned and pushed the Oakleys up onto his head.

"His and his friend's. Took everything I had to hold myself back." Doyle rolled over and forced himself to a sitting position. He dry-heaved a couple times, then managed to stick his head between his bent knees and sip a couple deep breaths. Some of the pain receded.

Harper offered his hand and eased Doyle to his feet. "Might be better if we weren't here long," Harper said. "Someone probably did call the police and there'll be a cruiser along in a few minutes. Unless you're wanting to swear out a complaint?"

"No," Doyle replied. "Me and the police, we got a long history of not understanding each other too well."

"Good," Harper said. "That way I don't have to break your heart by refusing to be a witness."

"You'd do that?" Doyle asked, weaving unsteadily and trying to ignore the pain gnawing at the bottom of his stomach.

"In a heartbeat. I don't owe you anything, and Terry's part of the community."

Doyle nodded in understanding. He was an outsider; Terry Whatever-His-Name-Was lived in the area. That was good to know, though, because it also meant the woman he'd seen in his vision probably also lived in the area. "You probably saved my life there. I thought he was going to kill me."

"Not Terry," Harper shook his head. "He may have put you in the hospital, but he wouldn't have killed you. Noticed you had a run-in with Mortie earlier."

"It's this new self-help audio tape I've been working on," Doyle said. "Helps you make new friends."

"How's that working out for you?"

"So far," Doyle said, touching his ribs, "I'm batting a thousand."

"Mortie is, anyway."

"I met you," Doyle pointed out. He glanced across the expanse of beach and spotted Mortie standing at one of the bait shop windows.

"I'm not your friend."

"Are you Terry's friend?"

"Not really."

Doyle nodded. "Is there a bar around here? I'll buy you a beer."

"How are the children in danger?" Angel asked. He sat at his desk. Cordelia sat on the office chair borrowed from the outside room, and Sister Juanita Canales occupied the client chair in front of the desk.

"Because a thing was taken from the church," the nun said.

"What thing?" Angel asked.

"I can't tell you everything about this thing without the *padre*'s permission."

"Then we can call him," Cordelia said. "If he says you can tell us, no problem, right?"

"Father Carlos is in no condition to talk on the phone," Sister Juanita replied. "He's in the hospital. Last night, when the thing that I can't tell you about was taken, the *padre* was attacked. He's in intensive care at the hospital."

"Who attacked Father Carlos?" Angel asked.

"A woman."

"Like a woman scorned woman?" Cordelia asked.

Sister Juanita gave Cordelia a disapproving look, like she'd just bitten into a lemon. "No. The *padre* is a good man."

"So who was the woman?" Angel asked.

"We don't know. Only Albula was there when this woman came in."

"Did Father Carlos know the woman?"

"We don't know." Sister Juanita sighed. "He's in a coma. Last night, the *padre* delivered a eulogy for an eight-year-old boy named Cristofer Segura." She shook her head. "His death was a sad thing. It is terrible to see the young die in such a horrible manner."

"That was the little boy with asthma, right?" Cordelia asked.

Suspicious surprise dawned in Sister Juanita's eyes. "How did you know?"

"Only from another case we're working on," Angel said.

"What case would that be?"

"We're not at liberty to say," Cordelia said before Angel could respond. She crossed her arms and returned the old nun's stare full measure.

"This is a matter of grave import," Sister Juanita said. "I would ask that you not trifle with this."

"I'm not," Cordelia replied evenly.

Sister Juanita gathered her skirts and stood. "Perhaps I've made an error in coming here." She headed for the door.

Angel stood quickly, wanting to find the right words to stop the nun's departure. "Sister, is this about the woman in black?"

The nun stopped moving for the door. She turned slowly and studied Angel. "You've seen her?"

"No, but I know about her. I'm helping a friend of mine—a detective with the Los Angeles Police Department—try to find the woman in black. She killed a group of Bleeding Hearts at a convenience store not far from the church. And a twelve-year-old boy."

"Yes," Sister Juanita said.

"She also killed two police officers last night."

The nun nodded. "I had heard that."

"Please," Angel said. "Tell me about it. If I can help, I will."

Sister Juanita hesitated for a moment, shot Cordelia a reproving glance, then seated herself again. "The *padre* was gravely injured last night. A wound to the side of his head. The woman hit him, you see, with a shovel."

"A shovel?" Angel asked. "Where did she get the shovel?"

The nun blinked. "Does it matter?"

"If she brought the shovel in, it might indicate more about her."

"Like maybe she's a gardener," Cordelia put in.

"She didn't bring the shovel in," Sister Juanita replied. "She found it down in the basement of the church and used it against the *padre.*"

"What were they doing in the church basement?" Cordelia asked.

"After the eulogy," the nun said, "a woman entered the church. The *padre* and Albula were cleaning up after everyone had left. Many people showed up." She gazed at Angel. "You know how it is with churches when it makes a community close."

"Yes," Angel told her. Memories of the times he'd gone to church with his parents and his sister rolled through his mind. There had been dinners and weddings and christenings, and dozens of other celebrations and wakes that had kept the community close. At the time, he'd had other interests pulling at him. Shortly after that, Darla had appeared.

"The *padre* likes his time alone in the church," Sister Juanita went on. "Especially after such a trying event as the death of a small parishioner."

"Cristofer's family went to church there?" Angel asked.

"His grandmother, yes. Cristofer's mother ran away shortly after the baby was born. Lavina Segura had no luck with family. You know how it is in some families."

The dark pain twisted inside Angel but he kept

his face placid. He nodded, not trusting his voice. Inside him, the demon darkness laughed, enjoying his agony.

"Lavina had two sons," Sister Juanita said. "Her oldest joined the merchant marine and fell in love with the sea and solitude. He chooses to have no children, and not to return to his home. The second boy died in the streets ten years ago, killed by one of the Latino gangs. Perhaps he was a gang member as well. To learn now could only break her heart more. Maria stayed with Lavina when she lost her husband to a weak heart two years after that. Then Maria left just after the baby was born. She's not been back." The nun paused. "All that Lavina had was Cristofer, and now he's gone."

Angel remained quiet, listening to the voice in the back of his mind. Pieces were sliding together back there and he had the sense of a pattern, but he couldn't quite see it.

"As I said," Sister Juanita went on, "the *padre* and Albula—she is Lavina's sister-in-law, married to Lavina's husband's brother—were cleaning when the woman came in."

"Albula never got a good look at the woman?" Angel asked.

"No. She wore a veil like she was in mourning."

"She wasn't at the eulogy?"

"Albula didn't think so. The woman talked like she had missed the eulogy and was shamed by that.

Albula left the church to leave the woman alone with the *padre*. They went to the confessional."

"Because she missed the eulogy?" Cordelia asked. "That's a lot of guilt."

"It was a subterfuge," Sister Juanita insisted. "The *padre* went into the confessional booth with the woman. Albula heard that, then she later heard the *padre* calling out for the woman. Alarmed, Albula went back into the church from the kitchen. She saw that the door to the basement was open. When she peered down into the darkness, she saw the woman hit Father Carlos with the shovel kept in the basement. Albula ran back to the *padre*'s office and called the police. By the time they got there, the woman was gone."

"Why did she go to the basement?" Angel asked.

The nun hesitated.

"Sister Juanita," Angel said softly, "I can't help you if I don't know more."

"Yes." The nun sighed. "What was told me was told me in confidence. Even the police do not know why the woman went down there."

"But you do," Angel said.

Sister Juanita knotted her trembling hands together in her lap. "Yes. Father Carlos was married for a very long time to a wonderful woman, though they were never blessed with children. I had the good fortune to know her. As she lay dying of cancer ten years ago, with Lavina Segura and I in attendance because the poor *padre* was beside himself in his grief and confusion, she told us of the secret room in the back of the basement. Until that time, we had never known of the room. And I have been at that church all my life."

"Was that what the woman was after?" Angel asked.

"That's all it could be."

"What was in the room?" Angel asked.

Sister Juanita shook her head. "I don't know. The *padre*'s wife, she didn't know either. She only told me that whatever was in that room held the power of a demon and that the *padre* had been made responsible for it by the *padre* before him."

Angel considered his options. Going to the church was possible despite his vampirism—he'd been in churches before—but the experiences were never entirely painless or without cost. He hesitated only a short time, though. "Could I see this room?"

The nun's hesitation lasted only little longer. "It could help you?"

"Yes."

"I suppose that is so." The nun shook her head. "Although how the *padre* could keep such a thing in the church is beyond me."

"He didn't," Angel pointed out. "Father Carlos was only given care of it. Maybe he didn't even know what it was. Have you been in the room?"

"Yes. But I saw nothing there."

"Then how do you know something was taken from it?" Cordelia asked.

"Would a secret door cover an empty room?" Sister Juanita asked. "Or would that woman have worked so hard to get by the *padre* to get into the room?" She shook her head and smoothed her skirts. "No. Something was in that room, but I have no clue as to what it might have been."

"I need to see the room," Angel said softly.

"Then we should go," the nun said. "There's nothing more I can tell you."

Angel glanced at his desk, trying to think of anything he might need, or how he was going to slip downstairs to his living quarters and take a couple weapons he might need.

The phone rang abruptly.

"Angel," he said into the receiver.

"Do you remember me?" a hoarse voice asked over the connection.

"You lost a friend last night." Angel recognized the homeless man's voice. "You should be in a hospital."

"Was. For a while. You get tired of lying around in those places. Especially when you're missing a friend. I've been out for a few hours an' thought I'd look around in some places I know just south of Los Angeles. Between where you found me an' Jimbo. There's a bunch of run-down warehouses in an old business district what ain't got quite tore down yet."

"I know them," Angel said. The area was a rat's maze of decrepit buildings and provided protection from direct sunlight for vampires and other night-skulkers.

"A group of young kids, runaways most of 'em," the old man said hoarsely, "have taken up in there. They're livin' hard on the streets, makin' their way at night. Rough trade, mostly. But a few minutes ago, I seen one of them unmarked eighteen-wheelers roll through the neighborhood."

"I'm on my way," Angel promised, glancing at Cordelia and Sister Juanita. "Get clear of the area."

"Can't do that, son," the man said. "I took time to call you, but I gotta get in there and warn them kids. Jimbo wouldn't expect me to do any less."

Before Angel could try to argue with the man, the connection broke and white noise swirled in his ear. He cradled the phone. "Something's come up." He walked from his office to join Cordelia and Sister Juanita. "I can be there in a little while. Cordelia, why don't you take my car over to the church and I'll meet up with the two of you there."

"All right."

"Take a look around in the room," Angel suggested, his mind racing as he felt the pressure of the clock hammering at him. "There should be a church logbook—a history—that Father Carlos keeps. Maybe it'll give us something to work with, too."

"Where are you going to be?" Cordelia asked.

"Along," Angel promised as he headed downstairs. "Soon." He paused for just an instant. "While you're in that room, Cordelia, be careful. There's no telling what might have been freed from there or what it might have left behind."

Downstairs in his private living quarters, Angel plucked weapons from the wall quickly. He'd made a mental list on the way down the circular stairs. He strapped on the wrist-mounted stake launchers, then added extra stakes inside his trenchcoat pockets, and took up a double-bitted battleax.

Armed and ready, Angel kicked aside the throw rug covering the trapdoor that led into the sewers beneath his chosen city. He pulled the ring to open the trapdoor and dropped through. He was running by the time he hit the pavement. Rats scurried away from him, squeaking in surprised fear.

Angel leaned into his run, lengthening his stride and using all the strength and speed available to him. His boots drummed the pavement so rapidly they sounded like machine-gun fire. He laid out the map of his path in his mind and kept pushing through the sweltering darkness, hoping he would arrive in time.

"Her name is Hannah Boyd. Her family is protective of her."

"Protective." Doyle worked his jaw gingerly. "Yeah, I got the protective part." He and Harper sat in a small bar farther south along the beach. Nets and fishing gear covered the walls, and boat lanterns made over into electrical fixtures provided the dim light that barely cut the smoke-hazed shadows that filled the bar.

"Hannah's a good-looking woman," Harper said, sipping his beer. He lounged on the other side of the booth they'd taken up in the back of the place.

Doyle pressed his own beer bottle to the side of his face. The chill helped stave off some of the pounding from the beating he'd taken. "From the quick look I got at the picture hanging in Rudy's bait shop, I'd agree with you."

"She's got a lot of guys chasing after her."

"Does Terry always tend to them himself?"

Harper grinned. "When one of them gets persistent enough."

"Hannah has a daughter. Seems to me Hannah's husband ought to be taking care of any would-be Lotharios. I mean, the ones the woman couldn't chase off herself."

Harper drained his bottle. "Hannah has no problem chasing off guys."

Doyle looked at the other man. "Oh man, we're talking personal experience here, aren't we?"

"Oh yeah." Harper nodded and grinned ruefully. "I knew she was a little out of my league, you know, but I had to try. Hannah has a little girl, but she doesn't have a husband. She also let me know she wasn't wanting to find one."

"Ouch."

"Yep," Harper agreed. "I'd rather have taken a beating than hear that. Terry kind of likes me. I go fishing with him and his father when they need an extra hand and I got time to spare. I'm a finish carpenter by trade. Do a lot of work on some of the cabin cruisers in the area. But I'm not overly ambitious. When I get a stake put back, I don't mind sitting back and letting life coast by for a while. Hannah's not interested in a guy like that."

"Maybe she's just a tough sell," Doyle said. "I'm thinking, maybe you shouldn't take it so hard." But the half-demon was thinking about his wife. Till he'd found out he was half-demon, he'd thought his life with her was about as perfect as it could get.

"Maybe she is," Harper agreed, "but she got hurt bad by her daughter's father."

"Nasty divorce?" Doyle signaled the bartender for two more beers.

"Never married," Harper answered, taking one of the beers.

"Where's the father?"

"Don't know. Did you know Hannah was a TV star?"

Doyle's interest pricked up at once. "No."

"Yeah, she was a TV star. Her career crashed about the same time she came up pregnant with her little girl."

"She act in anything I might have seen?" Doyle asked.

"You ever see a show called *Daring High: The School for Spies?*" Harper asked.

Doyle forgot about the pains and aches of his beatings. "I've heard of it."

"Hannah was on that show," Harper told him. "That's where she met the father of her baby. Guy ended up marrying one of the other women in the show, though."

"Did he know about the baby?" Doyle asked.

"No. Hannah was written out of the show, probably because the guy's wife was jealous of her. This guy had some kind of pull with the people producing the show."

"Why didn't Hannah say anything about the baby?"

"You'd have to know Hannah," Harper said. "Her family is really tight. She thinks the world of her little girl. You couldn't ask for a better mother. I don't think her family knows who the father is. I mean, I don't think they know as much as I do."

"That it was someone on that show?"

"Yeah." Harper shrugged. "I think they suspect, but Hannah hasn't told them."

"How did you find out?"

"She told me. Like I said, I was really close to her for a while."

"So why are you telling me?"

"Because I don't buy that you just happened to see Hannah and decided to make a play for her. I don't think you've ever seen Hannah. You didn't know Terry till he was on you. One thing I do know, you don't get to know Hannah unless you get to know Terry."

Doyle waited quietly.

"I'm laying my cards on the table," Harper said, "so that you know what you're looking at. Then I'm going to ask you what you want with Hannah. If I don't like the answer you give me, I'm going to take you out back of this bar and give you a beating that will make what Terry did to you seem like love taps."

Doyle sipped his beer again, feeling his already-split lip burn as the liquid poured over it. He glanced at the door.

Harper shook his head. "I'll bet I'm faster than you are, and I didn't take a beating an hour ago."

And then it's a footrace across the sand in the heat of the day. Doyle sighed and sat back in the booth. He reached inside his shirt pocket and flipped a business card onto the table.

Harper looked down at the card. "You carry around a drawing of a rat?" He glanced back up at Doyle.

"Not a rat. That's an angel." At least, Cordelia always insisted it was. "I work for a detective agency."

"You're a private eye?"

"My friend is. I'm more of the assistant type."

"Let me see some ID."

"I'm not the private eye. My friend is. I operate

under his license." *Or,* Doyle thought, *I would if Angel had one.* "I'm here because I think Hannah may be in trouble."

"What kind of trouble?"

"I can't tell you any more than that," Doyle said. "If I knew, I'd tell you."

Harper looked doubtful and the anger never left his face. "You want to give me a reason why I should let you walk out of here?"

"Because I'm working to make the trouble go away," Doyle said as convincingly as he could. "If that's not enough for you, let me finish my beer, then you can take me out back and beat on me all you want."

"Beating on you isn't going to help, is it?" Harper asked.

"Terry didn't get much."

"He wasn't finished."

"Well, you see, I was."

Harper nodded. "You think you're that tough?"

"Life's made me that way," Doyle said, "one beating at a time."

"Then why buy into other people's troubles through this business of yours?"

"It's not me," Doyle said. "It's my friend. He bought into this kind of grief a long time ago. It's a lot of weight. I'm helping him shift the load."

Harper showed Doyle a lopsided grin that was devoid of humor. "Why have friends like that?"

"Remember the way you talked about Hannah earlier? About how she was family to you?"

Harper nodded.

"That's the way it is between me and Angel. Despite all the easy ways out that are there for him, he does the right thing."

"People like that," Harper said wistfully, "they keep you anchored, don't they? I mean, maybe if you didn't know them, you couldn't be as strong yourself."

"Yeah," Doyle agreed.

Harper raised his beer bottle to clink against Doyle's. "To those people."

"To those people." Doyle drank to the toast.

Harper gazed at the half-demon. "Are you guys any good?"

Doyle answered without hesitation. "I always bet on us for the tough ones."

Harper took the card from the table. "I'm keeping this. And I'm keeping a close eye on Hannah."

"If you see anything suspicious going on," Doyle said, "don't hesitate to call."

"Where are you going to be?"

Doyle stood up a little unsteadily. His head still throbbed from the beating he'd taken. "Trying to find the trouble headed this way and stop it before it gets here." He offered his hand.

Harper took it. "You'll let me know?"

"Yeah. After all, you saved me from Terry."

A grin spread across Harper's face. "You never fought back against Terry. I'm beginning to think maybe I saved him."

"Don't give up on Hannah. If she told you more than she's told anyone else, there's a reason for that. Sometimes these women we fall kind of hard for, maybe it takes them a while to come around, you know?" Doyle thought of Cordelia as he said that. "And if it works for you, give me a call and let me know." He headed for the door.

CHAPTER THIRTEEN

"Hey. Wake up there, girl."

Struggling through the layers of fog choking her brain from staying out too late last night and drinking, Cindy cracked her eyes open slightly. Plywood covered the windows, but muted daylight still flooded the warehouse where she slept on rags she'd taken from Dumpsters around the neighborhood. It wasn't even the daylight of early evening, when she usually got up, which meant it was way the hell too early for her to wake up. She closed her eyes again.

"Hey, c'mon now!" This time whoever was talking to her grabbed her arm and shook it. "You got to wake up, girl!"

Cop? Cindy wondered, and that thought filled her with fear. She'd been in the city for almost two months this time. The last time the juvie officials had taken her back home to Indiana, it had taken her three weeks to escape her mother and abusive stepfather and return to Los Angeles. Even hungover as she was, she knew enough to be afraid of that.

She opened her eyes wider this time. She snuffled and blinked at the old homeless man that had hold of her arm. "You're . . . you're old and disgusting," she told him.

"Yeah, well you ain't no prize yourself, kid," the old man said. He glanced fearfully over his shoulder.

That look was one of the first Cindy had learned when she'd started making her way on the streets. Someone else's fear could turn into hers in a heartbeat.

"Get up," the old man commanded, "or you're gonna die."

Cindy noticed the white bandages on the old man's arms and figured he was an alcoholic just released from some rehab. "Who are you?"

"The guy tryin' to save your life. Now get up." The old man pulled again.

This time Cindy let him pull her to her feet. She looked around the warehouse. Nearly thirty kids had started flopping in the warehouse over the last few weeks. Some of them she knew by first name, but most of them she still didn't know. Four other kids were awake now, pulling at kids still stoned and drunk, trying to get them to their feet.

"What's going on?" Cindy asked the old man.

"Got trouble comin'," the old man said.

Cindy pushed him away, letting him know she could stand on her own feet. The old man went to the next makeshift bed and started shaking the kid there.

"What kind of trouble?" Cindy asked, still wobbly.

"Bad kind," the old man said. "Wake one of them other kids. Hurry."

Even as Cindy turned to the next pallet of rags, she heard footsteps echo on the wooden stairs from the level below. Nobody stayed on the bottom floor of the warehouse. The cops didn't much care for climbing the stairs and checking the second floor, and as long as they didn't have any lights on or barrel fires at night, no one knew they were there.

A group of men wearing biker leathers topped the stairs and stepped out onto the second floor.

The old man cursed and bent down for a broken stick. He stepped forward uncertainly, putting himself between the new arrivals and the boys and girls in the flophouse.

The men moved into a semicircle. Then their faces changed and became nightmarish, filled with gleaming fangs. Cindy screamed, recognizing then what they were and why they'd come from stories she'd heard on the street, but she knew no one would hear.

*   *   *

"Mr. Doyle?"

Turning from the window and the downtown Beverly Hills view, Doyle glanced at the receptionist who had detained him in the office building. She was pretty but distant, probably efficient as well. Even though she tried to hide it, Doyle knew she disapproved of him. He didn't blame her. Bruises from the earlier beating he'd received from Terry Boyd had started to show, and his clothing wasn't quite up to the dressed-down look in the offices.

"Mr. Heath will see you now," the receptionist said, gesturing toward the back offices. "Through the hallway here and straight back. Mr. Heath's office is at the back."

"Thank you," Doyle said politely, and headed in that direction. The immaculate hallway ended only a short distance ahead. Walls on either side held framed stills from television productions—television movies, straight-to-video releases, and series work—that Adrian Heath had been involved with. Doyle didn't recognize half of them, but he took the time to look at them all. Halfway down, he found what he was looking for.

Hannah Boyd wasn't listed as Hannah Boyd in the credit clip below the picture. She was listed as Hannah Fletcher and she'd played Dinah Swift, one of the students at *Daring High*. But the resemblance between that photograph and the one in Rudy's bait shop was unmistakable.

The office door opened and Adrian Heath stepped out with an anxious look. He wore khaki slacks and a dark green silk shirt. "I thought you'd gotten lost."

Doyle shook his head and regretted it. "Not quite."

"You said you didn't want to go into anything on the phone," Adrian said.

"No," Doyle agreed. "I was thinking maybe it would be better if we talked here at your office." He'd tried to call the office before showing up on Adrian's doorstep but had only gotten the answering machine. He'd have felt better if he could have talked to Angel first, but time was of the essence every time he got a vision.

Adrian lowered his voice. "Have you found her?"

"Not yet. But I got to talk to you about something else that's come up since we started investigating." Doyle reached out and took the framed picture from the wall. "Maybe we should finish this in your office instead of the hallway."

"Do be careful, Miss Chase. Those stairs can be quite steep."

No kidding. Cordelia raised the battery-powered lantern in her hand to drive back the shadows that filled the small basement at the bottom of the stairs Sister Juanita had been referring to. A sense of foreboding raked at the back of Cordelia's mind. It almost felt like her apartment had felt when she'd first moved in with Dennis the ghost—like someone was watching her every move.

She reached the bottom of the stairs and stopped. Lifting the lantern high again, she only saw neat shelves containing canned goods in Mason jars and yard implements. A coiled hose occupied a hook over a yellow mop bucket. The room smelled of potpourri and pine-scented detergent.

Sister Juanita, armed with a lantern of her own from the church's office upstairs, followed Cordelia more slowly.

Curious and hesitant at the same time, Cordelia shone the camera around, highlighting each wall in turn. *Boy, they really wanted to keep that secret room secret.*

"It's on the back wall, Miss Chase," Sister Juanita said. After coming down the stairs, her breathing sounded labored.

Stepping closer to the back wall, Cordelia began a closer search. *Where is Angel? The icky parts of these cases are his by rights. Not mine. I don't have anything I'm supposed to redeem myself from.* Her lantern beam moved across the grained wood. "I can't find it."

She's lying to you, a cold voice rasped in Cordelia's mind.

All pimply from the chill that poured through her, Cordelia spun suddenly and glanced over her shoulder. "Who said that?"

The beam only showed the neat arrangements of gardening implements.

"Who said what?" Sister Juanita asked.

"Didn't you hear that voice?" Cordelia asked.

"I didn't hear anything except you telling me that you couldn't find it. If you'll allow me, I'll open the door and show it to you."

Cordelia took a step back and watched the nun reach up high onto the wall. She strained for a moment, even going up on her toes but couldn't reach what she strove for.

"I can't get it," Sister Juanita said finally. "I'm not tall enough."

She's lying, the cold voice hissed. *She's only fooling you. Making a fool of you.*

"You don't hear that voice?" Cordelia shone her lantern into the nun's face.

"Could you please redirect that light, Miss Chase?"

Reluctantly, Cordelia took the light from the old nun's eyes and glanced around the basement again. "There's someone else down here with us," Cordelia insisted.

"I assure you, there's no one at the church but us. Albula won't be in till later to do some of the cleaning, and Gabriel finished the yard work this morning."

There's someone else in here. The voice creeped Cordelia out. *It's no problem. I can handle this. There were worse things in Sunnydale. And it can't be nearly as bad as the same time that Terri Hunter and I wore the same dress to—*

"The switch," Sister Juanita instructed, "is on the wall. Where it meets the ceiling. If you reach up there, you'll feel a small obstruction."

Steeling herself, Cordelia reached up.

Are you going to do her bidding? the voice taunted. *Your station in life is far above hers. Why should you do something she tells you to do like some common servant?*

Cordelia slid her fingers along the wall. "You've never heard voices down here?"

"Only when there was someone upstairs talking so loudly I could hear them down here." Sister Juanita frowned. "Are you sure you feel up to this, Miss Chase?"

"I'm fine," Cordelia replied. *But I'm happy there's a stake in my purse. Just in case any weirdness gets started. And no, I'm definitely not looking for any weirdness. A day without weirdness is a day . . . a day where everything is normal and that would be just peachy.*

"Perhaps we should wait on your friend. He seemed to think whatever the call was about wouldn't take too long."

"Everything will be fine, Sister Juanita," Cordelia said. Calling the sister "sister" was kind of weird. Cordelia had never had a sister, just two parents.

And they lied to you, didn't they, Cordelia? the

sibilant voice asked. *Treated you like a princess, then they turned their backs on you and left you to fend for yourself.*

Cordelia's hand trembled. In a way, her parents had turned their backs on her after their financial troubles. She felt the concealed button under her fingers.

You were always your father's little girl. You were supposed to be the apple of his eye. But he lied to you.

Cordelia breathed in to calm herself as she pressed the button. She almost decided to take the nun's suggestion that they wait for Angel, but her pride wouldn't let her.

The door popped open, and the hollow echo on the other side of the wall let Cordelia know about the space there. She stood for a moment, one foot braced against the wall so whatever might be inside couldn't come charging out of the room.

"Is something wrong?" Sister Juanita asked.

Besides this weird voice talking to me? Cordelia glanced at the nun, still blocking the door. "Are you sure you're not hearing things?"

"I hear nothing."

Maybe she's partially deaf, Cordelia thought. *And maybe I'm imagining things.* She forced herself to breathe out, then slid her foot back from the door. She pulled it open slightly, telling herself that if something inside slammed against the door she wouldn't be surprised. At least, not much.

Your father never cared for you, the voice said. *He only pretended to. As long as he thought you were his possession, he was content to have you. But when you turned your attentions somewhere else, demanded his love when you needed it most, he turned away.*

That wasn't exactly what had happened back in Sunnydale, Cordelia knew. Her father had lost everything to the IRS for not taking care of his tax situation. And he'd never told her or her mother until it was way past too late. As a result, Cordelia had had no choice but to leave Sunnydale rather than bear the disgrace that would have come once everyone found out what had happened. Her life there had ended.

She was still angry with her father over that. So angry that—

You should make him sorry for the things that he has done to you.

Shaking, Cordelia pulled the door open and shone the lantern inside. The beam played over the small room, catching streams of dust eddying about. Carefully mortised stones created the walls, ceiling, and floor. The room stood completely empty.

Cordelia entered cautiously. Anger filled her and stirred within her like a live thing. She kept remembering her father, thinking about the way he had disrupted her life. Both her parents had maintained high expectations of her.

They had expectations of you, but they felt they owed none to you themselves.

Trembling, breathing deeply as the anger worked within her, Cordelia shone the lantern beam on the floor and walls, trying to find some indication of what had been held inside the room.

Years and years of dust covered the floor.

Cordelia shone the beam down across the floor. *There should be footprints,* she thought. However, the layer of accumulated dust remained smooth.

There is hatred and rage within you, Cordelia Chase, the voice said. *Those things can be used. I can give you the revenge you seek against those who have wronged you.*

Frightened, Cordelia shoved herself back. Before she could step from the room, the door closed behind her. She pushed against it with her free hand, but it didn't budge.

"Miss Chase?" Sister Juanita called from the other side of the door.

"Help!" Cordelia slammed her hand against the door. "The door's stuck!"

Stay, the voice commanded. *Stay and I can give you all that you desire. Everything is within my power.*

Cordelia rammed her shoulder into the door but only succeeded in hurting herself and nearly breaking the lantern. Not wanting to be left locked up in the dark, she placed the lantern on the floor. As though gripped by a sudden windstorm, the dust whirled up from the floor and covered her in a cloud. It stung her face, hands, and arms, choking her. She slitted her eyes and stumbled away from the driving dust. Her foot knocked the lantern over.

The light went out, leaving her alone in the dark.

Now, the voice cried, *now let me show you all that I can give you!*

Angel came up through the sewer manhole behind the warehouse address the old homeless man had given him over the phone. The afternoon sun streamed down from in front of the building, leaving the alley behind it safely swaddled in shadows.

Before Angel could push the manhole cover back into place, he heard a girl scream inside the warehouse. He hefted the battleax in both hands and ran for the door between two retractable bay doors. Thankfully, the door was open.

Inside, a sweeping glance told him that the first floor was empty. Only a few broken pallets, some empty cardboard boxes and bags of litter from take-out places covered the floor. A wooden stairway along the left wall caught his attention just as the second frightened scream ripped through the warehouse.

"Stay away from her!" someone yelled.

Angel recognized the old man's voice even as he ran for the stairway. He kept his human appearance, thinking it might give him an edge against the vampires above because they would think he was human for a moment, and because he wanted the potential victims to think that he was fighting *for* them and not *over* them.

At the top of the stairs, he saw seven vampires advancing on a group of homeless kids. Not hesitating, Angel charged the vampires. Their attention was focused on the kids; they didn't hear him coming up behind them.

The old man waved his wooden shard threateningly.

"You're stupid, old man," one of the vampires said.

The old man lunged at the vampire with the stick, but the vampire caught the stick easily.

"Don't kill him," another vampire said. "As long as his heart's still pumping, we can bleed him out. He'll still be worth a little *ka-ching, ka-ching.*"

Setting himself, Angel swung the battleax. The keen edge sliced through the neck of the vampire in front of him. The head leaped clear of the shoulders and tumbled through the air for just a moment before turning to dust along with the rest of the body.

Before the head had turned to dust, though, it flew far enough forward to attract the attention of the other vampires. They turned on Angel, faces shifting to masks of snarling rage. Two of them charged at once.

Instead of falling back as the two vampires had undoubtedly expected him to do, Angel stepped forward. He popped the vampire on the left in the face with the long ax handle, staggering him and driving him back. Still moving, Angel ducked the other vampire's attack, stepped forward again to go beneath the vampire's arm, then swung the battleax one-handed, striking that vampire's head off as well.

Another vampire charged at Angel, reaching for him from only inches away as Angel lifted his left arm and twisted. The wrist-mounted launcher shot a stake out that pierced the vampire's heart. The headlong charge didn't break off, but it was only the dead creature's dust that blew over Angel.

Before he could get set again, one of the surviving vampires grabbed the ax handle then head-butted Angel in the face. Staggered, Angel fell back, pain filling his head from the blow. The dark demon shifted within Angel, demanding its release. No one in the warehouse could stand against it, and its hunger made it scream in the back of Angel's head.

The vampire tore the battleax from Angel's hand and howled in triumph.

Dizzy from the head blow, Angel realized the vampires standing before him were relative new-borns to their unlife. He didn't expect them to have much in the way of trained fighting abilities, but their strength, speed, and numbers couldn't be discounted.

The vampire that had taken the ax charged, swiping at Angel like he was chopping wood. Angel dodged, stepping back, knowing he had the attention of all the vampires now. No one else in the warehouse offered them a threat, and with them fighting so close to the stairway, there was no escape for the homeless kids. Angel was the only chance they had of making it out of the building alive.

Angel dodged again, the heavy blade missing his head only by inches.

"You scared?" the vampire taunted. He wore the Diablos' leathers and was big and broad. He shoved the ax at Angel, trying to catch Angel's face on the blade.

Angel used his left hand like a sword, parrying the battleax's wooden haft to the side while standing his ground. The vampire poked the ax again, but was parried once more. Growing annoyed and overly confident, the vampire struck again and again, moving faster and faster, committing more and more of his body weight to the attack.

Moving quickly, Angel kept on parrying, turning the ax away from him at the last second, making the defense look easy.

"C'mon, Skeeter," one of the other vampires encouraged. "Take him and be done with it."

Angel let a small smile twist his lips as he parried another attack, gazing at the vampire trying to kill him. Despite how the battle looked, Angel was playing with his attacker instead of the other way around, and the vampire knew it even if his companions didn't.

The vampire stepped forward, leaning heavily, and thrust the battleax at Angel's head. Angel slapped the ax to the right, choosing that moment to carry the attack to his opponents. He shook his right hand, releasing the stake into it, grabbing it easily as he stepped forward.

Angel caught hold of the battleax's handle in his left hand, arm tight across his own body now, as he swept the stake in his right hand in an upward blow, disguising the motion from the other vampires with his own body. The stake slid through the vampire's chest, penetrating the heart, with a flat *thunk!*

As the vampire turned to dust, Angel pulled the freed battleax around in a tight blur. The blade cleaved the head from the vampire standing practically at the other vampire's shoulder. Then there were only two vampires left in the warehouse.

They moved back instantly.

Angel used both hands on the battleax, whirling the weapon before him in a glittering array of steel and wood. Both vampires turned and fled. Instantly, Angel threw the battleax haft-first, plunging it through Skeeter's chest and ripping through the heart. Unwilling to let the other vampire go free, Angel slipped one of the stakes from his trenchcoat pockets and pursued him.

The vampire started to plunge down the wooden staircase, but Angel slammed into him in a full-body tackle. Angel used the vampire to cushion the crash against the wall beyond. Angel stayed on top of the falling vampire, pinning him to the floor and placing the tip of the stake against the vampire's chest.

Angel waited, letting the vampire take in the stake and the position it was in. "I want to know where your base of operations is."

"Go to hell," the vampire spat.

"Already been there," Angel said. He shoved the stake into the vampire's chest, narrowly missing the heart.

The vampire screamed in pain.

"I can make this last a long time," Angel promised. He left the stake in the vampire's flesh and took out another one.

The vampire writhed, but wasn't strong enough to get away.

"I want to know where you guys are based," Angel said. He drove another stake through the vampire's chest on the other side of his dead heart. "I don't have a lot of time." He took another stake from his trenchcoat pocket. "I've got a lot of stakes, but if I run out because you're being stubborn, I'll tear the wood off the steps and go again."

The vampire cursed.

Angel slammed the stake through the vampire's

shoulder. "Your choice." He took yet another stake from his trenchcoat pocket, aware that the old man and the homeless kids were watching him. He turned off his feelings, not caring what they thought about him. Every night the blood-delivery operation was left intact added to the body count.

Gasping in pain, the vampire ground out, "Corinth Studios."

Angel recognized it as an old movie studio lot that had been shut down nearly ten years before and was now being rezoned as a residential district. Mercilessly, Angel plunged his last stake through the vampire's heart. The vampire turned to dust beneath him.

Angel pushed himself to his feet wearily. He crossed the warehouse and picked up the battleax, aware that every eye in the building was on him. He glanced at the old man and nodded. "You did good."

"You saved them," the old man said.

"*We* saved them," Angel said. He looked around the room. "We saved them for now. They've still got to save themselves." When he got the chance, he intended to call Kate Lockley and let her know about the nest of homeless kids. Kate could get the juvenile division into the area to try to clean it up. Maybe some of the kids could be given the help they needed. It wasn't all about the demons on the street; a lot of those kids had demons in their heads, and Angel knew those intimately as well.

"At least," the old man said, "this way they get the chance—"

Without warning, the sound of a woman crying in mortal anguish filled the warehouse.

Angel spun around, watching incredulously as a woman dressed all in black climbed up the stairs. She was beautiful even with tears covering her face.

"Children," the woman in black cried. "Come to me, my children. Let me adore you."

The homeless kids immediately withdrew. Some of them cursed and called the woman in black names.

"I saw her!" one of the girls screamed. "I saw her last night! She's the one who killed those two police officers!"

"Don't run from me!" Steel rang in the woman in black's voice. "Don't you dare run from me! Get over here! I paid for you with my suffering and my betrayal! You come to me now!" And despite the cascade of tears, the woman in black began to laugh madly; and the sound remained trapped inside the warehouse, rolling in on itself.

CHAPTER FOURTEEN

"How did you find out about Hannah Boyd?"

Doyle sat in a chair on the other side of Adrian Heath's huge desk in his private office. He felt uncomfortable talking about the woman. *God knows I've got enough of my own personal demons I want to keep hidden.* "Kind of came up while we were checking around."

Adrian glanced back at the framed photograph on his desk. "There aren't many people in this town who know about this. And it's not the first time something like this has happened." He paused. "But it was the first time something like this happened to me. Have you met Hannah?"

"No," Doyle said. "I've only seen her in pictures."

"You can tell from a picture that she's beautiful. But there's more to Hannah than that." Adrian stood up behind his desk and started pacing. The office was large and spacious. More television stills and award plaques covered the walls. Adrian and Marisa Heath had donated to several local funds and charity drives.

Doyle waited patiently. With all his experience in listening to people in dives and bars, at the high and low points of their lives, he knew he couldn't go directly at Adrian to get the answers he needed. The answers would come from him in layers, like an onion, when he was ready to give them.

"Hannah's also a very talented actress," Adrian went on. "And she's fun to be around. When you work in television and spend the kind of hours those people do at it, do you know primarily who they're going to meet?"

"Other people working those shows," Doyle said.

"That's right. And a show's producer, if he or she is really involved in that show, is in the same boat. I've dated lots of women who have been on my shows. But I never took advantage of my position. I guess you'll have to believe me on that."

"I do," Doyle responded, and the truth of the matter—surprisingly—was, he did.

"Hannah let me know she was interested in me," Adrian said. "There was little hesitation on my part." He turned and gazed out the window at the rolling hills that held the familiar HOLLYWOOD sign. It could barely be seen by Doyle in the distance, a jumble of letters off to the right. "We dated hot and heavy for most of a summer, then—just as easily as she'd let me know she was interested—she told me she didn't want to see me anymore."

"*She* dropped *you?*"

Adrian turned toward the half-demon with a small smile. "You sound surprised."

"The way I heard it, you dropped her, and dropped her from the show."

"I wouldn't have dropped her from the show even if I'd decided I didn't want to see her anymore," Adrian said. "She was one of the reasons *Daring High* pulled in the ratings it did. The show was never quite the same after she left."

Doyle hesitated. "I know this isn't politically correct, but—"

"Why did she dump me?" Adrian laughed. "Because she was the first one of us to realize what we had was a short-term physical relationship at best. One of those chemical things nature does just to keep you guessing about life. Trying to stay together would have been the wrong thing to do. I wasn't objective enough at the time to see it the way Hannah did. But she's always known what she's wanted. Anyone who knows her will tell you that."

Doyle considered, then realized there was no politically correct way to ask what he needed to ask. And he was aware that he was dropping a bomb if Adrian hadn't known. "Did you know about the baby?"

"Not until ten months ago. Hannah kept that to herself. She didn't want me to have any part of the baby."

"Why?"

"We were on fall break when Hannah found out she was pregnant, by then Marisa and I were seeing each other, even talking of marriage." He shook his head at the memory. "Have you ever been that in love, Doyle? So much in love that every minute of your day seemed consumed with obsessing about the other person?"

Doyle wanted to say no, knew that probably most other people would have said no. But he remembered Harry, and he remembered how things had been with her. It still hurt to think about. "Yeah, I know what you're talking about."

"Hannah saw that going on between Marisa and me," Adrian said. "When I confronted her about the baby later, after I found out, she told me that she hadn't come to me because she was happy for me and thought the baby would only be confusing. For all of us."

"If you'd known, do you think it would have been any different?"

"I don't know," Adrian replied. "I like to think that it wouldn't have changed things between Marisa and me. Hannah still wasn't prepared to commit to me. She's too much her own person. Except with her baby. You can hear it in her voice."

"You've talked with her?"

"We're friendly, but not chummy. She doesn't want me around her daughter."

"That's gotta be hard to take."

"It's been confusing, to say the least. Hannah insists that it's for the best."

"But you're not so sure?"

"That little girl is my daughter, Doyle, and I haven't gotten to know her for the past three years. How do you just go introduce yourself to a child and say, 'I'm your daddy'?"

"I don't know," Doyle admitted. But he was thinking about his mother. Was that why she hadn't come up to tell him he was a half-demon? Because she didn't know how? It hurt now to think of all the fears she must have held inside, hoping that maybe the demon part of him wouldn't manifest itself.

"Neither do I." Adrian gazed out the window.

Doyle tried to push thoughts of his mother and Harry from his mind. He wanted a bar and a lot of drinks. He wanted to watch the ponies run or the Lakers play or the Kings play and get so caught up in all of it he couldn't dwell on things or try to make sense of them. Families helped and families hurt. One didn't come without the other. And the loneliest place to be in the world was anywhere without family.

Clearing his throat, Doyle asked the question he most dreaded. "Did Marisa know about Hannah and—" He stumbled over whether or not to say *your daughter*, then felt even more embarrassed to say anything at all when the silence stretched out.

"Marisa," Adrian said, "is the one who told me about Hannah and the baby."

Doyle sat back in his chair, surprised. "How did she find out?"

"She ran into a mutual friend from *Daring High*," Adrian answered.

"It must have been quite a shock for Marisa."

"It was," Adrian admitted. "Things got rocky there for a bit, but they straightened out as they always did between us." He paused. "Until this. Marisa talked to Hannah a time or two. They ended up fighting. Marisa thought that I should get to see my daughter, and Hannah told her there was no legal proof that I was the father."

"She didn't put you on the birth certificate?" Doyle asked.

"No. Which means that if I want to see my daughter, there's a lot of nasty legal action ahead."

"What are you going to do?"

"I haven't decided. Things at home got a little more frustrating. Marisa started talking about us having a child. I agreed. But it just didn't happen for us. She had a miscarriage about two months ago. It hurt her terribly."

"You didn't mention this when we talked last night," Doyle pointed out.

"This seemed . . . private." Adrian sighed. "Marisa was very upset about the miscarriage. She told me that it was her fault, that it was punishment for what she'd done."

"Do you know what she meant by that?"

Adrian shook his head. "I was there the day the doctor told Marisa that she was pregnant, and that she should have no trouble carrying the baby full term. He said her earlier pregnancy had shown no signs of any problems."

"Her earlier pregnancy?"

"The doctor was certain that Marisa had had a baby before."

"Doctors usually know those kinds of things. What did Marisa say?"

"She told me later that the doctor was mistaken but she didn't want to argue with him. I've heard horror stories from other women about obstetricians who basically took over their lives once they were pregnant. They tell me you don't dare correct a doctor like that. Marisa told me she had miscarried the first baby eight years ago."

Doyle turned the information around in his mind. It didn't help him with anything he was working out about Marisa Heath's disappearance, but maybe Angel or Cordelia could make something of it. However, he had established to his satisfaction how he'd happened to have the vision of Hannah Boyd aboard Adrian's yacht since they were obviously connected. But he still didn't know what danger Angel was supposed to protect the young woman from.

Standing, Doyle started to excuse himself.

"Aren't you going to ask about the business records?" Adrian asked in surprise.

"The business records?" Doyle repeated.

"I thought that was what you were here for," Adrian said. "I only found out myself today. I called and left a message at Angel's office."

"Found out what?"

"A few days before she left, Marisa came into the office and checked through my business records. Actually, I still think of them as my grandfather's business records. They belong to businesses that my grandfather inherited from his father, and boards that my grandfather handpicked are still managing them. I have very little to do with them."

"Why would Marisa look over your business records?"

"I have no idea. She's never been interested before. My personal assistant here at the office only told me this morning. Since Marisa went missing Friday, my assistant didn't know Marisa was gone. I only told her this morning. According to my assistant, Marisa seemed to be very upset Friday when she was here."

"Why?"

"I don't know. But Marisa did leave this behind."

Adrian pulled out a desk drawer and took out a folded newspaper page.

Doyle took the page and spread it across the desk. "What was she looking at?"

"The only thing I can even think it might be is this." Adrian tapped a story in the center of the page.

Doyle scanned the article. *Protesters in Huntington Park Claim Pollution Responsible in Death of 8-Year-Old.* The picture of the smiling boy's face beside the headline almost broke Doyle's heart.

"One of the companies the protesters claim is responsible for that boy's death belongs to me."

"Were you aware of the pollution issue?"

Adrian nodded. "That group has been claiming that for years. But the company board assures me we're well within the EPA guidelines."

"Marisa never discussed your grandfather's— *your* businesses—before?"

"No."

"Your name is mentioned in the paper," Doyle said, scanning the article. "Maybe that's the first she knew of it."

"But why would it matter?"

"I don't know," Doyle replied. "Maybe this had nothing to do with her leaving." *But even as a betting man and as much as I love long shots, I wouldn't put money on the chances of that.* "Can I have this?"

❖   ❖   ❖

Cordelia dropped to her knees in the secret room in the basement of the old church. The dust pelting her face went away and became a soothing caress instead. Even when she opened her eyes, though, she saw only darkness.

You don't have to be afraid of me, Cordelia.

"I am afraid of you," Cordelia said into the dark. "I'm afraid of you and I'm mad at you, and if I get my hands on you, boy, are you going to regret the mad part."

I don't want you to be angry with me.

"Well, you're *way* too late for that."

I can help you change your life. I can make you powerful.

"You're saying I'm not?" Feeding on her anger, Cordelia forced herself to her feet. "Then you haven't been hanging around in the right demon circles, because there are vampires and other assorted little hellspawn that are afraid of me."

I'm not a demon.

"Well, if you're a ghost I'm not impressed with that bit either." Cordelia turned, trying to spot some glimmer of light. "I live with a ghost named Dennis. His own mother killed him and walled him up in my apartment. Dennis took a little training, but he's a good guy now. Even helps out at parties. And with Dennis around, you know, you just never lose the remote for the television."

Accept me.

"Why? So you can mess with my head and turn me into some bug-munching zombie?" Cordelia trembled. "Okay, major *ewwww* with that last thought. I mean, the whole concept of having little bug legs and antennas and gucky bug guts under my fingernails is just making me that much more angry."

Your father, your family, betrayed you. Let me take care of you.

Cordelia stepped forward in the darkness, trying to find the door again. Two steps later, though, she still hadn't touched anything solid. *Where did the walls go? They can't have just disappeared!*

Without warning, a cold blast of wind rattled through Cordelia. Images flickered through her head, recalling holidays home with her family and the way her father had treated her. He'd constantly acted like she was better than all the other kids at school, that she shouldn't even be hanging with anyone who wasn't her equal in social standing.

Your mother never cared about you, either. She only pretended to because it helped her to preserve her image in front of the other women. She pretended to be your family.

In the darkness of her mind, Cordelia was convinced that what the voice told her was true. Her parents had concerned themselves with their own wants and needs. Cordelia had only been an accessory to them. And in that moment, all the pain and anger she'd carefully locked away inside herself spilled loose inside her heart and her mind.

For one soul-searing moment, Cordelia felt totally alone in the world.

Come to me and let me comfort you. You have no family, but I can be your family.

Cordelia turned toward the voice, finally able to pinpoint it in the darkness.

A woman's face pushed through the shadows, gradually becoming visible. She was beautiful, her heart-shaped face the color of alabaster, eyes dark as coal, her nose thin and aquiline. *Everyone should have a family, Cordelia. Join me and we will make those people who pretended to be your family hurt for the way they have treated you.* A hand slid out of the darkness and turned palm-up in invitation. *Take my hand and let me comfort you.*

Cordelia knew she shouldn't take the woman's hand, but she couldn't think of a reason not to. It would feel good to belong. She hadn't belonged with anyone in a long time.

You've never belonged to anyone the way you could belong to me.

Panicked, but feeling twice removed from the feeling, Cordelia remembered family photographs she'd taken. Every time she painstakingly built them in her mind's eye, her mother and father melted away from them, leaving her stranded and alone in the Christmas pictures, the fall pictures, the spring pictures—always alone.

Those were false images, the voice said. The hand extended farther toward Cordelia. *Come to me. Let me show you the truth. You never need to be alone again.*

Cordelia reached for the offered hand. It was terrible to be alone. She knew that. She'd spent her life primarily alone despite all the hangers-on she'd had at Sunnydale High. In the end she'd had to turn to Buffy and her friends for company. And that had led into Xander's arms for a while. Maybe that hadn't been meant to be, but for a time it was true. Since she'd been in Los Angeles, there hadn't been anyone who cared about her.

No one, the voice agreed, reading her thoughts.

No one, Cordelia thought, losing herself to the painful loneliness, *no one*—"Except Angel," she said aloud. She stared straight into the woman's face. "Angel has been there for me since day one. Well, since he came to L.A. and found me here. And Doyle's there, too."

You're fooling yourself. Let me comfort you.

Cordelia shook her head, shaking off the fugue that had held her in thrall. "No, you're lying." She took her hand back. "Angel's my family now, and Doyle—well, Doyle's like a favorite cousin." But she remembered how Doyle was always bantering with her, always paying her attention, even during arguments that she made him lose. *Okay, maybe Doyle's something more than a cousin*. She didn't want to deal with that issue at the moment.

Cordelia—

"No, you can just stay away from me," Cordelia said, stepping back. "This is one of those soul-stealing tricks you demons like to work on so much. Well, I'm not going to play your little game. I'm done." Her next step took her back into the wall behind her.

"Miss Chase!"

Recognizing Sister Juanita's voice, Cordelia turned and pounded on the wall. The light in the small room dimmed, and when Cordelia glanced over her shoulder the woman's glowing face and hand were gone.

The door opened suddenly and Cordelia almost fell out.

"All you all right, Miss Chase?" Sister Juanita's face was a mask of concern.

"I'm fine," Cordelia assured the woman. Holding the door to the secret room open, she turned around and looked inside.

The dust still covered the floor on the inside of the room, but Cordelia's footprints marred the smooth texture now. In the middle of the floor, however, she could now see a small toad carved from obsidian. The black gem glittered in the lantern light.

Drawn by the toad, Cordelia cautiously reentered the room. She stared down at the gemstone creature, halfway expecting it to hop at her. When it didn't, she nudged it with a toe. The obsidian toad slid through the dust. Still, she didn't want to touch it.

Cordelia retreated to the shelves against the basement wall and took down a broom and a dustpan. She swept the obsidian toad into the dustpan, then dumped it into a trash bag. She didn't immediately feel better, but it was a start.

"Get them out of here," Angel told the old man standing beside him. Angel held the woman in black's stare, pacing her at every turn to let her know she wouldn't reach the children without a fight. He held the battleax in both hands.

"How?" the old man asked.

"Through one of the windows if you have to," Angel said. "We're only one floor up. Even dropping and breaking a leg won't be as bad as what could happen here."

"You can't stop me." Tears glittered on the woman in black's face. She let loose a short burst of laughter again, eliciting fearful curses from the street kids working feverishly to tear away the plywood sealing the windows from outside. Thankfully, that end of the warehouse only let in a little sunlight that barely inched across the scarred concrete floor.

"I can't let you have them," Angel said. He stayed in motion, not knowing what the woman in black was capable of. He felt the wrongness of her now, even farther off the scale than anything pure demon or half-demon that he'd encountered.

The woman in black lifted her arms. Suddenly winds filled the warehouse, whipping dirt and debris from the floor. The piles of rags the street kids had been using for beds exploded into multicolored confetti whirlwinds that twisted across the warehouse.

"You are a man," the woman in black declared. "No man can stop me." She shifted to the left.

Angel stepped with the woman in black, moving through a defensive kata, always presenting himself in a position of power and movement. The battleax moved in his hands as if it were a part of him. He drew on two hundred and fifty years of fighting demons and reading about the creatures of power that moved between this world and the world that had been. When man had evolved and spread over the globe, so many demon races had experienced genocide or displacement.

Even the demons that were supposedly extinct were often found waiting or lairing in side-pockets of reality or other planes of existence. Angel had studied a great number of them, and had killed several of them over the years, with and without his soul. He'd never seen anything like the woman in black. She exuded power, raw and unstoppable.

Abruptly, she stepped up into the raging wind that clawed at Angel's clothing. She floated in the air, flying on it somehow, controlling her movements with the ease of a hawk holding its position in a gale wind. She turned her head and squinted her eyes at him. With her hair whipping around her from the wind and the maniacal laughter trebling from her lips, she looked unreal. "You're not human, are you?"

Angel didn't answer. "How are we doing back there?" he asked the old man.

"Getting there," the old man promised. Nails screeched as they pulled free of timbers. "Some of 'em have made their way to the ground."

"Call the police," Angel ordered. He wasn't happy about the idea. Maybe he was only calling up more victims for the woman in black.

She came at him without warning, following a sudden gust of wind that blew her at Angel. Stepping back, keeping himself centered, Angel whipped the battleax.

The woman in black lashed at him with a hand.

Quick as he was, Angel wasn't entirely able to fend off the blow. Her sharp fingernails tore through his trenchcoat sleeve and ripped into his flesh beneath. Her touch burned like acid.

Grunting with the pain, Angel shifted again, swinging the ax handle like a staff. He feinted at her head, then chopped at her knees, hoping to break them into shards of bone that wouldn't hold her weight. He felt certain she couldn't keep riding the winds forever.

However, she was even faster than he was. The ax handle only cut through empty air as she drew back with blinding speed. She laughed at him in earnest then, but it was the mocking sound of insanity mixed with pure, sweet torment.

The demon inside Angel reveled in the sound of the woman in black's pain. And Angel knew despite the circumstances of her visit to the warehouse that she was in pain. He knew that sound from both sides.

The woman in black regarded Angel again. "You *are* interesting, vampire."

Angel moved warily, keeping the battleax at the ready, shifting from foot to foot and presenting first one shoulder then the other to lure her out. He always moved to take advantage of her movement, seeking a way to turn it against her.

"How long have you lived?" the woman in black asked.

"I died young," Angel replied.

"Really?" The woman in black peered more closely at him. "Is that what I see that is so different from the others of your kind I have met over the years?" As soon as her question finished, she burst into the uncontrollable weeping and hysteric laughing. The noise rolled through the warehouse, drawing more curses from the street kids still scrambling for safety.

"They probably didn't challenge you," Angel said.

"They didn't," the woman in black agreed. "We met and preyed on our separate victims. But I have always been different from them. I am owed my due. A vampire simply chooses to feed."

"How are you owed?" Angel asked.

"Because of all that I gave up in the name of love." A loud, anguished wail blasted from her, echoing over the warehouse, but it was followed again by the unnerving laughter. "Have you ever sacrificed in the name of love?"

"No," Angel said forcefully, hoping to drive a wedge between them that the woman in black couldn't cross with her warped thinking. They were nothing alike.

"Have you ever known love?" the woman in black asked.

Angel kept moving and kept silent. He turned the battleax in his hands, using the bright sheen on the double-bitted head to see the reflection of the warehouse behind him. It was even easier because he wasn't reflected in it.

Almost all of the street kids had cleared the

building. Only a handful of them and the old man remained.

"You have known love, haven't you?" the woman in black taunted. She shoved her head closer, well within striking distance.

Angel reacted at once, deciding between heart-beats to chance it.

CHAPTER FIFTEEN

The woman in black lifted an arm to defend herself. The battleax handle slammed against her forearm and it was like hitting a brick wall. Still, the woman in black allowed the winds holding her up to drag her away again. Angel didn't show his surprise at the exchange.

"This girl that you loved," the woman in black said, "was she as pretty as me?" She lifted her long arms over her head, emphasizing the curves of her body. Then she twirled in the air, moving in a slow cadence that evoked a primitive response buried deep in Angel's brain.

Watch her stomach, Angel told himself. *She can feint with her head, legs and arms, but she can't feint with her stomach.*

The woman in black stopped moving. "You haven't answered my question, vampire."

"You haven't asked me one that I was interested in," Angel countered.

"You're like all men," the woman in black complained. "So ready to wound with words, to chip away at the confidence and well-being of those who would only love you."

"You kill people," Angel argued.

"Only those that I'm entitled to kill." The woman in black glanced over Angel's shoulder. "The world owes me its children." She smiled. "Look at them cowering back there. Not an innocent among them, yet they know what I am, what blood price I am owed."

"Why don't you tell me?" Angel said.

"Ah, vampire, if you were but a child again," the woman in black said, "you would know me."

She struck suddenly in a blinding flurry of blows that Angel barely managed to block. The battleax handle cracked in his grip and he knew even the hardened wood couldn't take much more punishment. As quickly as she'd attacked, the woman in black drew back.

"I am death," the woman in black stated. "I am the death of innocence. But I come by it naturally, you see, because first it died in me." She paused, laughing uncontrollably for a moment again as fresh tears cascaded down her face. "That's what a part of you fears in me, doesn't it, vampire? You've still got some innocence left in you."

"No," Angel said, thinking of all the years he'd spent killing people as Angelus.

"Oh, but I think that you do. Did you give yourself to a vampire so that you might live forever?"

"No."

"Immortality, I have been told, is the price men have paid their souls for all their lives. Deals are struck with demons. Painters and musicians and writers work so hard to stretch and perfect their craft that they might share in that immortality." The woman in black regarded Angel with suspicious dark eyes. "Or was it love?"

Angel remained silent, but he couldn't help thinking of Darla. At one time, he'd loved her literally more than life itself.

The woman in black's eyes flashed. "That was it, wasn't it? You were in love with the one who betrayed you!"

Angel stepped forward and swung the battleax at her waist.

With a gesture, the howling winds pulled the woman in black from the path of Angel's blade and almost knocked him down. He retained his balance with effort.

"She took your life from you," the woman in black said, "and what she could of your innocence. But why didn't she get it all? Vampires usually do."

"You like the sound of your own voice," Angel suggested, wishing he had a means of carrying the battle to the woman in black. "Maybe you should get your own talk show."

"You intrigue me, vampire. That's the only reason I'm letting you live." The woman in black laughed for a moment, then regained control of herself. "What secrets do you have?" She darted forward, her arm elongating till it was three times its original size.

Angel tried to avoid the woman in black's fingers, but she was too fast. He barely felt her arm graze the battleax haft, then her fingers stabbed deeply into his brain.

A firebomb of agony detonated in Angel's skull. He dropped the battleax from nerveless fingers and fell to his knees. With the next wave of pain, he went blind.

"Ah," the woman in black congratulated herself, "here it is. This is the difference. You have a soul. And it's *yours*. What did you do to deserve this punishment?"

Although he didn't want to, Angel suddenly remembered the Gypsy girl he'd chosen as the night's prey. He'd spent hours torturing her before he killed her. Then he remembered how it had felt when the curse put on him by the Gypsies had returned his soul to him. All the despair and grief of a hundred and fifty years of wanton slaying had returned to him and stayed for the last hundred years.

"There is more, isn't there?" the woman in black

taunted. "There is more and I will have it. I don't suffer alone, do I?"

Angel yelled in pain as the woman's fingers dug even more deeply into his skull, reaching further back into his memories. Without warning, he began reliving the night he'd returned to his home, to his family, after rising from the grave where Darla's crimson kisses had put him. That was when he'd found out a vampire's victim went to the grave with anger and returned with the same. Love didn't follow a person into the grave when he or she was turned, and it never crawled out of the grave with him or her.

No! he shouted inside his mind, trying desperately to turn off the memories or pull himself free of the woman in black. Instead, he relived that night. He'd tracked down each person in the house, each member of his family, and he'd killed them. His mother's and sister's dying screams echoed in his mind, followed by his father's curses. They had all feared and hated him at the end.

"You murdered your family?" the woman in black asked. She licked her lips, then licked the fresh tears from her cheeks. She laughed, her whole body shaking with the effort. "You and I are not so dissimilar, are we, vampire?"

Angel looked up at the woman in black. Whatever she'd done to him had left him unable to leap up and seize that slender neck in his hands. If he could have gotten to her, he knew he would have released the demon hunger inside himself on her.

"What other secrets do you hide, vampire?" the woman in black asked as she regarded him with renewed interest. "Perhaps we shall find out at another time."

"What do you want?" Angel's voice was a weak, hoarse rasp.

"What do I want?" The woman in black threw back her head and laughed. "I want the children. They are owed me. The world treated me unkindly, and love betrayed me. I will have my vengeance. If I am to have nothing else, I will have that."

"Not the children," Angel said.

"Because now you see yourself as some kind of avenger?" The woman in black laughed and wiped at her tears. "Don't you remember the children you preyed on, Angel? Your sister? Someone named Drusilla? Their avengers came for you, didn't they? Only to die by your hand as well." The wind died and the woman in black settled back to the floor.

Angel struggled to get to his feet, barely able to stand once he did. The pain danced like lightning inside his skull, reaving and ripping at his motor control over his body and his consciousness. He glanced back at the warehouse wall.

All of the street kids were gone. Only the old man remained there.

"You saved these children, vampire," the woman

in black said, "but if there'd been an innocent among them, I would have taken him or her. And you would not have stopped me. Go right your wrongs and serve your penance, and continue to fool yourself by crossing your true nature." Her eyes flashed fire. "But don't presume to meddle in my affairs again." She turned sharply and walked away.

Angel tried to go after her, but knew even if he caught her that he was in no shape to do anything. He remained standing and trembling as she went down the wooden stairway.

Her laughter and her sobbing mocked him.

By the time the paralysis lifted enough that he could navigate the stairs, the woman in black had disappeared. His cell phone rang in his coat pocket. He answered it, stepping into the shadows outside the warehouse as he peered in both directions along the street. Not even the street kids he and the old man had rescued remained in sight.

"Hello," he answered.

"Angel," Cordelia said. "Where are you?"

"It doesn't matter," Angel said tiredly. "Are you still at the church?"

"Yeah. Look, something really creepy just happened here. I . . . I just wanted to make sure you were all right."

"I'm fine," Angel replied, but he didn't feel that way. The woman in black had stirred up memories that would haunt his sleep for a long time. "Are you okay?"

"Yeah," Cordelia said, but her voice sounded hollow and Angel knew she'd had a bad experience as well. "Sister Juanita told me the hospital just called a few minutes ago. Father Carlos has regained consciousness. They're allowing limited visitation." She paused. "If you're up to it. You don't sound like yourself."

"It's the cell phone connection," Angel said, knowing full well that it wasn't. "Where's Doyle?"

"At the office. He just called me."

"Pick him up," Angel instructed, "and meet me at the hospital." There were still a couple hours of daylight left, too much to risk riding in the car. The sewers were his safest route to the hospital. He broke the connection and shoved the phone back into his pocket.

When he turned around, he saw the old man standing in the warehouse doorway behind him. "Is she gone?" the old man asked.

Angel nodded.

"Those things that she said about you," the old man asked, "was they true? About you killing your family and all them people?"

"Yes," Angel said dryly, not knowing how the old man was going to react. Even Buffy and her friends had had a hard time dealing with all the evil he'd done as Angelus.

"That's part of how she beat you back there," the old man said after a moment. "She used your past against you."

Angel didn't say anything.

"But you're not alone, are you?" The old man gazed at Angel intently. "That other young man I saw you with last night? He's more than just somebody you work with. He's a friend." The rheumy old eyes searched Angel's. "And you got more friends than that. Despite whatever bad things you might have once done."

"I've been lucky," Angel said.

The old man shook his head. "One thing I've learned. You don't get lucky with friends. You earn 'em. Just like you earned yours." He let out a breath. "That woman beat you back there partially because you let her get to you through your past. What you got to realize is you ain't that man anymore."

Angel started to disagree. He still remained very much that man, the demon's hunger still infested him, and sometimes it had lusted for his friends.

"Oh, I ain't sayin' it ain't a battle," the old man went on. "Me an' Jimbo, we knew all about such things. There was plenty of reasons for us to hate ourselves. We lost our families, too. Part of it was the war, what it done to us, what it changed us into. But part of it was our own faults because of what we done instead of facin' ourselves."

"You don't know what I've done," Angel said.

"It don't matter." The old man came closer to Angel and laid a withered hand on his broad shoulder. "I'm gonna tell you a secret, Mr. Angel, something it took me an' Jimbo nearly a couple lifetimes to learn. A man don't have to live in his past. He's expected to learn from it and maybe even atone for it, but he don't have to live there. An' that's part of what you're still doing. What you owe yourself an' these friends of yours is knowing one day you got up an' you wasn't that man anymore. You chose a different path. And you been buildin' this new man you've become ever since that day. Don't you let nobody tear that man down."

The old man's eyes misted and his hand on Angel's shoulder trembled.

"That's how me an' Jimbo got along in this world," the old man said hoarsely. "Maybe we didn't turn out to be much worth a damn when you put what we did in the scales that people measure a man's life by, but we knew we wasn't the men we used to be. An' that's gotta mean something. I gotta believe that."

"It does," Angel said.

Angel took the stairwell up to the fourth floor of the hospital. When he reached the nurse's station in the west wing, he found Doyle, Cordelia, and Sister Juanita seated in a crowded waiting area filled with families and small children.

"How is Father Carlos doing?" Angel asked the nun.

Sister Juanita got to her feet. "The doctor says he expects the *padre* to make a full recovery, but he will need his rest to do so. However, we will be allowed to speak with the *padre* for a short time. The doctor is concerned for Father Carlos and doesn't want him overtired." She paused authoritatively. "Nor do I."

"It's important that I speak with him," Angel said. "I've met the woman in black. I couldn't stop her. She's still out hunting."

Cordelia touched the torn sleeve of Angel's trenchcoat. "Are you all right?"

"I'm fine," Angel replied. "Thanks." He gazed at Cordelia. "You didn't sound like yourself over the phone either."

"Whatever this thing is," Cordelia said, "*whoever* it is, it tries to be your friend." She quickly related her experiences in the basement's secret room. "It concentrates on your loneliness and tries to do like a mind-whammy on you. Luckily, it didn't stand a chance against me. I mean, I've never felt lonely a day in my life."

Angel looked at Cordelia, knowing that despite what she said now, she'd faced some of her own demons in that room. "Let's see the toad."

Cordelia took a trash bag from her purse and opened it.

Hesitantly, Angel reached for the obsidian carving.

"I really don't think picking it up is a good idea," Cordelia said.

Warily, Angel flicked a forefinger against the black gemstone. It was colder than the air-conditioning around them, and even that brief touch told him that the obsidian toad contained a wealth of powerful energy. He took the trash bag from Cordelia and folded it into his pocket. Cordelia didn't seem to resent its loss in the slightest.

"So we don't know if the woman who attacked Father Carlos is using whatever she found there, or if it's using her," Angel said.

"My vote is that it's using her," Cordelia said. "I mean, maybe she went there after it, thinking it would do one thing and not the other, but I don't think you can control something like that." She frowned. "And how could it be trying to possess me—or whatever it was doing—at the same time it was attacking you?"

"Echo," Angel said.

"What echo?" Cordelia asked.

"The toad," Angel said. "Whatever that entity is— the woman in black—it was housed or leashed by this. If an object has to hold that much power over a long period of time, it takes on some of the qualities of its occupant."

"So it became its own person?"

"In the same way a ventriloquist's dummy is its own person, you might say," Doyle said. "It's not capable of taking off on its own, but it can snare someone to do that."

Angel nodded. "Whatever residual power is in the obsidian toad is only a shadow of whatever the woman in black is."

"Then it's strong," Cordelia said.

"Yeah," Angel agreed. "Really strong."

"What would it have done to me if it had gotten me?" Cordelia asked.

"Some objects like that," Angel said, "absorb the life-force of other things. Or they take over whomever they come in contact with."

Cordelia looked disgusted. "You mean I could have been that toad-thing's zombie toy?"

"You aren't," Angel pointed out. "Where's Father Carlos's room?"

"This way," Sister Juanita said. "I visited him briefly this morning."

Angel fell in behind Sister Juanita and glanced at Doyle. "What did you find out about the woman you saw in your vision? Do you know what's threatening her?"

"Can't say for sure what's after her," Doyle admitted, "though I've got a suspicion." He took a map from his pocket. "Me, I'm not one to believe in coincidences, right? I mean, unless it's just part of an unlucky period I'm going through. So I took a peek at the news to track this woman in black we've been hearing about."

"I'm with you." Angel had been thinking along similar lines. Especially since he was certain he knew the identity of the woman who'd attacked Father Carlos.

Doyle held the L.A. area map out. "The woman in black is headed in a definite direction." He held up the map briefly, then tapped the three areas where the woman had been seen. "The convenience store you and I were at. The downtown area where she killed the two police officers. She also showed up at an elementary school earlier." All the Xs lined up, heading from the Huntington Park area at an angle toward San Pedro. "Where was the warehouse where you saw her?"

Angel touched an area in front of the last X, between that location and San Pedro.

"Still in a straight line," Doyle said, nodding. He put the map away.

"The woman in your vision?"

"Lives in San Pedro. I thought at first that I had the vision on Adrian's yacht because we were around that area. Remember that I told you she had a child?"

Angel nodded.

"This woman used to work in television as an actress. Guess who the baby's father is."

Angel put it together as Sister Juanita halted in front of room 436. "Adrian."

"Got it in one." Doyle grinned. "The plot thickens, doesn't it?"

"Did Marisa know?" Cordelia asked.

Sister Juanita waited expectantly at the door.

"She's the one who told Adrian he was a daddy," Doyle said.

"The day she disappeared?" Cordelia asked.

"Ten months ago." Doyle took another paper from his pocket. "The day she disappeared, Marisa went into Adrian's offices, checked on some of the business holdings that her husband had. They belonged to his grandfather but were passed on to him."

"The businesses in Huntington Park?" Cordelia asked.

Angel took the folded paper and opened it. He scanned the newspaper page, realizing it was the same one Cordelia had shown him on the computer back in the office. He studied the boy's face in the picture. *Innocence. The thing that draws the woman in black.*

"You knew about them businesses?" Doyle looked surprised.

"When I did the background check on Adrian," Cordelia replied.

"Marisa also had this newspaper article," Doyle said.

"Why?" Cordelia asked, peering over Angel's shoulder.

Doyle shrugged. "Beats me. Adrian didn't know either."

"I know why she had it," Angel said quietly. He folded the paper and returned it to Doyle. He nodded to Sister Juanita and opened the door, then followed her inside.

The stink of hospital antiseptics and thick pollen of flowers filled Angel's nose. The afternoon sunlight left a pool that reached a third of the way into the room but wasn't going to present too much of a problem. Flowers and plants filled tables and chairs around the room. Smiley-faced balloons drifted in the breeze created by the air-conditioning.

Father Carlos lay on the bed. With the white linen over him and the hospital monitors and IV tubes attached to him, he looked small and skeletal. His head turned as the door opened and he made a snuffling noise when the tubes in his nose twisted against the pillow. "Sister Juanita," he greeted in a whisper-thin voice. He raised a trembling hand.

The nun crossed the room to the bed and took the old *padre*'s hand, patting it affectionately. "Father Carlos, I am very pleased to hear that you are doing better."

"A mild heart attack, they tell me." Father Carlos dismissed the severity of the attack with a shake of his head. "Coupled with the injury to my head, it knocked me off my feet for a while. But I shall be back to the church for this Sunday's service."

"You'll do no such thing," Sister Juanita replied. "You'll lie in that bed and rest."

The *padre* smiled, his flesh looking ashen and gray. "I'll be lazy after I am dead, not before." He looked past her. "I don't know your friends."

Sister Juanita hesitated, looking at Angel for guidance.

Angel stepped forward. "We're not exactly friends."

"Oh?" The *padre* touched a small wooden crucifix at his side.

"We've come about the woman in black."

A frightened and sad expression filled Father Carlos's face. He lay back on the bed as if his strength had deserted him. "She is real, then?"

"Yes," Sister Juanita answered. "I am sorry, Father Carlos."

"Why? You've done nothing wrong."

"I know how you take on the troubles of the church," the nun replied, "and I would not bring you one more such burden had I a choice. Especially at this time."

The old *padre* glanced up at Angel and evidently made a decision about whatever it was he sensed about him. He put the crucifix away. "She has harmed children, then?"

Angel answered without hesitation. Lying would serve no one. "Yes."

"How many?"

Angel shook his head. Knowing numbers wouldn't help and might add to the old man's burden. "More if we don't stop her."

"Do you know what she is?"

"An elemental," Angel replied. "That's my best guess."

Father Carlos nodded morosely. "That is what she is called in the documents. You know of such things?"

"I've had some experience with them," Angel replied.

"As you may know," the old *padre* said, "elementals are created in nature. In some of the reading I have done, it's been suggested that they were spirit-forms of emotions, of needs and wants. They took form predominantly among forested lands, places where many things grew together and needed to be shielded from predators. Usually they protected animals and the land from demons and, eventually, mankind. Spirit-forms guided deer herds from attackers and were thought to haunt certain parts of forests where the chain of life was most necessary to keep the world intact during the beginning."

"I've read about those things," Angel said. "A lot of arcane scholars believed that the elementals in the beginning of civilization weren't sentient, that they were merely forces that strove to keep the balance of life."

"Yes," Father Carlos said. "They were believed to be truly neutral aspects of our world. They knew neither good nor evil. They only knew to protect with whatever means they had. But that changed when the elementals started existing with the demons and humans that rose up in this world. They took on the attributes of the demons and men. Sometimes they took on the aspects of women."

"The woman in black," Angel said. "We don't have much time."

Father Carlos took a rattling breath, closed his eyes for a moment, then opened them again. "More than three hundred years ago, when the Spanish first came into California, one of the priests of the church I serve came from Spain. There he had been high-ranking and privileged, but he ran afoul of a cardinal who had sent him to the Spanish colonies."

Sister Juanita poured a glass of water from the bedside carafe and handed it to Father Carlos. The old man drank the water slowly.

"My church," Father Carlos said, "is an offshoot of the Catholics and Lutherans. Priests are permitted to marry and father children. This priest came among the people in this area and he found a woman who caught his eye and took away some of his loneliness. She was little more than a girl in her years and ways. She was beautiful and unspoiled, and dreamt of a life much larger than the village she'd grown up in. She loved the priest with all her heart and more than anything wanted to be his wife, to have the chance to see these faraway places he had seen. But the priest, though it shames me to say this of one of my own order, didn't care about her in the same manner. She was the balm he took for himself to ease his wounded ego. All he wanted to do was return to Spain, and to the station among the Castilian courts."

"That's an old story," Cordelia muttered.

"Yes," Father Carlos agreed. "One too often found still. But at the time, no one knew the repercussions this one woman-child's love for this priest would have." He sipped more water. "Though he didn't marry her, the priest fathered three children by the woman. They were all bright and intelligent, and I would like to believe that he cared for them in some way because they were of his blood, and of the church where I shepherd my own flock. In time, the church in Spain relented and the priest was offered a chance to go back there."

"But he didn't want to take the woman," Cordelia said.

"No," Father Carlos said sadly. "How could he go back to that way of life with a wife who possessed only rudimentary social skills? He refused to take the woman, even went so far as to tell her that her presence and the presence of their children would only shame him and very probably end his career. He would not let that happen."

"Oh," Sister Juanita said, shaking her head in sympathy, "that poor girl."

"In the beginning, yes," Father Carlos said, "she was a very pitiful and wretched thing. The whole community felt her sorrow and pain, but every attempt they made to draw her back to them only made the woman's pain greater. And not all of them welcomed her back. Several delighted in her fall from the priest's favor. As the priest's consort, you see, she had also made enemies among the village by taking liberties with her station."

Voices passed by in the outside hall. Angel glanced at the small alarm clock beside the old *padre's* bed. Time passed too quickly.

"On the day that the Spanish ship arrived to take the priest back to the Old World and the castles and courts that he longed for," Father Carlos said, "the woman led her three children down to the river that had birthed the community all those years ago. You see, her grief over the priest and his rejection of her had driven her mad. She believed that it was the children, not herself, that the priest was ashamed of. There is some speculation in the journal entries I have read that the priest even told her that he would have taken her had it not been for their children, who were even less socially refined than she. However it came to pass, the woman believed that the children stood between her and the priest's love, and between her and the world that waited for her. So she decided to remove that obstacle."

"No . . ." Cordelia's voice sounded weak and strangled.

Even after all the things he had seen done, all the things that he had done as Angelus, a cold chill filled Angel. It was hard not to walk away. Only the realization that more children would die if he didn't stay gave him the strength to listen to the story.

"The children were small," Father Carlos said. "It must have been easy to hold them under the water. And she did this to each child in turn, till there were three corpses where children had been only moments before. Even though her anger had sustained her through her murders, the pain that wracked her when she realized what she had done was even greater. She stumbled back into town, insane and crying, calling out for the priest."

Doyle cursed and Angel saw pain haunting the half-demon's eyes.

"When he finally understood what she was telling him, finally understood the horror of what she had done," Father Carlos went on, "the priest went to the bodies of his children. Although he was partially to blame for their deaths—and maybe even because of that very thing, knowing how heavily such a thing can weigh in the eyes of God—he turned on the woman, disavowing any love he might have ever felt. He went aboard the ship and didn't even stay to arrange for the burial of his children. The villagers had to take care of that."

Sister Juanita crossed herself.

"After the funerals, the woman understood more of what she had done, but there was no undoing of it. The ship sailed and took the priest far from the woman. Her children lay interred in graves. And the village ceased to be a home for her, only a place that she dwelt and wandered through, eating scraps like a dog. The villagers began calling her *La Llorona.*"

"The Weeping Woman," Angel said, locking the mythology in now. Several cultures had adopted the belief of the Weeping Woman who had murdered her children.

"You see," Father Carlos said, "even before this poor woman murdered her children, there were stories of women who did such things. Those stories were true as well. Women who had children by other men while their husbands were away on ships or at war sometimes smothered children or drowned them so their husbands wouldn't have to know. But this *La Llorona* became something even more fearful."

Angel waited impatiently, but knew he needed to know everything.

"After a year or two of her madness and desolation, unable to comfortably stay in the village and having nowhere to go, the woman believed the only thing she could do was take her own life." Father Carlos sipped water again. "She climbed to the top of a mountain and prepared to throw herself off. Though she was certain several villagers had seen her go, and this is borne out by the fact that several villagers did make journal entries about seeing her leave that day, no one showed up at the mountain to stop her—"

The door to the room opened and a middle-aged nurse carrying a clipboard poked her head in. "I'm sorry, but Doctor left orders that Mr. Oliveria not be disturbed for long."

"We only need a few more minutes," Angel said.

The nurse shook her head. "I'm sorry, but—"

"Nurse!" Sister Juanita's voice was stern and unforgiving.

The nurse took in the nun's black-and-white habit and immediately grew silent.

"He did ask nicely," Sister Juanita pointed out, "and we are not quite done now. I don't think we need to discuss this any further, do you?"

The nurse hesitated only a moment. "No, sister. A few minutes more won't hurt."

"Good," Sister Juanita said.

The nurse retreated.

"Wow," Cordelia said. "I've never seen a nurse back down so quickly."

"Sister Juanita," Father Carlos said quietly, "has amazing powers of persuasion. It's a gift." A smile flickered at his lips, then quickly died away. "That day that *La Llorona* picked to die, an air elemental came to her." His eyes focused on Angel's. "As you know, elementals often take the shape of the four forces of nature: earth, air, fire, and water."

The Eastern beliefs listed five, Angel knew, including metal, but the actual spectrum of elemental manifestation was probably broader than that. However, the air elemental angle explained the power the woman in black had to call winds into being.

"The air elemental was bitter with loneliness as well, and in this they recognized each other," Father Carlos continued, "but the elemental had great power. It seized the woman when she flung herself from the mountain. Frustrated and scared and lonely herself, the woman accepted the air elemental into her, bonding with it so completely that no one could find the seams where one ended and the other began ever again. Powerful and vengeful, *La Llorona* returned to the village where the woman had lived. She arrived in the night and she took the children, slaying all of them, laughing and weeping the whole time."

"Why did she kill the children in the village?" Cordelia asked.

Father Carlos shook his head. "No one may say. Perhaps this had always been the air elemental's hunger, or perhaps it was the woman's own madness manifesting itself. *La Llorona* claimed that she had given up her children to a world that had betrayed her and that the world owed her its children. She killed adults that tried to stop her as well, offering mercy to none. But it was the children she stalked."

"But they stopped her," Cordelia said. "They had to have. Otherwise *La Llorona* would not have been held in the basement of your church all these years."

"Someone did stop her," the old *padre* agreed. "But it wasn't until years later and hundreds of children had been killed. *La Llorona* wandered along the west coast down into Mexico and up to British Columbia. However, she always returned from these journeys to the village where she had been born and—in a sense—died. During her last visit, the priest who was at the church then had learned of a means that had sometimes been used in the past to bind air elementals. He created a toad-gem that—"

Angel took the garbage bag from his trenchcoat pocket. He opened the bag, using the plastic itself to keep from touching the stone, and revealed the obsidian toad.

"That's it," Father Carlos whispered. "That is the gem he used to trap *La Llorona*. It's referred to as a captor-gem in the documents. The toad shape was chosen because of the mutability of the creature it bound. As toads change—from an egg to a tadpole to an amphibious creature to a toad—the trapped creature changes also. Once *La Llorona* was captured, the gem was locked away in the secret room in the church's basement."

"Great," Cordelia said, "then all we have to do is find this elemental-demon thing and work the toad mojo on it."

"No," Father Carlos said. "It will take more than that."

"The person who freed *La Llorona* will have to trap her," Angel said.

"Should have known this wasn't going to be easy," Doyle groaned.

The old *padre* nodded. "Yes. Once a force of evil has been set free of a captor-gem, as long as the person who released it remains alive, they have to trap it again."

"How?" Angel asked.

"The captor-gem can only be released by someone who wants to use the power of the creature trapped inside. In this case, I think that the person who released *La Llorona* came seeking revenge. Against others."

"And against herself," Angel said. "She blames herself for what happened."

"How can you say that?" Sister Juanita demanded. "You talk like you know who this woman is who attacked him. The *padre* did not even see her well."

Angel locked eyes with the old man. "He recognized her."

Father Carlos looked away and said nothing.

"*Padre*," Sister Juanita said, "tell me he's not speaking the truth."

"You told me yourself that only two people learned of the secret room in the church's basement when Father Carlos's wife passed away," Angel told the nun.

Father Carlos looked at Sister Juanita. "That is how you knew?"

"*Padre*," Sister Juanita whispered, "Pilar told us about your burden."

"Who did Pilar tell?" Father Carlos demanded.

"There was Lavina Segura and myself there that day. Pilar only told us that there was a terrible demon locked in the secret room."

"Lavina Segura?" A confused expression filled Father Carlos's face, then understanding dawned as well. "So that was how she knew."

"Who, *padre*?" Sister Juanita asked. "Who was this woman who attacked you? Surely you can't be saying that Lavina Segura attacked you and released this thing."

The *padre* shook his head, unable to speak.

Angel knew the man was conflicted due to his oath regarding the sacrament of reconciliation. "It was Maria Segura."

"Maria?" Sister Juanita looked as though she couldn't believe it. "Cristofer's mother? But she has been gone for eight years. Even Lavina had given her up for dead."

"It was Maria that night," Father Carlos said softly. "I almost recognized her at first, but she had changed so much. She'd grown and her features had changed. It wasn't until she hit me down in the basement that it came to me who she was. She released *La Llorona*." He glanced at Angel. "She has to capture the demon again."

"How can she recapture the demon?" Angel asked.

Father Carlos shook his head. "Forgiveness, my son. She will have to forgive those whom she seeks vengeance on. And she will have to forgive herself as well."

"That all sounds fine and dandy," Doyle commented dryly, "but we're not exactly set up time-wise to handle a long-term self-forgiveness treatment. Isn't there another way?"

Father Carlos shook his head. "That is the nature of a captor-gem and those bound within them. As long as the one who released *La Llorona* is alive, it will be that person's responsibility to reinvoke the spell to trap her."

Doyle looked around. "Hey, maybe I'm a little out of line for asking, so forgive me here, but if Maria winds up dead fighting this thing—provided we can find her and get her to face it—that means the rest of us then have a shot at this rebinding ceremony, right?"

The old *padre* hesitated. "Yes, but I would not want Maria harmed."

"Do you know where Maria is?" Cordelia asked.

Father Carlos shook his head. "I don't know where for sure, but I have learned that when a child is in need or is scared, there is usually one place they always return to."

"I'll need her mother's address," Angel said.

Hesitation weighed heavily on the *padre's* features.

"All you're going to do is delay me," Angel promised. "I'll come back and let you know how many lives that delay cost."

"You're a hard man," Father Carlos said sadly.

"Yeah."

"But it's going to take a hard man to do what you have to do." Father Carlos gave Angel the address. "I wish you Godspeed. Take care of Maria—if you can. In spite of her circumstances and her son's death, she's hardly more than a child herself in many ways."

Angel didn't make any promises. At this point, there was no way of knowing what promises he could keep. No matter what it took, no more innocent blood would be shed.

The menace of *La Llorona* ended tonight.

CHAPTER SIXTEEN

Sunset painted the western skies a deep purple, and the last true rays of the sun had vanished minutes before as twilight settled in over the city.

Doyle pulled the convertible over to the curb in front of the old, modest three-bedroom home in the Huntington Park area. Angel sat in the backseat. On the way over, while the sun had still been out, he'd remained under a heavy canvas tarp to protect him from the direct sunlight. Cordelia rode in the passenger seat.

The flower gardens out in front of the address Father Carlos had given them were carefully tended, and a wooden porch swing sat under the eaves. The lawn showed a lot of care, and the sounds of sporadic mowers sputtered nearby. Lawn ornaments in the shape of giant plastic yellow and white daisies and red and black woodpeckers spun in the breeze and homemade birdfeeders hung from tree branches.

A middle-aged woman worked in the flowerbed to the left of the porch. She was petite, with black and gray hair hacked off at shoulder length. She wore jeans and a light sweater. A straw sunhat with partial mosquito netting shielded her head to keep the bugs from her face. She pushed her trowel into the flowerbed, got to her feet, and gazed suspiciously at the three people in the convertible.

Angel clambered out of the backseat and walked toward her, flanked by Doyle and Cordelia.

The woman confronted them at the front steps, stopping near the cordless phone she'd left on the railing. "May I help you?" she asked.

Angel hesitated for a moment. There was no easy way to say what they'd come to do. "Mrs. Segura?"

The woman paused, then gave a tight nod.

"I've just come from Father Carlos's bedside at the hospital."

No emotion showed on the woman's face.

"He talked to me," Angel said, "and let me know what happened to him last night."

"The *padre* is going to be all right?" Lavina asked.

"The doctor expects him to make a full recovery," Angel said. He was conscious of the neighbors standing on their own front porches.

The men were dressed in undershirts for the most part, street tattoos visible on their arms and chests, and some of them smoked, burning bright orange coals in the descending night. Women, teens, and children watched as well, and a pocket of stillness seemed to settle over the immediate area. It was the typical reaction of a close-knit neighborhood to a stranger in their midst, an extended family protecting one of their own.

Angel knew if he made any overt move to get into the house that most of the men and teenage boys would rally to Lavina Segura's aid while the others called the police. If the situation weren't handled properly, they'd be mobbed and maybe even arrested. He didn't look around and he spoke loud enough for most of the people in the general area to hear.

"Father Carlos is going to be fine," Angel said again, emphasizing that if he wasn't one of them, at least they had some of the same interests.

"Thank God." Some of the tension left Lavina then. Weakly, she sat on the steps, but did not move from Angel's path. "You came all this way to tell me this? Sister Juanita has my phone number."

"I came this far," Angel said, "to get Maria."

"My daughter?" The tension returned to Lavina's face. "But she has been gone for eight years and more. Everyone who knows me knows that."

"She came back," Angel said. "Maria was at the church last night. Father Carlos saw her."

"That is impossible."

"She was there," Angel said.

Lavina stood slowly, obviously not trusting her legs. She gripped the step railing tightly. "I do not know you."

"Call Sister Juanita at the hospital," Angel suggested. "Ask her about me. Ask her what Father Carlos told us about last night and Maria."

Lavina shook her head. "No. I want you to leave my property."

"Father Carlos knows that Maria freed *La Llorona.*" Angel heard the startled whispers of the fearful name from the lips of several of the neighbors. He also saw the shadow moving behind the screen door inside the house. The lights had been left off in the living room, but someone had switched off the steady drone of television voices.

"No. She did no such thing."

"Sister Juanita admitted that you and she learned about the demon that was kept in the room in the church's basement from Father Carlos's deceased wife," Angel went on. He had no choice about handling the situation gently. All the truths had to be laid out, and all the lies exposed.

"I've been there," Cordelia said gently. "The demon is real. Look, Mrs. Segura, what happened to Cristofer wasn't easy on anyone. It had to have been especially hard on Maria."

"Maria was not there," Lavina insisted. "Don't you think I would have known my own daughter?

Don't you think it shamed me to see that my own daughter didn't come to her son's funeral?"

"Sometimes," Doyle said, "our lives take these funny little twists." He shrugged. "Not real funny, I suppose, because I've been through a few of them. Seems like no matter how hard you run or how far you go, you can't get away from fate."

"My daughter wouldn't—" Lavina's voice broke.

"Maria was upset over Cristofer's death," Angel said softly, still conscious of all the people watching him. He knew the woman was aware of the audience, too. So was the person inside the house. "She felt guilty about leaving him with you, and she felt even more guilty about the part she and her husband played in his death."

"You wouldn't know what my daughter felt," Lavina snapped. "How could you even guess what she has been through?"

"I know about guilt," Angel said. "I know it moved her last night and it's moving you to protect her now."

Lavina stood and pointed. "Leave my house!"

"It's too late for that," Cordelia said.

"Ma'am," Doyle said, "I got to tell you: We may be Maria's last hope."

"*La Llorona* isn't going to go away," Angel said. "Father Carlos told me that the person who released *La Llorona* has to be the one who binds her again. Only Maria can do that."

"I told you Maria is not here!" Lavina's voice escalated.

"*La Llorona* has already taken the life of one innocent child who I can name," Angel said. "Benito Rodrigo in the convenience store. Maybe you knew him."

The boy's name echoed around the neighborhood in the whispers of parents and children. Benito evidently had been known throughout the area, or at least the story of his death.

"*La Llorona* killed a man at the elementary school today," Doyle said. "She would have taken children if she'd been able. How much guilt do you want Maria to bear before she faces up to what she's done?"

The whispering coming from the neighbors grew fiercer. Some of it turned angry.

"Eight years ago," Angel went on, knowing they had to keep the situation under control or it would get volatile, "Maria had a baby but no husband. She knew how hard her life would be, and she was scared. It wasn't what she wanted."

Tears ran down Lavina's face. "Don't talk to me. Leave my house. Leave my house *now!*"

"I'm sorry," Angel apologized. He pushed his guilt over the confrontation with the woman away from him. Giving in to it wouldn't get Maria. "I can't. If I don't act, more children will die. I don't want their blood on my hands. I don't want it on Maria's, and I don't want it on yours."

"It is *La Llorona* who is doing the killing," Lavina said hoarsely.

"But it was Maria who freed her." Angel's vision was sharp enough to see the slight movement beyond the screen door. A light glowed in another room behind the slight feminine figure standing there.

"No!"

"Maria knew because you knew. Maybe she heard you and Sister Juanita talking about it when Father Carlos's wife passed away. I don't know. We'd have to ask her. That's not important anyway. What is important is stopping *La Llorona*."

"She did not do this."

"Eight years ago," Angel said, "Maria left home, left her baby, and left you. She went into L.A. and took up acting. It was probably something she was always good at, something that she'd always wanted to do. She took on another name and became Marisa Smith."

"You didn't mention any of this in the car," Cordelia whispered. There hadn't been time for the whole story, so she and Doyle still had a few surprises coming.

Angel ignored Cordelia's complaint. There'd be time enough for explanations later. "Marisa Smith became something of a success," he went on. "She walked away from Maria Segura and changed her hair and makeup enough that she wasn't even recognized by anyone from the old neighborhood when she was on television. She acted in a television series, and she went on to marry a wealthy man named Adrian Heath."

"Now *that*," Cordelia whispered, "*that* you should have told me, Angel."

"You don't know what you're talking about," Lavina said loudly. "These are all lies."

"No," Angel said, "it's the truth. Ten months ago, Maria, as Marisa, found out her husband had a baby by another woman. It was from a time before her marriage; her husband didn't know until she told him. But the baby made Marisa afraid again. What if her husband, knowing that baby existed, pulled away from her and abandoned her? Maria already knew how hard it was to leave a child behind."

Trembling, Lavina sat in the porch swing. "Please go."

"I can't," Angel said. "Marisa tried to have a child with her husband, hoping to keep him with her. She didn't know that he loved her and was going to stay with her no matter what. She couldn't trust that. Especially not if he somehow found out she'd abandoned her own family and child, and that everything she'd told him about her past was a lie. Maybe someday she hoped that she'd be able to tell him the whole truth."

Lavina's shoulders quaked as she cried. "It is not

easy to be a mother in these times. You don't know what it's like for so many young girls to become a mother and yet be tempted by what seems so possible in life."

"Maria became a success," Angel said. "Maybe it wouldn't have happened any other way if she hadn't left. But she didn't leave completely. No one can walk away from their family completely free of the ties there." He knew that from experience. Even though his own family had died by his hands, they were never far from his thoughts. In the early days after his soul was returned to him, he'd thought that alone was going to kill him.

The shadow on the other side of the screen door shifted again.

"Marisa had a miscarriage a few months ago," Angel said, drawing on the information Doyle had given him in the car. "She probably thought it was some kind of punishment. Then, a week ago, she learned of Cristofer's death from an asthma attack. A newspaper article came out, blaming your grandson's—her son's—death on the companies in the area that are causing air pollution. That article also named the owners of those companies. One of those owners was Adrian Heath, her husband."

"No," Lavina said weakly. "None of this is true. You are lying."

"I can only imagine how that made her feel," Angel said. "She had left Cristofer in your care, then gone off to find a better life for herself. Part of that life was funded by the very business that may have had a hand in killing her son. In her pain and anger, she remembered the story she'd overheard about the demon trapped in the secret room of the church basement. She couldn't show up at the funeral, so she waited outside until it was over. She knew Father Carlos was inside the church, but she couldn't wait any longer. She went inside and spoke with Father Carlos, distracted him long enough to go to the basement, and opened the door of the secret room to release *La Llorona*—"

"She would never do such a thing!" Lavina insisted.

The screen door opened and Marisa Heath stepped out onto the small porch. "Enough, Mama. Please." She wore her hair pulled back in a ponytail now, as well as designer jeans and a pullover top.

The older woman looked at her daughter. "Maria, you shouldn't have come out here."

Angel listened to the flurry of conversations that raced around the surrounding houses.

"What would you have me do, Mama?" Marisa asked. "Hide from the truth longer?" Tears ran down her cheeks. "I can't hide anymore. I've tried. There's no place to go that I don't see Cristofer's face."

Lavina crossed to her daughter and hugged her fiercely. "Please go back in the house."

Marisa shook her head. "I can't," she cried softly. "I'm so sorry." She held her mother for a moment, then looked at Angel. "Everything you're saying is true. I freed *La Llorona* from the secret room in the church basement, but I thought she would destroy me. I was too weak to destroy myself. I thought about it, but I just couldn't do it. If I hadn't been so weak, then maybe Benito would still be alive."

Curses echoed around the neighborhood and Angel knew they were standing on a powder keg. Doyle and Cordelia shifted around him, recognizing the new threat, too. "Marisa," Angel said, "why don't you come with us?"

Marisa wept openly. "I didn't know that the creature locked inside the room was insane. But when it entered my mind, I knew. You could hear her laughing and crying." She closed her eyes for a moment. "I saw her drown her own children. I felt them dying with my own hands. No one should have to do that." She gulped a quick breath. "I tried to break away from her, but I couldn't. She held on to me too tightly. I thought—I hoped—that she would kill me. But she let me live. I don't know why."

"Because she needs you," Angel said. "She needs you alive to help make her strong. Guilt can't survive on its own. It has to have victims in order to thrive, and the greatest victims are those who have done the greatest wrongs and realize that." He spoke to her from the heart, knowing all about guilt. *"La Llorona is* guilt, Marisa, and it won't stop unless you stop it. *She* won't stop unless you stop her."

"I can't," Marisa said. "She's too strong."

"I can help you," Angel said. "There are things about *La Llorona* that you didn't know."

Marisa shook her head. "I'm afraid. God help me, when I first found out about Cristofer, and that the companies Adrian owned, companies that I have been living off, had everything to do with his death, I wanted to die. But when she was inside my mind, showing me all the things that she showed me, I became afraid of dying." She wiped at her eyes. "I want to live."

"Then live," Angel said. "But you can't do it with the guilt. If you don't do something to offset the guilt, you're going to die inside. You don't deserve that. And it won't bring Cristofer back." He remembered how he'd stood over his family's bodies. "Nothing ever brings them back when they're gone. But you can live, and if you live right, them being gone will mean something if it changes you."

Marisa shook her head again and started to turn away at her mother's beckoning.

"La Llorona left you alive," Angel said, tensing. "But *La Llorona* also learned about Hannah Boyd and her child from you. Maybe you were thinking about Hannah and her little girl when you were

blaming yourself and Adrian for Cristofer's death, or maybe she just dug it out of you. I don't know. But I do know that *La Llorona* is going toward San Pedro. And I think it's to kill Hannah and her child, acting on the threat they presented to your marriage. Maybe when someone frees *La Llorona* her personality adopts part of the person who frees her. Or maybe *La Llorona* isn't complete unless she's working through someone else's pain and anger. But I do know that she's headed for Hannah."

"You must go away," Lavina said weakly, pulling at her daughter.

"I can't," Angel said. "Only Marisa can stop *La Llorona*." He looked up at the young woman. "I need you to help me save them. If you don't, they're going to die tonight. *La Llorona* may have reached Hannah Boyd's home already."

"Marisa can't help you against a demon," Lavina said. "She's lucky to have escaped with her own life, and now you would have her throw it away."

Angel stared quietly at the young woman. "Please. The guilt is yours, and only you can remove it. This would be a step in the right direction. It will keep any other guilt from piling up on you."

"You need to go," Lavina said harshly. "You need to go or I will call—"

"No, Mama," Marisa said. She pushed herself away from her mother. "What he says is true. I don't know if he's right about my ability to stop *La Llorona*, but I know I can't stand by and do nothing. You can't hide me from my responsibility in this. I will go with them."

"No!" Lavina stood and ran to her daughter. She gripped Marisa's shoulders. "You can't go with them! You are only a child, Maria!"

Tears slid down Marisa's face. "Everything he has said so far is true, Mama. If he says that I am the only one who can stop *La Llorona*, then that must be true as well." She pulled her mother to her and hugged her tightly. Then she looked at Angel. "I am the only one who can stop *La Llorona*?"

"Yes," Angel replied.

Marisa nodded. She pulled her mother to her tighter and kissed her cheek. "I must go, Mama."

"No," Lavina wailed. "I lost you those years ago, and I lost Cristofer only a week ago. I cannot bear to lose you again, Maria. Don't you understand that?"

"And would you have me stay, Mama," Marisa asked in a soft voice, "knowing that because I stayed more mothers and fathers lost their children?"

Lavina had no answer.

"I love you, Mama, and I'm sorry for the pain I caused you then and the pain I'm causing you now." Gently, Marisa disentangled herself from her mother and walked down the steps to join Angel.

* * *

"Hey, I thought I told you this morning to never show your face around here again! I guess maybe I didn't make myself plain enough!"

Angel watched the big man behind the bait shop counter reach under the counter and bring out a baseball bat. "Mortie?" Angel asked Doyle.

"Yeah," the half-demon replied. "Big, isn't he?"

"Yeah," Angel said, squaring off as the man came toward him. Cordelia and Marisa stood behind them as every person in the bait shop turned to watch the action.

Evidently the bait shop was a gathering place for the locals after the sun went down. Groups sat around tables outside and the nearby beach to watch the ships and boats out in the harbor.

Angel and Doyle had tried the address for Hannah Boyd's apartment when they'd first reached San Pedro, but the place had been empty. One of her neighbors suggested that she might be at Rudy's bait shop. Sometimes she piloted rental boats for some of the tourist businesses in the harbor, and other times she simply went to the bait shop to hang.

"Get out of here!" Mortie roared, fisting the base-ball bat menacingly as he approached.

Angel spread his hands. "We just want to talk. We need to find Hannah Boyd. She's in trouble."

"Uh uh," Mortie said. "Told your little friend there that nobody was going to bother Hannah. I meant it, too."

Another man joined Mortie, and from his build, Angel guessed it was Terry Boyd, Hannah's brother. "I got your back, Mortie," Terry growled.

"Get out," Mortie ordered.

"Can't leave," Angel replied. So far, there'd been no sign of *La Llorona*, but he knew that the elemental had to be close by. The warehouse was only a few hours' walking distance from the harbor. Around the beach at this time of evening, there were a lot of kids who were potential victims.

"You're leaving." Mortie swung the baseball bat.

Angel caught the bat as it blurred toward him, then stopped it between himself and the big man. Mortie's eyes widened in shock, and Terry launched himself at Doyle in the same instant, taking the half-demon down to the ground. Angel seized Terry by the back of his jacket, pulled him off Doyle, and threw him at Mortie. Both of the men fell to the ground.

Everything in the bait shop stopped and all eyes centered on Angel, Doyle, Cordelia, and Marisa.

"Okay," Angel said, "now that we have that out of our systems." He gazed around the room and tossed the baseball bat away. "We're looking for Hannah Boyd. She's in trouble. We're only here to help her."

"I know where she is, Doyle," a voice called from behind.

Angel turned and saw a man standing in the doorway.

"This is Harper," Doyle said. "The guy I told you about."

"Where's Hannah?" Angel asked.

Harper shook his head. "What kind of trouble is she in?"

"Kind?" Cordelia exploded. "You're worried about what *kind* of trouble she's in? By the time we get through explaining it to you she could be dead is what kind!" She approached Harper. "If you know where she's at, we need to know."

Harper hesitated only a moment, glanced at the two men lying on the bait shop floor, then back at the group in front of him. "Hannah's out in the harbor. I just took her out to a yacht called *League Strider.*"

"That's Adrian's yacht," Marisa said in surprise. But Angel heard the hurt and anger in her voice as well. "What's he doing here?"

"He came to see Hannah," Harper replied. "Says he's looking for his wife and thought Hannah might have some idea where she was."

"Can you take us there?" Angel asked.

Harper jerked a thumb over his shoulder. "My boat's still out there."

"Let's go."

Harper led the way outside.

A warning siren drew Angel's attention to the north end of the beach. As he watched, a police car drove out of a parking area with its flashing lights on and headed across the beach. The beach crowd gave way reluctantly as the police car prowled through their midst. The Angel's Gate Lighthouse sounded mournfully out in the harbor.

"Angel . . ." Cordelia said.

"I see her," Angel replied, spotting the woman in black as the police car headlights cut her out of the darkness.

The woman in black ignored the lights, the siren, and the people moving away from her. Her focus remained riveted on the harbor.

Angel glanced out at the night-drenched ocean and scanned the dozens of small craft. There were several that were big enough to be Adrian Heath's yacht. "Can you find *League Strider* out there?"

"Yeah," Harper replied. "Who's she?" He pointed at the woman in black.

"That's who is after Hannah," Cordelia said.

"The police will stop her," Harper said.

"No they won't," Doyle said.

"She's just one—"

La Llorona waved her hands without turning toward the police car. Winds whipped up suddenly and sucked clouds of sand from the beach. The sand blew over the police car, burying it from sight for a moment. In the next moment, the police car roared in front of the woman in black. Moving easily, *La Llorona* shattered the driver's side window, reached in, and hauled out a full-grown man easily in one hand. Her mocking laughter and anguished cries alternately drowned out even the lighthouse's dirge.

"Move," Angel ordered, grabbing Harper by the arm to start the man in motion.

Without the driver, the police car kept rolling across the beach till it rolled out onto a pier and nose-dived onto a pleasure boat moored below. The car broke through the boat and the two vehicles sank in a tangle. Only a few seconds later, the ocean curlers lapped over the flashing light bar as the wrecks continued to sink.

Angel stayed beside Marisa as they ran. The woman was tense and she kept gazing over her shoulder at the woman in black.

"I'm supposed to be able to send her back into that gem?" Marisa asked.

"You can," Angel said.

"How?"

"I'll help you."

"Here," Harper called out, running along the dock and pointing to a powerboat.

Angel helped Marisa and Cordelia into the powerboat while Doyle kicked the mooring ropes loose and Harper keyed the engine. The engine caught just as the half-demon leaped down into the powerboat.

On the shore, *La Llorona* tossed aside the policeman she'd grabbed from the car. The way the policeman landed told Angel that the guy was either dead or unconscious.

Harper opened the throttle and the sound of the engines blatted over the harbor as the powerboat came around in a tight semicircle. Doyle joined the man at the controls.

"What are we doing?" Marisa asked. "Couldn't we try to stop her from the shore?"

Angel shook his head. "Father Carlos said you'd have to be in close to *La Llorona* to make this work."

"We could draw her in to me." Marisa held on to the powerboat's railing tightly, her body jerking as the powerboat hull slammed against the waves.

"No. She'll go for Hannah first. And if Hannah's baby is there, *La Llorona* will want to go there even more."

"What is Adrian doing here?"

"I don't know," Angel said. "You can't think about that right now."

Harper steered the powerboat expertly, cutting between other sail craft. But if Harbor Patrol spotted them, Angel knew the authorities would try to pull them over.

Marisa stared at the ocean, her mind obviously on her husband's sudden appearance with Hannah Boyd.

"Do you love Adrian?" Angel asked.

Marisa shot him an angry, pained look. "Of course I do."

"Then trust him."

Tears filled Marisa's eyes and she started to cry.

"I'm confused, Angel. I don't know what to think about him. Or even about myself. I can't help remembering the pollution from his plant helped kill my son!"

Angel looked at the woman. "Marisa, there's nothing you can do about that. Cristofer is gone, but there are a lot of other children out there. Start here, start now. If you can trap *La Llorona* again, you can save hundreds of children. If you talk to Adrian, maybe something can be done about the pollution from his plant that will save other children in your old neighborhood. Who knows? If Adrian is able to change his company, maybe those other companies will consider making changes, too. You could change the whole neighborhood."

"Cristofer shouldn't have died," Marisa said. "He was too young to die. He was only a baby."

Angel thought of his younger sister who had died at his hands. "Children are always too young to die."

"I left him there to die," Marisa said. "What you told my mother was true. I thought more of myself than I did of my child. I put myself and what I wanted ahead of him."

"You can't do anything about that," Angel said. "No matter how much you regret it, no matter how much you wish it had never happened, it did."

Marisa shook her head. "I can't." She looked up at Angel. "Let *La Llorona* kill me."

"*La Llorona* won't kill you," Angel said. "She needs you alive so that she can stay here in this world."

"I have to live?"

Angel remembered what Father Carlos had said about Marisa's death, that if the woman were dead, anyone could use the captor-gem to trap *La Llorona*. But he said, "Yes. Dying's easy, Marisa. It's living that's hard to do. And, if anything, you owe it to your son to make a difference with your life." And as he said that, Angel knew he was speaking to himself as well. "We all work toward some kind of redemption in our lives. This is yours to do."

Marisa nodded wordlessly. "Tell me what I have to do."

Angel took the obsidian toad from his trenchcoat pocket and folded it into Marisa's hands. "Forgive yourself, Marisa. That's all you have to do. Forgive yourself for what you think you did to Cristofer. Start now and be the best person you can be. And when you have forgiven yourself, command *La Llorona* to take her place back in this gem."

"I don't know how," Marisa said hoarsely.

"You can," Angel said. "It won't be easy, but you can. You may never get over the guilt, but you can stop hating yourself. I promise you that." He paused. "I know it can be done."

"Oh man," Doyle said over the throbbing power-boat engine. "Now that bites."

Glancing up into the dark sky, Angel saw *La Llorona* walking on the water and out into the harbor. Even as he watched, the elemental waved her hands and the wind lifted her from the water and carried her across the harbor. Foggy spume blasted from the ocean's surface as she sped across it.

"Where's *League Strider?*" Angel asked.

"There," Harper replied, pointing.

Angel glanced ahead and watched as Harper neatly steered the powerboat in beside the yacht. *La Llorona*'s course was taking her directly to the yacht.

"Cordelia," Angel called, "stay with Marisa. Help her—help her—" *Help her believe?* Angel knew it couldn't be done. A person learned to believe on his or her own, in the things that he or she chose to. By leaving *La Llorona*'s fate up to Marisa, he might be dooming them all.

"I've got her," Cordelia said, stepping up beside the woman.

Marisa turned the obsidian toad over in her hands. Then she looked back up at the elemental speeding across the harbor, hanging in the air.

Angel took a fishing gaff from a toolbox beside the control area as he passed and ran forward along the powerboat's prow. The throbbing engines made speech almost impossible. "Pull it in close again," he yelled to Harper.

Harper gunned the engine and swept in close to the yacht, matching the powerboat's speed to the yacht's.

Angel gathered himself on the powerboat's prow, feeling the boat shift as Doyle joined him.

"You got a plan?" the half-demon asked.

"Save everybody," Angel answered.

"I like it," Doyle said, wiping spray from his face. "Got kind of an even-handedness about it. And simple, too. You got to give it that."

Angel scanned the yacht's deck nearly six feet above them. The leap wasn't all that hard, even from the prow of a speedboat. Adrian stood at the railing with two security guys. A woman with spiky platinum blond hair stood at his side, holding the hand of a little girl who was pointing at the powerboat.

Glancing to his left, Angel saw that *La Llorona* was only a hundred yards out and closing fast. He timed the choppy beat of the powerboat crossing the waves, set himself, and leaped. Catching the yacht's railing, he pulled himself up, watching as Adrian, Hannah Boyd, and the little girl stepped back from him. The little girl reached for her mother and clung to her leg. The two security guys stepped forward, pistols in their hands.

"Freeze, buddy!" one of the security guards roared. The other one held a Halogen flashlight on Angel.

Angel put his hand up, blocking the light from his eyes. "Adrian!" he yelled. "It's Angel!"

"Angel?"

Through his spread fingers, Angel saw Adrian step forward. He looked at Angel hard, then waved the security men aside. The flashlight beam moved away, swinging out into the harbor.

"What are you doing here?" Adrian asked.

"Trying to protect Hannah from that," Angel answered, pointing at *La Llorona*. The elemental flew across the water, leaving a twisting mass of ten-foot waves behind her.

"What is it?" Adrian asked.

"Long story," Angel replied, reaching down to help Doyle, who'd also jumped for the yacht. He pulled the half-demon onto the yacht's deck.

"Where is Marisa? From the way Doyle talked I thought she might be trying to harm Hannah. That's why I came out here."

"She's in the powerboat with Cordelia." Angel stepped forward, moving onto the yacht's semi-lighted deck where *La Llorona* could see him. The security guard branded her with his flashlight beam, making her laughing and weeping expression of madness stand out against the night and the black sea.

"Mr. Heath," the other security guard yelled, "permission to fire!"

Adrian looked at Angel. "That . . . that *thing* is going to try to hurt Hannah?"

"Yes," Angel replied, trying to get the feel of the rolling deck beneath his feet. He'd fought from ship decks before, but the last time had been a long time ago.

"Fire!" Adrian yelled.

The security guards opened up at once, and the sharp reports of their weapons broke through the thunder of the yacht's and powerboat's engines. If any of the bullets hit *La Llorona*, she didn't show it. She streaked straight for the yacht without hesitation. The security guards kept firing, their weapons throwing foot-long flames from the muzzles.

Angel grabbed Adrian and shoved him into motion. "Get Hannah and her daughter below. Now!"

The ten-foot waves caught up with the yacht, rocking it violently. Seawater slopped over the railing and spewed across the deck. Adrian slipped twice and got back up both times.

Still cackling and crying, *La Llorona* flew up beside the yacht, drawing the attention of both security guards. They never saw the monster wave break free of the heaving ocean till it was too late. The rolling mountain of water slammed into both men and knocked them against the railing on the other side of the yacht.

Angel hung on to the railing and rode out the rough water. Then he stepped out onto the yacht's deck, brandishing the fishing gaff in front of him, getting the heft and feel of the impromptu weapon.

"Vampire!" *La Llorona* cackled with mournful glee.

"We've got some unfinished business," Angel shot back. He fell into a martial arts stance automatically, getting his balance despite the drenched deck.

The elemental came for him at once. "You're a fool, vampire. I let you live earlier. I won't be so generous this time." She threw her head back and laughed, then cried out in anguish. Without warning, she attacked.

Angel leaped to the side and lashed out with the fishing gaff. The hooked blade hung in *La Llorona*'s side and tore through. Even as he tried to set himself, the harsh winds that the elemental controlled rocked into him, blowing him off-balance. He retained his footing with difficulty, barely setting himself before his opponent came back around.

He blocked her attack, turning her blows with his forearms, unable to get enough room to use the gaff again. Her side still bled but didn't appear to have much of an effect on her. Doyle attacked her from the rear, lashing up from the deck with an oar that caught her across the back.

Snarling viciously, *La Llorona* whirled on Doyle and knocked him backward.

Angel struck with the gaff again, burying it deep into the elemental's thigh.

La Llorona laughed in response, high-pitched and wild, accompanying the warning blast from Angel's Gate Lighthouse. She turned back to Angel, madness gleaming in her eyes.

"I will have the children," she promised with insane zeal. "They are owed to me by this world. I will have what is mine. Once they are gone, my world can be perfect. I can use their lives to sustain my own. They will keep me company in my thoughts."

Angel yanked on the fishing gaff, trying desperately to pull the elemental down to his level. Realizing that he couldn't overcome the power that kept her aloft, he tried to climb up to her.

La Llorona raked Angel's face with her fingernails in a fierce slap. "Did you know that the voices of the children I kill stay with me always?"

Staggered by the blow and the pain, Angel couldn't dodge her next blow. The impact drove him from her, tearing free the fishing gaff because he refused to let it go. He landed hard on the deck and unconsciousness lapped at his mind, trying to drain it down into the darkness.

"They sing to me," *La Llorona* said, flying higher. "I listen to their voices and they sing to me." She wept and laughed, then wept again. "And though I listen to them, I can never hear the voices of my own children. They were taken from me. Do you know what it's like to search so long for your children, yet hate them at the same time?"

Angel pushed himself to his feet.

"She's crazy," Doyle said, wiping blood from his mouth.

La Llorona hung in the winds above them. The same wind that tore at Angel's and Doyle's clothing held her aloft as gently as a feather. She gestured, and suddenly a waterspout erupted ahead of the yacht on the starboard side. The water whirled rapidly, twisting and turning into a dancing funnel. Before Angel could set himself or shout out a warning, the waterspout slammed into the yacht.

Caught amidships, *League Strider* rose up high on the starboard side. Water crashed over her prow and became a sluicing tide that rushed over the deck. Both security guards washed over the railing. Adrian had Hannah and her daughter at the door leading belowdecks but hadn't made it inside. They started to slide, driven by a wall of water.

Angel slid across the deck and held on to the railing with his free hand. For a moment he was looking down on Harper's powerboat, thinking they were about to smash onto it as the waterspout drove them toward the speedboat. But Harper had reflexes and the presence of mind to steer away from the yacht as it came down sideways.

Doyle came yelling, barely managing to catch the railing beside Angel.

However, Adrian, Hannah, and her little girl slid across the deck and spilled into the ocean. Angel caught just a glimpse of the little girl's blond head a moment before it disappeared below the ocean surface. *If the yacht goes down,* Angel thought, *the undertow will take us all down with it.* Only he and Doyle could probably survive it.

"Doyle," Angel called as the yacht started to roll back over to starboard, "get the girl!"

"On my way!" The half-demon released the railing and dropped into the water not far from where the little girl had gone in.

Riding the yacht back to level, Angel gathered himself and took a fresh hold on the fishing gaff. He was drenched and freezing. His eyes stung from the chill and the salt. He scanned the sky and spotted *La Llorona* swooping down toward the little blond-haired girl as she bobbed to the surface only a few feet from Doyle.

La Llorona closed on the little girl like a fisher-hawk, fingers ready to scoop her from the water or perhaps kill her there and then.

Angel ran and leaped for the attacking elemental. He collided with her in mid-flight, roping one arm around her waist and driving the fishing gaff home in the back of her head. He'd hoped the blow might stun her, or at least wound her so severely that she'd retreat at least for a moment.

La Llorona squalled in pain, then laughed mania-

319

cally. Her body shuddered in convulsive heaves from the laughter. Then they hit the water and went under. When she came back up, Angel still clinging to her back, she'd become an old crone. Her flesh was covered with lesions and hung loosely from her frame.

They'd landed only a few feet from the little girl. Doyle swam for the child as Hannah Boyd screamed for her daughter. The little girl managed to tread water, but she shrieked for her mother, spluttering as a wave momentarily covered her over.

"Doyle!" Angel yelled in warning.

The half-demon turned, but *La Llorona* struck with blinding speed, striking him on the side of the head with a bone-cracking thud. Doyle disappeared beneath the waves without a sound.

"My child!" *La Llorona* shrieked as she swam toward the water with single-minded intensity. "Give me my child!"

Angel trusted the fishing gaff buried deep in the elemental's skull. He let go of *La Llorona*'s waist and yanked himself forward, wrapping his free arm around her throat as he closed his legs around her waist.

La Llorona reached for the child, falling only inches short of her target.

Then another body hit the water near the little girl.

Angel watched helplessly, pulling back on the

fishing gaff with all his strength and clamping down tight on his opponent's throat. A normal person would have been dead, but the elemental continued to fight against him.

La Llorona's arm swept forward again. Just as her arm was about to reach the little girl, Marisa Heath surfaced. She caught the elemental's arm and deflected it. At the same time, she slapped the obsidian toad against *La Llorona*'s forehead.

"No!" Marisa told *La Llorona*. "No more children!"

Angel held more tightly to the elemental's head, then grabbed *La Llorona*'s other arm as she tried to strike Marisa.

"You're going back!" Marisa cried.

"You called me here," *La Llorona* croaked in dark fury.

Hannah Boyd swam to her crying child and pulled her away. Only a few feet away, Doyle surfaced groggily, dog-paddling weakly to keep himself afloat.

"I was wrong," Marisa said, tears mixing with the seawater washing over her face. "I was selfish."

"Your husband killed your child!" *La Llorona* screamed. "You can still have your revenge! I will give you that!"

"Revenge won't bring Cristofer back and it won't take away the things I did to him," Marisa said angrily. "You're going back!"

Abruptly, the obsidian toad glowed virulent purple, expanding a bubble of light nearly three feet across. In the next instant, *La Llorona* was sucked into the captor-gem. She screamed angrily and laughed, bellowing in pain the whole time till she was gone.

Angel slid under the water for a moment once the buoyant elemental was no longer there. He swam for the surface, catching hold of Marisa, who slumped exhaustedly against him and was already starting to sink.

Harper pulled the powerboat around and Angel quickly passed Marisa up to Cordelia. He stayed in the water and helped Doyle collect Hannah and her daughter. Adrian made the swim to the powerboat, but had to cling to the side till Harper could help pull him aboard.

Once everyone was on board the powerboat, Angel and Doyle pulled themselves aboard.

"I did it," Marisa said when she saw Angel come up. "I didn't think it was possible, but I did it!"

Angel shook water from his face. "I know." He glanced at the powerboat's stern and saw Adrian sitting there, obviously not knowing what to think or to do. Cordelia kept him company, but Adrian only had eyes for his wife. Doyle helped Hannah find a dry blanket for her little girl, talking easily to both of them, using the charm he always had.

Tears still ran down Marisa's face as she looked at

Angel. "But the pain of Cristofer's death and what I did, it's still there."

"That part won't go away," Angel said. "But it gets a little better with every day that passes. That's what redemption is all about: getting better a little bit at a time. It's slow, but there's no other way. And it gives you something to live for when you get to thinking there's absolutely nothing to live for."

"I don't know that I believe that as strongly as you," Marisa said.

"You will," Angel said. "In time."

She glanced back at her husband, who returned her gaze but made no move toward her. "What do I do?" she asked. "What do I do about Adrian?"

"He's scared and he's hurt," Angel said.

"Why is he staying away from me?"

"Because he's giving you the space you need to decide what you want to do," Angel said. "That takes a lot of strength for a guy to do. Don't confuse what you're seeing in him. He still doesn't know why you left. He doesn't know about Maria Segura or her son. I didn't tell him." He paused, looking into Marisa's eyes. "He loves you, Marisa, and he loves you enough to let you go if that's what you want."

"That's not what I want," Marisa said, shivering against the cold and the fear that gripped her.

"Then let him know that. You're the one who has

to make the next move. He came this far. He was ready to stand by you if you needed him. And I'd say he still is."

Marisa hesitated. "There's so much I need to tell him."

"Trust him," Angel said. "You need your family, Marisa. No matter how hard it gets between you, he's your family and your mother's your family. Family is the strongest thing there is in the world, but it has to be built from both sides. He can love you whether you love him or not, but can you go through life without loving him?"

"No," Marisa whispered. "No, I can't."

"Then don't. It's that simple."

Marisa glanced at Angel. "Thank you." She headed back to Adrian, walking slowly at first.

Angel watched as Adrian stood uncertainly, then reached out and pulled Marisa into him with both arms when she ran toward him. They held each other tightly with quiet desperation.

Looking away to give the couple a moment of privacy, Angel watched Doyle and Cordelia helping the others and knew that what he'd told Marisa was true. Family did help smooth the rough and rocky parts of life and unlife. With family, there was always someone to share the triumphs and tragedies with, the guilt and the redemption. And later on tonight or tomorrow, there was still the blood-supply ring operating out of Corinth Studios that had to be shut down. When he faced that, Angel knew he wouldn't be alone.

For one silent moment, Angel gave thanks for the family that he had been given in the city that he'd adopted.

About the Author

Mel Odom lives in Moore, Oklahoma, and is the author of several books in the *Angel, Buffy the Vampire Slayer, Sabrina the Teenage Witch* and other media-related series. His new book, *The Rover,* a hardcover fantasy novel, is coming out in July. His e-mail address is mel@melodom.net.

Buffy
the vampire slayer™

"Well, we could grind our
enemies into powder with a
sledgehammer, but gosh,
we did that last night."

—Xander

As long as there have been vampires,
there has been the Slayer. One girl
in all the world, to find them where
they gather and to stop the spread of
their evil and the swell of their numbers.

LOOK FOR A NEW TITLE
EVERY MONTH!

Based on the hit TV series created by
Joss Whedon

2400-01

BASED ON THE HIT TV SERIES

Prue, Piper, and Phoebe Halliwell
didn't think the magical incantation
would really work. But it did.
Now Prue can move things with her
mind, Piper can freeze time, and
Phoebe can see the future. They are
the most powerful of witches—
the Charmed Ones.

**Available from Pocket Pulse
Published by Pocket Books**